Sister Blackberry

Melissa Newman, Ed.D.

Published by
Martin Sisters Publishing Company
www.martinsisterspublishing.com
Martin Sisters Publishing ©2022
Reprinted with rights and permissions from original printing and publisher
Whiskey Creek Press ©2009

ISBN: 978-1-62553-105-6
Literary Fiction
Printed in the United States of America
Martin Sisters Publishing

DEDICATION

For my mother, whose colorful life fueled my imagination.
Nellie Louise Martin-Dozier, 1936-2001.

1950 Cleveland's Depot on Chester, Cleveland, Ohio

The cover photo was retrieved from the Cleveland Public Library Collection

PREFACE

Sister Blackberry's final words dried on paper in the spring of 2006, the book was first published by a since-sold publisher in 2008, and then published again by Martin Sisters Publishing in 2022.

I was trained and working as a journalist for over a decade when I wrote the first words for what would be my first novel. I searched for two years for a publisher and found a mid-list house that was a perfect home for my work. "Sister Blackberry" and my second novel, "House of Cleaving," lived with this publishing house until the company sold in 2015. I had a choice to make – get my rights back or move my work with the new publisher that was, at that time, unknown to me. I chose the latter and waited for the right time to re-release "Sister Blackberry."

Because this was my first novel and I had learned some things since that first keystroke, I was tempted to rewrite the whole book. But there was something about this story – raw in content and in literary expertise – that resonated with people and still does.

This story is as relevant today as it was then, in many ways, more so. Some light editing and some new words here for the preface and on the back cover are all that is changed about this work. I fought the editor in me that had a burning desire to rip it up and start over – I'm glad I didn't. So here she is again, my first novel, "Sister Blackberry."

I have often been asked how the story of Sister Blackberry was born – this is both an easy and complicated question.

The easy answer is that it was a dream. The more complicated piece is how that dream became a story.

When I was a young journalist covering everything from

murder to government corruption to community events at a small newspaper in eastern Kentucky, I got a phone call one afternoon from a trusted source at the local courthouse.

"You need to get over here," the voice said. "A court case was just filed – you're gonna want to know about this one."

The voice gave the Circuit Court Civil Action case number, so I'd know where to look.

I knew something was happening and I knew it was big for our small town. I could tell by the way folks were looking at me as I walked down the hallway to the court's public filing office. Once inside, one of the ladies cut her eyes at me and then at Judge's door. I quickly surmised that the file I was looking for was on the Judge's desk. It wasn't uncommon for a sensitive file to be with Judge, and I had been granted permission to take a peek in the past. So, I walked right in and asked for it, specifically, by case number. Judge's administrative assistant (we called them secretaries back then) was pleasant as usual – a hometown girl, just like me. I knew her well. Judge had his door open and heard what I was asking for and promptly entered the foyer to address me straight on. The mostly one-sided conversation went something like this … "that file is on my desk; you are not getting it; it's a juvenile case" … I started to speak, but Judge stopped me … "no, I don't want to hear it – you're not getting it."

I left the Judge's office not knowing quite what I was looking for, only that it must have been a big, but I knew if I hung around the courthouse long enough, I'd get some information, so that's just what I did. Within the hour, I learned that a family had filed suit against a local school district because their male student, who was attending school dressed as a female, had been expelled.

Even though it was a small town, and I was entangled in happenings about town most of the time, I never uncovered the identity of this family or the child, even though I tried time and again. For that, I still hold a great deal of respect our small but capable court system in my hometown.

The frustration of a young reporter who can't get a story is like heartburn that won't go away. It's all consuming —all you can think about.

And just the way heartburn can bring about vivid dreams – thinking of Charles Dickens' "A Christmas Carol" when Ebenezer Scrooge accuses the ghost of Jacob Marley of being "a bit of undigested beef" – this frustration I was experiencing manifested itself as a fully formed story about a young woman with physical gender ambiguity.

While most dreams are splintered in meaning and lack the cohesiveness of waking life, this full story, this full dream, came to me as a family saga wrapped in three generations of secrets and those family members who became entangled in half-truths and omissions of historical facts.

Of all people, why did the Universe choose me to hold this heartbreaking saga that could provide a deeper understanding of human misery, compassion, hatefulness, greed that can still offer so much hope? I truly still don't know. I researched, I read, and I interviewed to be as factual as possible within this work of fiction.

I was a confident writer and believed that I was perfectly capable of penning this saga. And I knew this story had to be told, but I had no lived experience with this subject matter. I am a white, middle class, heterosexual, female with one husband, two children, and at the time I had two cats and a dog.

I am not a part of the LBGTQ+ community and before this story, this dream, I had no knowledge or understanding. I have been very honest about who I am when groups call and inquire about a reading or personal appearance. Some continue with bookings and some cancel. I get it.

When the novel first launched, I traveled for events and readings – from Cleveland to Atlanta to New Orleans and Chicago, at least one person would always speak up about knowing someone who had been born with physical gender ambiguity.

Every. Single. Time.

This thing that we all think is so uncommon, is not that sparse at all – at least in the fandom of "Sister Blackberry."

In the past I'd sometimes find myself wishing this story had been gifted to someone with a better understanding or personal experience. Then again, maybe there exists the power of change in the dissonance between writer and subject – just maybe hearing someone like me with so much compassion and empathy for this community can open more powerful conversations.

What I do know is that when I woke from that dream, this story commanded that I share it. I had experienced, just for a sliver of time, the life of this person – the pain, the struggles, the yearning to belong and be loved – and it changed me.

My hope is that it changes you, too.

CHAPTER ONE

Rayes County, 1936

The fence rows were lined with briars. Viola picked a few of the best-hidden sweets and put them in her pocket. She ate them as she walked along the fence at the property line until she came to the Cole farm. Across the field, she could see Janie in the back yard, hanging clothes on the line. A quick smile came to Viola's face, and a tickle in her belly made her laugh a little. She hadn't seen Janie for four days. Back at her own farm there was plenty of work to keep her busy—the garden, the laundry, the chickens. But Viola was tired of all that today. She missed her friend.

"HEY!" she shouted across the field. At first, Janie didn't look, but after a second yell, she glanced toward the field. Viola gathered her skirt up in one hand and ran toward Janie, waving her hands as her shoes scraped against the tall grass. She ran behind the barn and around the part of the fence where she always crossed.

Janie came to the fence to help Viola over. "I've missed you," she said, pulling Viola's arm as she scaled the split rails. Once she was on the other side, the women hugged, their bellies mashing against one another.

"How you been?" Janie asked. "Has he been kicking a lot?"

"Yes, kicking up a storm," Viola said. "How 'bout yours?"

"I have to go to the bathroom a lot. I guess that's from all the kicking." Janie looked up toward the porch. "C'mon. Let me get you some water. It's hot out here." She went inside for drinking cups. Viola held the door and then followed behind her.

A trip through the house landed them out back by the well pump. They filled their cups and sat down in the outside chairs. Viola stared at Janie's face. There was a bruise under her cheekbone, and she had some red marks on her neck.

"Has Bick been home?"

"Yeah…" Janie answered. "He came home for two days. Did you see him come in?"

"No, just askin'," Viola said. She wiped her hair off her forehead with the bottom of her dress, and as she did, the berries turned upside down and fell to the ground from her pocket. "Oh, I forgot. I picked these on the way."

"Mmm. They look so ripe," Janie said as she grabbed one and popped it in her mouth. "Maybe one day next week when the men leave again, we can make some pies at your house."

"Mmm. Is Bick going to be home in time for the baby?"

"Yes, I think so," Janie replied. "Even so, this baby isn't waiting for him."

"Have you got a name yet?"

"I don't know. Brother Caslin said it's going to be a boy, ya know. I think I'll name him Robert, after my grandfather."

"But what if it's a girl?" Viola asked.

"I doubt that. Brother Caslin's been delivering babies for a while, and if he says it's going to be a boy, then it probably will be a boy. No sense in questioning it."

Janie talked about Brother Caslin a lot. She and Bick attended the Pentecostal Church. Voila was Baptist and didn't agree with Janie all the time on religion, but she bit her tongue most times. She had heard from the people at her own church that the Pentecostals spoke in tongues and claimed that the Lord spoke through them. She had seen people do this when she was a young girl. Once, a lady came to pray for her father when he was sick with pneumonia. She brought a cooked dish of green beans and new potatoes, a few biscuits, and some tomatoes fresh from her garden. Viola loved fresh tomatoes. The lady prayed for her father and at the end began to speak in a muffled voice. She got louder near the end, but Viola couldn't understand what she was saying. The lady's rolled back in her head as she mumbled. When she left, Viola's mother explained that if the Lord wanted to say something, he'd most likely say it so everyone could understand—not in words that did not exist.

Viola had seen Brother Caslin in town and at community meetings, picnics and such. He always gave her a funny feeling. She wasn't scared of him, but she didn't want to be around him for too long either. Her mother had always told her to pay attention to those feelings she had about people. She said being a good judge of character was a gift not to be taken lightly.

She never understood Bick's and Janie's total trust in Brother Caslin. They thought he was always right, no matter how wrong and narrow-minded Viola thought he was.

The couple of times Viola had seen Brother Caslin's wife, Sarah, she always looked worried. She was jumpy and scared like a little rabbit, never more than two feet from her husband at all times. When he went to gather with the men for conversations about politics, religion, and what not, she'd stand behind him.

Viola had heard Janie talk about the church but tried not to speak her opinion. People in town were always saying that Caslin's church handled snakes. Viola had only asked Janie once about that. She'd snapped at Viola and told her that faith came in a lot of different forms. This led Viola to think it was true. It didn't sound like a denial.

It didn't matter. She knew Janie was a true Christian, always thinking of others. Viola had been no exception to this kindness. But Janie's husband believed women should do what their husbands told them. Viola was a little more independent than Bick was comfortable with. He said it was because of Viola that Janie had never gotten the Holy Ghost, and until Janie stopped thinking of her as a friend, the Holy Ghost would never speak through her.

Janie had at least shared that much with her friend.

Viola worried about Janie and had thought often about telling her they couldn't be friends anymore. She suspected that Bick would hit Janie when he found out she and Viola had been together. There weren't as many bruises and marks since Janie had gotten pregnant, but there were still signs. Viola couldn't figure out how someone as sweet as Janie could be married to a man who would hit her. And what about the baby? Would Bick hit the baby? Viola wondered. She had wanted several times to have a talk with Bick about his actions, but Den warned her better of it, said it would just lead to more trouble than it was worth. Den had given up on what he referred to as his childish name—Dennis—when he and Viola married, mostly for practical purposes like name signing. Still, even if the childish name was gone, the child was still present and would jokingly boast about how lucky Viola was to have such a good husband. It was hard for her to keep her mouth shut. The more marks she saw on Janie, the harder it was.

Brother Caslin and Sarah would be the ones to deliver Janie's baby. They birthed all the babies in the congregation. Viola was kind of envious of that. At least Janie knew who would be there for the birth. Viola was afraid of being alone when her baby came. Still, she couldn't help but think her friend should have a doctor there.

"Are you scared, Janie?" she asked.

"No. You?"

"Yes," Viola said. "What if Den doesn't make it home in time for the baby?"

"Don't worry. I'll keep a watch on you."

"I do have the doctor in town looking out for me. I wouldn't want anything to go wrong."

"Like what?" Janie asked.

"Well, anything. The baby could not want to come out or the cord could be wrapped around its neck. I've heard of that before. The doctor's nurse comes to see me every month to check things out underneath. When she thinks I've opened up enough, then I'll go stay in town at the clinic until the baby comes. That's the only way Den felt safe leaving me at home alone."

"Can't he take some time away from work?"

"No, he'll lose his spot in the mine," Viola said. "There are people waiting in line for those jobs down there. We can't live without the coal money anymore."

They talked until the sky turned orange with the evening sun, about the babies that would soon be theirs.

"I have to go into town tomorrow," Viola said as the sun was setting. "Will you go with me?"

"Okay," Janie said. "Why are we going?"

"I have business at the bank with Mr. Mills. Well, it's Den's business, but I have to drop off some papers to the bank. I'm going to drive the truck."

Janie laughed. "I still can't believe he lets you drive that truck."

"When I have to. He's never home. And it's important that the papers be there tomorrow." Viola's forehead furrowed as she looked out toward her farm. "Everything will work out for us?" It came out more like a question than a statement. "God does look out for our every need, doesn't he?"

"Of course he does, Viola. You believe that?"

"Yeah, I just wanted to hear you say it."

"What is it?" asked Janie. "Why are you so worried?"

"It's just that…I spend my life alone so much of the time. I work at the farm all day and then sleep at night. Is this all there is?"

"Viola, wait until that precious baby gets here. Your purpose will change. You'll have plenty to do and plenty of love. Things are going to change for both of us when these babies get here. God love 'em both."

"Yeah." Viola's eyes glazed over with tears. "Well, I guess I'd better get back before dark. Meet me at the house and we'll go after we eat."

Viola saw Janie watching her as she walked back behind the barn toward her farm. She struggled a little to get over the fence but cleared it nicely even without Janie's help.

*

Janie brought biscuits and eggs to begin the trip into town. She and Viola cooked the eggs and ate their breakfast.

After Viola had taken her business at the bank, they headed back toward the truck. There was an auction taking place on the steps of the courthouse. Someone else had lost their farm, and today it was being sold. Viola had seen these before. It always made her sad.

"What are they doing?" Janie asked.

"They're selling someone's farm. It's when someone gets money from the bank and then can't pay it back. The bank takes their farm."

"I've heard Bick talk about that, but I've never seen it happen."

There he was, Judge Baker, at the top of the steps. A crowd gathered around him. Janie and Viola gathered with the crowd to watch for few moments.

"It's 23 acres, more or less," Judge Baker announced to the crowd. "It's quite the little gem, so dig deep. This one's a find."

Viola and Janie stood shoulder to shoulder as they watched the bidding. They didn't recognize most of the men who bid on the Taylor property. They all looked very important, dressed in suits. Not like Rayes County men at all.

"Wonder where they are?" Janie asked.

"Who?"

"The Taylors."

Viola imagined the Taylors wouldn't have been able to bear the sight of their home auctioned. That was probably why they were making themselves scarce.

"Oh, I don't know," Viola said as the two women looked all around the square.

Seated on a bench around the side of the steps was Langley, dressed in his usual garb: a straw hat with a flower poked through one of the holes on the side, a long skirt, and a scarf around his neck. School children who were walking to the school yard yelled at him and made fun. Langley yelled back a couple of times but then just twisted his body around, so he didn't have to look at them anymore.

"Why does he do that?" Janie asked Viola.

"Some people say he's not right in the head. There's something wrong with him."

"Brother Caslin says he's possessed with the Devil. You'd think he'd be worried about his soul and trying to get into Heaven instead of trying to look like a woman."

"Janie, don't say things like that. Maybe he just doesn't know any better. He doesn't have anyone to look after him."

"He has the Lord, and if he knew and believed in him, then he wouldn't be that way," Janie said sharply.

This was one of those moments when Viola had to bite her tongue. She'd heard every sermon that Brother Caslin had preached that summer—not in person but through the voice of her friend. She was sure that if Brother Caslin ever told Janie the sky was green and the grass was blue, Janie would have believed it and then preached it to Viola.

Viola always listened and remembered what her mother used to tell her. "To each his own," she would say.

"God gave Langley a simple mind, Janie, and we should show him simple kindness." Viola and her last word would sometimes get her into trouble, but not this time. Janie either didn't hear or just accepted the last comment without quoting verse from Caslin. Janie looked around and didn't see her friend right away ... "Janie! Hey, Janie!" Viola yelled, trying to find her. Viola spent the next few seconds in a panic as she searched for Janie, then spotted her.

"Where did you go? I thought I'd lost you in this crowd," Janie said, wiping the sweat off her forehead.

"We just got shuffled around a bit," Viola said, looking over at the bank and then down at the paperwork Mr. Mills had given her. "But I'm ready to go now."

Janie knew that she and Bick didn't owe the bank anything, but she wondered if Viola and Den did. Maybe that was Viola's business with the bank. Janie was afraid to ask but all day had tried to catch a peek of the sealed envelope Viola carried with her.

Even when Viola had handed the papers to Mr. Mills, Janie was trying to find one last clue as to what was in this mix that had to be delivered just in time today. Mr. Mills had seen that Janie was trying to peer over Viola's shoulder and gave her a stern look as Viola looked in her pocketbook for a bank ledger.

Janie was ashamed and didn't look up again until she and Viola walked out the door. She was still feeling a little embarrassed, but she was sure her friend hadn't noticed that Janie was trying to get a peek

Both women were ready for a short rest before heading home. It certainly was hot, and although the air was wet enough to drink, it could never quench a thirst. Janie had brought a bottle of water wrapped in some cloth in her pocketbook. The two leaned against the truck and shared the water. It wasn't cold, but it wasn't really warm. Neither of them cared. It was wet, and they were both thirsty.

Janie was about two or three weeks from having her baby, and Viola was about the same. Bick was coming home sometime soon, but Den probably wouldn't be home for a while. Janie knew Viola was scared. Her mother and father had both passed on. Viola was an only child. She was alone, and Janie could sense her friend's fear. Janie knew Viola envied her in a strange way. Maybe because Bick was always home more than Den.

"Don't worry," Janie said, coming out of her thoughts. She looked at her friend's worried face. "I'm going to take care of you."

"I know," Viola said quietly, rubbing her swollen belly.

"Let's go," Janie said.

Once Janie had been delivered back to her house and Viola was back at the farm, she went inside and immediately got a drink and laid down to take a nap, claiming exhaustion.

*

Viola opened her eyes to the morning sun in her face through the curtains. She was as tired today as she'd been all week. The trip to town had taken all her energy, but that had been two days ago. Her belly felt tighter than ever this morning. She got up and made her way to the bathroom and then into the kitchen., staring out the window while she drank a cup of water. She wondered if Bick had come home to Janie. She wouldn't know for sure until church time, when she would see them go down the road in the truck. Even if she couldn't see the truck or hear the engine, she could always see the dirt billowing up from the back as they went.

She hadn't seen Janie in two days, and Den wasn't coming home this week. She kept telling herself that if the baby came, Janie would take care of her until Den came home. Still, she was scared. She started out the back door to the garden for some fresh tomatoes when she felt a pain in her lower back. She ignored it and went on out the door. It was already hot out, and the air was just as thick as it had been every day that summer.

"It's going to rain today little one," Viola said, patting her belly. "Listen. Do you hear it? That's the rain crow." She felt nothing when she spoke to her unborn child. It just didn't seem real. She wondered why she wasn't as excited about her baby as Janie was about hers. It was as if she couldn't imagine having one. She wondered if it was a sign that something might be wrong.

Back inside, Viola began to clean up in the kitchen, looking out the window periodically to see if Janie and Bick were going to church. It was almost nine o'clock. They should be going down the lane by now.

She watched for a few minutes longer and, sure enough, saw the clay-colored dust cloud. Strangely, it was a comfort to her. It made Viola feel a little safer knowing that Bick was home for a couple of days. At least there was another person who knew she might need help. She'd never cared much for Bick, but Janie seemed to love him dearly. There had to be some good in him.

Day turned into night, and Viola's pains were coming more often. She hadn't seen Bick and Janie go back out the road for night services, but it had been raining all day, and the drops had most likely fastened the dust to the road. She was making her way to the bedroom when she felt the water gush between her legs. She knew what this meant: it was time. Her knees buckled under her, and she began to cry uncontrollably.

"Oh, dear God. Oh, dear God." She sat down on the bed and sobbed as the pain that had been in her back moved into her legs and belly. "I've got to go," she said to herself, thinking she could make it to Janie and Bick's place.

Viola pulled herself together enough to get out the back door. She could feel the ground moving beneath her, and then everything went black. The last thing she felt was her head hitting the hard ground.

CHAPTER TWO

Sunday evening, just as the sun had begun to lay its face on the back side of the mountain and the fog began to rest in the bottom, Janie put away the supper dishes and got ready to head out to the church house with Bick. She took a long, hard look toward Viola's farm to see if she could spot her outside., but it was too far away.

She worried about Viola but was afraid to tell her husband. He had only gotten home last night; she didn't want to start trouble with him. He didn't like Viola much, mostly because she was Baptist. Janie so wished Viola would come to church with them so she could share their friendship with her husband. But for now, it would have to remain a secret between the two women.

Janie's and Bick's farm was thick around the edges with briars that kept the horses corralled within the confines of the old fencing and made Janie feel safe. It served, for Bick, as a reminder of all that was his—land, barn, and home all outlined in branches and leaves. The old place was well defined, everything where it should be and always was.

Janie whisked around the kitchen, sweeping the last crumb from supper off her new linoleum. When the sun peeked through the kitchen window just before setting completely over the mountain, Janie's new linoleum sparkled like starlight. It had gold speckles laid upon the whitest white she'd ever seen. Janie imagined Heaven's stairway lined with linoleum just like hers. It would have to be. It was so beautiful. Viola had laughed at Janie's comparison between her linoleum and Heaven. Thinking of the day they laughed about it made Janie smile.

She swept her hair, wet with sweat, off her forehead as she leaned over with dustpan in hand to scoop the last of the dirt from the floor. When she rose up, the room began to spin, and everything in the kitchen turned black for a moment. She stood silent and motionless until the spell passed. These spells came often as the day for the baby to come got closer.

The screen door slammed with a loud pop as Bick came back into the house. Janie opened her eyes, and sure enough, the spell was over.

"You ready, Jane?" Bick asked.

"I reckon I am," she said with a smile as she placed the broom and dustpan in their regular corner.

The ride to church seemed bumpier than usual, she thought.

"I thought the magistrate was supposed to get us some new gravel out here?"

"Oh, that'll be the day," Bick said with a sarcastic laugh. "One of these days this ol' truck is gonna fall in a pothole so deep the devil might have to try his hand at drivin'."

Janie laughed so hard she knew she would have to make a beeline straight for the bathroom when they got to church. *Just imagine,* she thought, *that ol' devil a-drivin' Bick's truck. Maybe he would catch his forked tail in the door and be done away with forever.* She laughed a little more on her way inside the church house. Her eyes darted across the pews as she wondered what the quickest path to bathroom would be. The bathroom at the church was new—at least the plumbing was new. Bick and some of the other men in the congregation had helped put the new lavatory and toilet in.

Joe John Mills met Bick at the church door as usual. They'd been buddies since they were kids and had stood at the church door waiting for a sermon for as long as any member of the congregation could remember.

"What's the matter with her?" Joe John asked Bick.

"Aww, anymore that's all she does is pee," Bick said with a snicker. "At least she's laughing. Most of the time she's crying, and I don't even know what for."

Once Janie was safe behind the bathroom door, she sat on the toilet with a sigh. "Lordy, Lordy, I thought I'd bust."

She felt a little funny. It seemed like she peed a lot more than she needed to. It just kept coming, even though she couldn't really feel it. She could hear it hit the toilet water.

"Finally," she said as she wiped and pulled up her panties. She straightened her skirt and brushed her hair back with her hand, trying to hurry before the whole congregation sat down and she had to interrupt.

Janie shut the door to the bathroom and there they all sat staring at her. She was too late. Now she would have to walk down the middle of the aisle. People were probably going to look at her.

She locked eyes with Bick, which made her a little more comfortable as she had to parade her big belly in front of the entire congregation. There he sat, Bible in hand and one eyebrow raised. Janie snuggled safely in next to him in their favorite pew. He held one part of the Bible and she held the other as Brother Caslin rustled around at the pulpit, putting his papers in order.

"Here we are again, brothers and sisters, inside the house of God, Hallelujah, Hallelujah," Brother Caslin said in his deep, wavering voice. Several *Amens* came from the front of the church, just like always. Janie felt warm inside as Brother Caslin continued his sermon.

This one was about Mary Magdalene. Janie had heard it done similarly before, but this time Brother Caslin delivered it with such style, the message of how only truly pure women would receive the gifts of God. Her favorite sermon was the one about worldly goods and how God didn't care what kind of car you drove, what kind of shoes you owned, or how much money you had.

Brother Caslin may have used his sermons more than once, but each time he added a little something extra to the message. Janie thought God must have told him if he left something important out, so he would do them again.

He never, however, left out the instructions about how to get to the Pearly Gates of Heaven. This usually came at the end of the sermon just before the calling of the lost and the backslid.

He never mentioned the stairway leading into Heaven. That was something Janie had made up on her own. She was sure that God wouldn't take her soul to Heaven without a stairway. She had a terrible fear of even cleaning the barn loft. God would lead her with a stairway, even he if had to make it just for her—and maybe a few other people who were afraid of high places.

Heaven, she thought as she looked up at the church ceiling. Then her thoughts turned to her new linoleum once again.

Bick had saved money all winter to buy Janie the new flooring. She didn't want the baby crawling around on the wood floor. It was sometimes splintery and rough and could hurt a little baby's tender skin.

Janie knew she wasn't supposed to be thinking about worldly goods during a church service. *But,* she thought, *if climbing to Heaven on a sparkly stairway reminds me of my shiny floor, then when I go home the shiny floor reminds me of Heaven — it must be alright with God.*

Janie squirmed around in the hard, wooden pew. Her back was beginning to hurt a little and wiggling around seemed to help.

Bick poked her in the ribs a little with his elbow. "Be still," he whispered.

"I can't," she whispered back with almost closed lips.

"Do ya gotta pee again?" he asked as he raised an eyebrow.

Janie halfway slapped him on the leg and turned her eyes back to Brother Caslin.

When the sermon was over and the lost souls and the backslid had made themselves right with God again, the congregation members rose to their feet and walked to the front of the church for hugs from the freshly cleansed. "Are You Washed in the Blood of the Lamb" was sung softly during this part of the service. That was the part Janie liked most about rededication.

The reborn were crying. There was always crying. Janie sometimes wondered how such a happy occasion could cause so many tears. Bick had told her once that they were tears of joy. She didn't really understand but accepted Bick's explanation anyway.

She made her way to the front of the church near the pulpit and hugged Ida and Loyola Brown, who had just rededicated their lives to Christ.

As Janie hugged Ida, she wondered what her sin had been. Ida was crying terribly. Her eyes were all red and swollen, and Loyola stood next to her with a handkerchief. He was crying, too. Janie couldn't understand what they could've done wrong in the eyes of

God. They were always at every church service. Then she remembered Bick telling her that those kinds of things were better left up to God to figure out. She felt ashamed of having nosy thoughts.

Brother Caslin and Sarah were waiting near the other side of the pulpit to shake hands with the men and hug the women. He didn't hug Janie right away, though. Instead, he grasped her belly firmly with both hands and looked up at the ceiling.

"Thank you, Lord Jesus, for this miracle we're about to receive." He hugged her tightly. Bick shook Brother Caslin's hand. "Feels like she's got about another week to hold on to that baby," Brother Caslin said.

"You sure?" Bick asked. "She looks like she's ready to pop."

"Well, only the Lord knows for sure," Brother Caslin quipped, "but I've been doing this a long time, and I say she's got another week."

Janie's stomach was churning. She wanted the baby now. She was tired of waiting. But she was scared, too. She wished that God would somehow make her go to sleep, and when she woke up, the baby would be in her arms. She knew better, though. Pain with birth was for sinners, and as much as she liked to ignore it, she was still a sinner in God's eyes until she made it to the Pearly Gates.

"Didn't I see you in town the other day with Dennis Garland's wife? What's her name? Uh, Viola?" Brother Caslin asked.

Janie was startled. She began to shake inside. She knew Bick would be mad. He glared at her, then back at Brother Caslin. Sick to her stomach, she sat down in the pew in front of her and stared out the window into the darkness outside. She watched as Bick gathered up their things and shook hands with the Deacons. She could feel her eyes getting warm, but she squeezed her eyelids together tightly to stop the flow. She knew crying would only make things worse. She could hear Brother Caslin and Sarah talking above her even though they tried to whisper.

"Why did you do that?" Sarah scolded her husband.

"I knew he had no idea she had been with that woman. She has to learn to obey her husband," Brother Caslin told his wife. "We have to look out for our brothers in the church."

*

On the ride home, Janie's back began to hurt worse than it had in church. "It feels like somebody's punching me in the back with a hot poker, Bick," she said.

"Maybe it's that ol' devil tryin' to push you out so he can have a ride in my truck." Bick laughed.

"It's not funny, Bick. It hurts," Janie said sternly. It was almost like he'd forgotten about the trip to town and Viola. She had thought and hoped for a long time that things would change when the baby came, and now, maybe they had changed.

"We'll get you home and lay you down," Bick said, getting more serious now. "But you know after this baby comes, there's gonna be a day of trouble."

"What do you mean?" She knew what he meant. Nothing was going to change—at least not anytime soon. He was mad about her going to town with Viola after she'd been told not to be with her. She should have told him. How stupid to think no one had seen her. "Bick, it doesn't have to be a day of trouble."

"Now, you know it does. I don't want you around that woman. First thing you know, she'll be making thoughts in your head about church again. If her husband had any control over her, she wouldn't be in town anyway, not without him."

"Viola is good and kind, and we do talk about God and church and good things." After that, all Janie could feel was a sharp sting on her face.

"I'm sorry," she sobbed. "I'm sorry."

CHAPTER THREE

Janie was sick with worry about what Bick might do. She wished he would just go ahead and get it over with. She couldn't sleep at all. She'd done wrong and she knew it. Being friends with Viola when her husband had told her not to was stupid. She knew she should just be happy with Bick and the farm. The ladies at church were nice, but they were exactly like her. Viola was different—interesting and different.

The pain was getting worse. She wondered if something was wrong with the baby. She was scared. Her mother had died when Janie's only brother was born. He'd died the next day. Janie prayed nothing was wrong.

Bick sat out on the front porch until Janie's cries were too much to bear. "I'm going to get Brother Caslin," he said, eyebrows scrunched together tightly.

"Yes!" was all Janie could blurt out. She lay there on the bed, wrenching in pain. She thought she was dying. "Oh God, please don't let me die," she prayed over and over.

It seemed like hours before Bick returned with Brother Caslin following behind.

It scared Janie even more to see Bick and Brother Caslin looking over her. They seemed worried. Sarah was in the kitchen, shouting with the Holy Ghost. Janie had a funny feeling that something awful was about to happen. It just didn't feel right. She remembered what Viola had told her about paying attention to bad and good feelings about things.

"What's wrong?" she grunted between the pains.

"Let's see," Brother Caslin answered.

He had Janie remove her underwear. Bick pulled her gown up around her waist and placed a blanket over her raised knees.

"This baby's coming tonight. Praise the Lord," Brother Caslin bellowed.

"But I thought you said it was going to be another week?" said Bick.

"The good Lord says it's a'comin tonight," Brother Caslin replied in a loud, scolding voice.

Bick couldn't stand to hear Janie scream like that. The torturing noise drove him into the kitchen, where he stood over the sink with a hand on each basin looking down into the drain. Sarah's prayers and shouting drove him out onto the porch. He prayed under his breath.

"It's a'comin'!" Brother Caslin cried.

A small, crackly cry filled the house.

"Praise Jesus!" Brother Caslin bellowed.

Bick raced into the bedroom. The baby was almost out, and Janie's howling cries were silent to his ears as watched the baby begin to leave her body.

The bedroom was dim. Only a small lamp by the bed shone mostly on Janie's face. Bick squinted his eyes to see over Brother Caslin's back.

He was hit with a force as Brother Caslin came to his feet. Bick stumbled back a step or two as Brother Caslin stood silent for only a few seconds. The baby lay on the bed, the cord still attached.

"Demon, demon, demon... God help us, Lord Jesus!" Brother Caslin squawked, tears running down his face. Bick could see Brother Caslin's eyes widening as he continued to curse the baby and pace around the room.

"God help you people. What have you done?" he bellowed in a way that seemed to echo through the house and up even into the mountain. "Guevedoche! Guevedoche!"

What is he saying? Janie wondered as panic began to well inside her. "Tell me what's wrong," she said. "Are you talking with the Holy Spirit?"

Those words came again and again. "Guevedoche, Guevedoche!"

Sarah entered the room, screaming. "OH, my God in Heaven, not here. Not here! The Devil followed us here?" she asked her husband as she lifted her hands to cover her face. She got no answer. "Are you sure? Maybe it's just swollen."

"No, it's guevedoche!" Brother Caslin screamed at her. "Take it outside."

Sarah didn't have to fight Janie for the baby. It was all so sudden. She cut the cord, pulled the baby from between its mother's legs, wrapped it quickly, and ran out the back door. Bick raced behind her, pulled her back to the ground, and took the baby.

Janie was crying and screaming her husband's name. She raised herself from the bed and ran out the back door, but Brother Caslin pulled her back in and knocked her down on her back.

"Take this demon and kill it, Bick Cole, or your soul will burn in Hell."

"No. No!" Bick screamed. "It's all in your head because you've seen it before. My baby's not that way."

Brother Caslin hit Bick in the jaw hard. He fell to the ground, and Sarah grabbed the baby out of his arms, running toward the barn as her husband held Bick down.

CHAPTER FOUR

Viola opened her eyes and saw the stars. She rolled over on her side and began to throw up. The pain in her back was unbearable.

"Janie, help!"

She had no idea how far she had gotten before she'd fallen. She must have fainted. The pains were constant, and she couldn't move. Suddenly, she felt the urge to push.

She felt something gush out, but she couldn't see. Viola threw up again and everything went black. She awoke to the pain again. It brought her up off her back, and when she pushed hard, she saw a head. Everything went black again.

When she opened her eyes once again, she thought she was dead. There was something between her legs. It felt cold. Through the pain, she rose up and saw her baby there. She pulled it to her chest, but it was so cold. She felt the urge to push again and did. After a big gush of blood and afterbirth, there it was. All of it. She began to shake the baby.

"No, God. No, God, please no," she said quietly, her tears falling on her newborn baby.

"HELP! God help us!" she screamed out over the field. She could see lights far away, so she gathered her strength and the baby and began walking. She was bent over in pain, and at times crawled on her knees. The closer she got to Bick and Janie's barn, the faster she crawled. Once she reached the fence, she put the baby over first and then crawled up behind.

"Bick!" she screamed when she saw him running out of the house toward the barn. He was chasing Sarah, who had something in her arms. In exhaustion, Viola shouted once more for help. She felt a rush of relief as she pulled herself up behind the barn, until she saw Bick rolling around on the ground fighting with someone. She knew something was wrong.

"Bick! Bick, bring my baby back!" Janie's voice floated out of the house into the stifling night.

Viola looked up toward the house and saw a shadow of someone in the doorway—someone struggling to get up off the floor. *Janie. Oh, my God, that's her baby,* Viola thought.

The baby was crying out, now unwrapped and lying there with Sarah holding a tobacco knife high over it. She spoke gibberish for a moment and then stopped suddenly. Viola froze and tried to make no noise. Her eyes were locked on Sarah's as if she were trying to will her to stop. Sarah's face was vacant, her eyes were filled with nothing, like a body with nothing inside. She brought the knife down over the baby's little chest and then looked slowly in Viola's direction. Viola shivered as the old woman stared at her deeply for what seemed an hour. Sarah then slowly moved her eyes back toward the baby and dropped the knife on the barn floor, then ran out of the barn.

"I'm leaving. The deed is done," she said to Brother Caslin. He followed quickly behind her.

"This family is cursed. Satan is here!" was the last thing he screamed as he and his wife ran to their truck.

Viola watched the headlights fade away. She could still hear Janie screaming and the baby crying. Bick held Janie as he cried, too. Viola looked down at her own baby, blue and cold now, and fell to the ground, sobbing over her child. Janie's baby cried and cried.

"God, forgive me for what I'm about to do," Viola said into the night sky.

She crawled across the barn floor, grabbed the edge of the shelf and lifted herself up. When she put her hand under the baby's head, it felt warm and soft. Just touching the child filled her with a sensation she'd never felt before. It was as if she'd touched an angel—an angel who was not supposed to be left here with these people.

Bick was coming back to the barn now; Viola had to hurry. She wrapped both babies in her skirt and ran as fast as she could toward the fence. She got as far away as she could and hid in a bush. She could see Janie and Bick through the barn's back window.

Bick helped his wife to the barn. They looked around and found nothing. No baby. It was gone. There was nothing.

"Where…" Bick said, and as quickly as he could get the words out, Janie had fallen to the ground.

CHAPTER FIVE

A baby's cry forced Viola to open her eyes. There it was, pink, soft, and perfect. A child—Janie's child—wrapped in a sheet from the extra bedroom. Viola held the baby close as she began to cry again.

"I don't know what happened at your house last night, little one, but I do know your mamma loves you, and I love you. Not to worry."

She couldn't get the image of her dead baby out of her mind, the sounds of Janie screaming and Sarah with the tobacco knife. What had gone so wrong? Had they all gone mad? What if Bick found out she'd taken the baby? What if Brother Caslin or even Janie had seen her out there by the barn?

Viola convinced herself that her secret was safe. She would keep it safe until it was safe—safe for Janie and safe for the baby.

"Oh, Janie," she muttered.

She sat up in the bed and began breast-feeding the child. In the mirror across the room, she saw herself—dirty, bloody. Mud was caked in her hair and made it hang long and heavy across her shoulders. Her thoughts demanded an answer for what she had seen the night before. Her own baby was dead and lifeless, waiting in the dresser drawer for a burial, as she allowed someone else's child to take its milk.

As the baby began to drift back off to sleep, Viola tried to lean her head over and close her eyes, but flashes from the barn kept coming to her. Sounds that weren't real startled her so that she would jump and wake the baby.

She was in so much pain; it hurt to move at all. There had been so much blood. She needed something to drink. Her mouth was dry, and her head felt like a boulder had hit her. Her face was black as soot, and pale streaks were only present where tears had eroded the grime. Her dress was bloody from top to bottom, and her womb was still gushing from the birth. She had gathered some linens from the night before and took them to bed with her. They were blood soaked and smelled of death. She knew she was going to die, to bleed to death. The dizziness would overtake her often. She just kept closing her eyes until it passed.

"Please, Lord Jesus, help me pass on through this day of blackness."

This was the beginning of a prayer she'd heard her mother pray a thousand times. *Even in the darkest of times, the Lord is there watching and making sure the light will return,* she'd say to Viola.

Viola couldn't imagine a blacker day than this. Her faith was waning as she looked outside. The sky was gray and disappointed, as though it were grieving right along with her. The storm would come, she knew. Maybe not today, but soon.

She took the sheet from her bed and wrapped it around the sleeping baby with both diagonal ends hanging off each side. She then tied the sheet around her waist with the baby upright, its head between her breasts, and walked over to the chifforobe where her dead baby lay wrapped in a bloodstained cloth.

She grabbed up the cold, damp bundle from the drawer and held it close, never looking underneath the garment. The thought of seeing what was rolled up in there was too terrifying. She didn't want to see it; she just wanted to forget.

As she shuffled through the house to the back door, she saw the baby's crib, new, never slept in. Her baby was dead. Through the kitchen window, she could see the fields, mist rising off the grain.

Viola had looked through that window for hours upon hours every day since she and Den had moved in. So many days in the field, walking, running, and playing. Viola closed her eyes and imagined it was spring again and the yellow wildflowers dotted the green blanket of earth and grain. When she and Den had married, they'd spent a special evening in that field, catching fireflies just before the sun went completely behind the trees.

Viola was shaken suddenly. "Den! Oh, my God. What will he say?"

If she explained to him that those mad people tried to kill the baby, he'd understand. But it was so unbelievable, so made-up sounding. She was sure he'd believe her. She was sure he'd do the right thing, but she didn't want to ask him to do that.

I can't tell him. This is my burden, mine and the Lord's. There's no sense bringing Den into the darkness of a lie that can't ever be told to anyone else. I'll carry it. I'll carry this child as my own until it's safe from Bick and those crazy people at that church, then I will help Janie raise it.

Viola caught her breath and opened the back door to walk toward the smokehouse. There, she gathered supplies—a hoe, a shovel, some rags, and a rake—and then walked out toward the field, heading toward the tree line and into the woods. It was already beginning to heat up. The mosquitoes buzzed around her ears and bit her uncovered neck. She covered the baby's head completely so the bugs couldn't bite the newborn.

The field smelled musty, and there was no breeze. The grain was as still as the trees. Except for the sound of her own steps and the grass scraping against her shoes, the earth was silent as if waiting for this act to pass so it could carry on once again.

Viola walked for at least half an hour into the woods, glancing from time to time—but only for a moment—at the bundle of cloth she carried. She still couldn't bear to look at what was inside.

She sat down to rest, placing the dead baby next to her on the ground. A small arm poked out from a gap in the cloth bundle. She gasped and quickly rolled the child back up into her arms, then headed back out on the path she made as she traveled. This time, she walked faster. Each part of the woods looked just like the rest. One more hill, one more ditch, and Viola saw the spot.

Just below the hill, as she stood in a rain-filled stream, she could see the Heavens in a perfect circle above the treetops. From that spot, her face straight up, she could see the gray sky.

The baby began to cry, and Viola's breasts began to leak. She set down her tools and her dead baby beside them and untied the sheet from around her waist so she could hold the baby to her breast. Her eyes fixed on the child as it sucked nourishment from her body. She couldn't stop staring at its face.

Once fed, the child settled back into its sheet sack. Viola tied the baby up tightly, cradled next to her body, and crawled up the hill to the final resting spot.

*

Viola gathered as many rough stones as she could find and encircled the child's grave with them. Her hands were blistered from digging with the shovel. The dirt was firm and packed hard.

"Please, Lord Jesus, take care of this child. Bless him with your all-encompassing love. Forgive me, Lord. You know why."

Viola's last prayer for her dead baby gave her little comfort as she headed home under the canopy of the woods. The Heavens were overcast. She had no idea what time it was. All she knew was that by tomorrow, it would be time to move on. No more grieving.

Viola was an old hand at pretend. She pretended her mother was still alive and just living far away. She'd sit and wonder what her mother would be doing at certain times of the day. She still heard her father's hearty laugh sometimes before she drifted off to sleep. The heavy memories of their deaths were packed away tightly in her mind, in the same place she would pack the memory of this day.

She was relieved to see the clearing ahead. "And this too shall pass," she said to the child still wrapped up close to her chest.

At home, Viola immediately began to unwrap the baby. Its eyes were open. It would spit out crackly cries from time to time. She wiped the baby clean and then began to undress from her muddy, blood-stained clothes. Viola washed until her skin was raw, and then she and the baby slept.

CHAPTER SIX

Janie had been up all night fighting Bick. She had beaten him until her fists were sore. Her eyes were swollen. She'd been in the barn turning over tables and rooting in the hay and dirt. There was no baby.

"Janie," Bick said softly. "I'm sorry."

"Why did they take our baby? Why?" Janie sobbed.

"They didn't take our baby. It's just gone. I saw them leave, and they didn't have our baby. I thought Sarah was going to kill her, but there was nothing out there. You saw, too."

"That word, *Guevedoche* … Janie, I've heard him talk about that. It's bad. It's bad, Janie."

"What is it, Bick? What's wrong with our baby?"

Bick looked down at the floor. "Janie, you don't want to know. It's evil. The baby's deformed."

"Did you see it?"

"No, but Caslin said it was… Something's wrong with it," Bick said. "Maybe the Lord just took it up, away from us. Maybe he just took it."

35

"Viola tried to tell me to get a doctor, and I told you. You didn't listen, Bick. You didn't listen," Janie said, sobbing softly.

"Viola doesn't have anything to do with us or our baby. It's none of her business what we do. She's a non-believer. You of all people should know that, Janie. That's probably what was wrong with the baby, you being out with her all the time."

"Leave me alone. I'm going back out there," Janie shouted, struggling to get away from her husband.

"Janie, there's nothing there. We've looked and looked."

"You go to Brother Caslin's and get our baby back, Bick Cole. You go!"

"They don't have the baby. Sarah didn't have it. I heard him crying after they left. I can't explain it, but I did."

"Then where is the baby?" Janie sobbed again. "Go get Viola. She'll help us."

"No," Bick scolded her. "It's none of anyone else's concern. Janie, I swear to God if you ever see that woman again, I'll kill you. You are never, never, *never*"—he yelled as he punched the ground to emphasize—"to tell anyone what happened here."

Janie knew he meant what he said. Her baby was gone, and now she could never see Viola again. Now that there was no baby inside her, Bick would show no mercy if she crossed him.

She hung her head with her face in her hands. She wanted to cry more but couldn't. The baby had been there and then gone just as quickly. All that pain, all that time, all that love for nothing. Her baby was deformed and now gone, probably dead.

Janie wanted someone to blame—Bick, Brother Caslin, God—anyone. She knew that Brother Caslin had delivered hundreds of babies. Why her? Why did this have to happen to her baby? She hated Brother Caslin and Sarah, too. She'd never seen them act so strangely. It was as if they had both gone mad.

Janie thought about the stories Brother Caslin had told Bick. He had been in medical school and traveled on a Christian Mission trip with some Methodists from up north. Sarah had gone with him as his nurse. The group included eight medical students and six nurses. When Caslin returned to the states, he'd had lots of stories for the men in his congregation about the savages that lived in the small villages. The word Guevedoche had come up a couple of times. Brother Caslin's job was to minister for the Lord and treat illnesses. Some of the stories were interesting, some frightening. Brother Caslin had delivered babies during his time there. He'd called them mud babies because of their color. He'd talked about the people there, mostly ignorant, poor, and dirty. Bick had told Janie time and again about how she shouldn't worry. He'd said Brother Caslin had saved many of the women who'd had breech babies. He'd told Bick he had saved plenty babies and then some— even some that shouldn't have been saved.

Brother Caslin had told Bick that the reason for so much misery at birth in New Guinea was that the people were ignorant to the teachings of Jesus. He said it would continue to be that way until the country was Christianized. Brother Caslin and his wife Sarah had spent several years there. Both of them had been Methodists at the time. They'd converted because the Methodists were too accepting of things outside the Bible. Brother Caslin believed the Bible and knew it line for line, word for word. He also believed that to help someone who wasn't following Christ was acceptable, but once someone had been shown the way and chose not to follow, his back was turned.

Only a handful of foreigners had converted to Christianity during his time in the overseas villages, and when they did covert, it wasn't to the religion that Brother Caslin held dear. It was a variation—a little of this and a little of that with Jesus crammed in the middle. Sarah wouldn't talk about her time with Brother Caslin overseas at all. Each time he'd bring it up, she'd walk away or change the subject. She had helped Brother Caslin deliver all those muddy babies. She was a midwife and even took some of the newborn savages to her own breast just to keep them alive. Brother Caslin had told Bick the reason they'd left, the reason they'd come to their church, the reason he'd left medical school.

Sarah had been attacked by someone in the village one night. She had been a friend to this village woman, teaching her how to garden and how to take care of her ailing mother and father. Late one night, the woman had attacked her like a man would try to attack a woman. That was about all Brother Caslin would say about why they'd left, other than that the village had been taken over by Satan and wasn't worth saving. He compared it to Sodom and Gomorra and said he and Sarah had turned and left, never looking back.

Janie tried to recall every detail of everything she'd heard about that word, but nothing made sense. She still couldn't figure why they thought her baby was evil like the muddy babies.

She trusted that Bick knew what he was doing. The rest of the young mothers in the congregation had had Brother Caslin deliver their babies. She had to trust that.

"I'm sorry," Janie whispered as she walked up behind Bick, who sat at the kitchen table. "It's not your fault. It's my fault."

Bick had thought long and hard about what they were going to say happened to the baby. It had to be stillborn. They would have to dig a grave; they would have to have a service. They agreed.

He turned to her with tears in his eyes and hugged her tightly around the waist. He sobbed into her belly as she stroked his hair.

"I love you, Janie." He stood up. "I'm sorry." He was always sorry. Janie knew he had a good heart but a hot temper. Still, she loved him. He put his arm around her back and led her into the bedroom. "Let's get you back to bed."

While Janie slept, Bick worried. He stepped out the back door, holding the screen so it wouldn't slam and wake Janie. The sky was gray with sorrow, and the air was already hot. Rain was coming, maybe even a storm. He knew what he had to do. He was going to see Brother Caslin. He went inside and looked at Janie lying there sleeping.

He didn't know what he was going to say to Brother Caslin once he got to the parsonage, but he knew he wanted some answers. He had never questioned his authority before, but today he was certain that was the only way to get answers.

There was so much going through his mind. He looked down at the floorboard of the truck several times at his rifle. He had no intention of killing his pastor, but if he couldn't get the answers he wanted, he would scare him a bit. Maybe, he thought, he could go get Joe John to help him.

Bick shook his head. He knew that was a bad idea. This was something he had to take care of on his own. No one, not even their friends, could know about this. He could still hear the baby crying and Janie screaming at him. The words that Sarah had spoken were ghostly. She had said them in a voice that Bick had never heard come out of her before, deep and raspy. He remembered her trembling with fear and crying to God for help.

Bick drove around the church house to the back and down the gravel and dirt road to Brother Caslin's parsonage. He and Sarah had lived there for years, and Sarah's garden was the envy of the entire female congregation. She worked in that garden from daylight until dark every day, except on the days there was church or someone sick to visit.

As Bick neared the house, he could see the front door open and the screen door flapping wildly in the wind.

He walked up on the porch, where a box with clothes hung out the side. He knocked on the door frame.

"Brother Caslin? You in there? Sarah?"

No sound came from inside the house. He stepped in. Various items were strewn about the house, but other than that, everything was still where it had always been. The back door was wide open just like the front. Bick cautiously entered the bedroom. All the sheets and blankets had been ripped from the bed, and the closet was empty.

He ran into the kitchen and opened the cabinets. Most of the dishes were still there, but some had been taken. Ground coffee was spilled out onto the cabinet, but there was no bag of coffee. The Caslins were gone. They had left in the night.

Bick sat down on the front porch steps and stared at the back of the church. Just last night they had all been in there together, happy and praising God. Now it was all gone. Bick began to cry and curse God.

"You just leave me here alone to fix all this, you son of a bitch!" Bick cursed the sky. "Always you leave me. *Always.*"

Bick threw rocks at the back of the church and then at Brother Caslin's house. He hurled them until he was too tired to look for any more to throw. He kicked the screen door and pulled it off its hinges, smashed the front windows with a long piece of wood from the now dilapidated door.

Bick hadn't made war with God like this since his brother had died. He trashed the house room by room, smashing out the windows as he went. The louder the glass shattered, the harder he hit the next one. He made his way back into the kitchen, slinging his wooden weapon again and again upon Caslin's home, but he stopped in his tracks when he shattered the glass in the back door.

Finally, Bick stood still. He was breathing hard, and his hands and arms were bloody with scratches and cuts. He reached up to the top of the back door he had just destroyed and pulled down an envelope that was taped there. It was sealed tightly and tied with a small piece of braided string.

His name was printed in dark lead pencil on the outside of the envelope. He opened it slowly.

Please understand this is God's way. You and Janie should not have any more children. Your baby had to die.

Bick read it and then read it again. But he didn't understand. His baby was not dead. It wasn't there at all. Sarah hadn't taken take it. He read the note again, then folded it neatly and placed it back in the envelope as delicately as he could, like it was a page from the Bible itself, then gently put the envelope in his pocket.

Caslin and Sarah hadn't taken the baby. He was sure of it. He had heard it crying even after they'd left. And there was no dead baby left in the barn. For some reason, though, Caslin thought the baby was dead. Bick was certain now. He knew better.

He got back into the truck, drove around the side of the church house, sat there for a moment, and then turned in the opposite direction of home.

He hadn't been to a bootlegger since he and his brother had gone years ago. That was a beating he'd never forget. His father had striped him red like a barber pole, and John, too. He'd seen his father drink plenty of times out in the fields. It was one of those things that a man just can't do without sometimes, he'd say.

*

"Well, looky comes here," Fred said when Bick got out of the truck.

"Are you a-comin' to pray fer me again? It's a little too early in the mornin' for a party."

Bick glared at the old man. Fred had been bootlegging in Rayes County for longer than anyone could remember. He made a pretty good living at it and always drove a nice car.

"Just give me a pint," Bick said flatly.

"Well, ain't that a fine how-do-ya-do. You was just here not three months ago tryin' to pray me into Heaven. You give up I guess, didn'?" Fred said, laughing.

One look at Bick's eyes told Fred he'd better shut up and get the pint.

"Here ya go. Now I'll take those greens you're a-holdin' there."

Bick didn't even count the money. He just handed Fred the bills he had taken from his pocket, took the pint, and walked back to the truck. Once inside, he immediately opened up the drink and took a huge swallow. It burned his throat and all the way down to his stomach and hurt his chest. He began to choke and spit.

"Lawsy day," Fred said as he watched Bick back out of his drive. "I'll be damned."

*

Once Bick was back home, he went inside to check on Janie. He peeked in the bedroom door. She was still sleeping, so he took off walking down the field, trying his best to avoid looking at the barn.

He could see the creek trail in the distance.

As a boy, Bick spent hours at that creek with his older brother, John. After chores on hot days, he and John would cool off by jumping from the tree limbs into the creek. It had only been a little over two years since the day he'd gotten the news of his brother's death. John had just married his sweetheart Virginia, and they had big plans. They were going to open up a general store and go head-to-head with the Canadys. John was going to offer more than just dry goods. Virginia was going to offer material and sell the new sewing machines like in the city.

Bick knew his brother could have made a go of it if he had lived through the mine cave-in. If only he had lived.

As children, the boys would stray away and always end up at the creek. It wasn't too far—only a few hundred yards past the tree line, down a hill, through a thicket, and over a fence. The greenery that lined the creek was furry with different shades of green, from Cedar to Pine and everything in between. The smell of wet rock, moss, and dirt wafted through the shaded area. Bick could breathe deep as he lay at the bank of the creek. Sometimes he and his brother would lie there for hours making up stories about the sky, God, and sometimes even the advertisements in catalogs—women in their undergarments. Every now and then, they'd even bring the catalog with them. They'd talk about all the things they'd buy and all the places they'd go and how a woman's breast would feel to touch.

Bick knew thinking of a woman's breast was wrong and not Christian-like, but he couldn't help it. Even the women at church weren't safe from the boys' wandering minds. Sometimes they'd come home from church and talk about whose were bigger and whose were pointier.

At the creek, they'd spend hours building up dams to hold the water for as long as they could. They would gather rocks—the bigger ones were better to start out with—then they'd use tins, filling them up with fine dirt and pebbles to shore up the dam. As fast as they could build, the water would begin to force its way through the tiniest cracks just as quickly. No matter how long they labored, the water would always win. Bick and John never gave in to complete defeat, as each summer day after chores, they'd begin damming up the creek again.

Bick's mother never worried about the boys until it started to get dark. Bick could still feel the sting of his mamma's switch each time they stayed out too late. After they'd gotten their beating from Mama, she got her beating by Paw. He'd smack her around a little and tell her that the one thing he asked, for everybody to be at the table for dinner, she was too stupid to do. The boys knew it was time to come home when the sun began to get an orange glow. By the time they would get back to the house, it was time for dinner. They only had to see their mama get smacked a couple of times before they made sure to be home on time.

Their father would be there waiting at the table. Bick's father worked the farm from sunup until sundown. Even though he worked all day on the land, the boys never saw him until dinner. He was a strong man, hands roughened by farm and weather. When he sat down to dinner, the lines in his face would be filled with dirt. At times he was almost as black as a coal miner. Bick's mother would bring him a wet washcloth, and he'd wipe it clean before grace.

Today, there were no sounds of laughter at the creek. There was no dam. The water, strong as ever, flowed as it pleased, undisturbed by little hands.

Bick never missed being a boy. He could hardly wait to become a man with a family of his own.

Today, all that had changed. He wanted to go as far back in time as he could imagine. He just wanted to be a boy again. He wanted John to be alive, and he wanted to go home just before sundown to see his father's farm-dirtied face and smell his mother's beans on the stove. Bick sat on a bent-over tree trunk with his eyes closed, breathing the wet air from the creek. He inhaled in as deeply as he could and opened his eyes, lightheaded from the alcohol. He'd almost finished it now.

He cried out to John for a little while and thought long and hard about going to join him.

"Damn you," he said to God as he drunkenly tried to skip a flat pebble down the creek.

On his way back through the woods, it began to thunder, and Bick could see flashes of white light coming over the mountain. Just as he cleared the thicket, it began to rain. He walked fast and then ran back to the house, passing the barn where he'd been the night before. He couldn't help but go toward it. Some of the fence behind the barn had been toppled over. He walked over and started stacking the rails but kept dropping them. Frustrated, he kicked at them and then fell to the ground, lying there in the grass for a minute or two, just looking at the sky with the rain falling on his face. Then he turned his head and saw it.

"Blood?" he said aloud.

There was blood on one of the rails, and there were long strands of black hair woven into the splinters. He pulled the hair out from between the splintered wood and held it up to the sky. It didn't feel like horse's mane. None of the horses had been hurt. Bick looked at the backside of the barn and then over toward the Garlands' farm.

*

When Bick came into the kitchen soaking wet, Janie was sitting at the table, eating a piece of leftover cornbread with a glass of milk.

"I got hungry," she said.

Bick grabbed himself a piece, sat down beside her, and took a drink of her milk.

Janie handed him a towel from the table, and he wiped his wet head with it. "What is that smell? Have you been drinking? *Bick*, you've been drinking. Oh, God help us," she bellowed and began to cry. "Don't you fall to pieces, Bick Cole. Oh, God, please forgive him." She got on her knees and began to pray.

"Oh, stop your bellerin'," Bick slurred. "God makes me sick."

Janie was stunned. "Please don't say that. It's going to be alright. I know, Bick. I know. We're going to have more children. I just know it. Maybe this one wasn't meant to be for us."

"Brother Caslin and Sarah are gone," Bick said, still slurring his words.

"What do you mean gone?"

"Just gone. Left in the night, probably right after they tried to kill our little deformed baby." Bick was half laughing over the situation.

"Where did they go?"

"I don't know, but all their clothes were gone and most of their stuff."

Her husband smelled of alcohol so much that Janie could barely stand the odor.

"Bick, you don't know what you're talking about. You're drunk."

He grabbed Janie by the back of the hair and held her head under his chin.

"Don't you talk back to me, you little whore. I crawl back in those mines every day and you're off flittin' around with that Garland woman. You make me sick. If this is anybody's fault, it's yours."

Bick shoved Janie's face into the wall. With her hair wrapped around his fist, he slammed and slammed, then slung her across the room. Janie's head hit the corner of the cabinet, and she was out.

"I'm going to get my baby back. Not your baby. MINE!"

CHAPTER SEVEN

The sound of the squeaky bedsprings shook Viola. She could feel his breath on her face. She screamed. There he was. She gasped for a breath.

"What's the matter with you?" Den said. "I didn't mean to scare you."

Viola's eyes darted around the room, and once she got her bearings, she exhaled and hugged her husband tight, tears rolling down her face.

"I guess you missed me?" Den asked.

The baby lay next to her. Den pointed and smiled, and she picked the baby up and pushed it into his chest.

"Go ahead," she whispered. "Take her." She was so relieved to see her husband. She was safe now, and so was the baby.

Den's eyes were wide, his hands almost as large as the baby's entire body.

"Here." Viola rose up a little. "Let me help you." She put her hands behind the baby's head, lifting as her husband lifted.

"When?"

"Monday, I think, or maybe it was night before last. I've lost track of time. What day is it?"

"Wednesday. Viola, we have to know when our baby was born."

"I know when she was born. Monday night. Now, you, how did you get home so early?"

"They had another team of men waiting to work, so I let one of them take my place so I could come home."

"You're not going to lose your—"

Den didn't let Viola finish the question. "Don't worry. The worker that took my place is definitely temporary. Stop worrying."

"When did the doc bring you home?"

"Who? Oh yeah, the nurse." Viola was still struggling to gather her thoughts.

"I had the baby here. I haven't been to the doctor yet."

"Oh, God, Viola. Are you okay?"

"Yeah, I'm fine now."

"Can you get up and around?" Den asked.

"Yes. How do you think I've been taking care of this baby?"

"I can't believe I'm a father. I left and then came home a daddy," Den said, looking at the child. "Is it a boy?"

"Umm, nope," Viola said.

"You mean we've got a little split-tail?" Den held the baby's hand in his fingers.

"I'm afraid so."

"I guess I'd better get the shotgun ready for all those little boys bound to be hangin' around," Den said laughing. "I'm going to sit here with this little doodlebug, and you go get dressed. We're going to the doctor."

"I don't need to go. It's all over now," Viola said.

"Yes, we have to go. And besides, I've already paid him to look after you. He's going to earn his money."

Viola was scared. What if the doctor could tell that she'd had a stillbirth? What if he could tell that this baby wasn't hers?

She stood in the hallway, watching Den with the baby. They looked so perfect together. The whole ordeal wasn't at all the way she had expected. Her own baby dead, bringing Janie's baby to her home, lying to her husband. She had to tell—just not now. She had to see Janie. She would understand why she'd done it.

This baby was not hers. She had saved it from certain death, but that didn't give her the right to call it her own. Viola held her hand to her mouth as the tears began to flow once more. A whimper would burst its way out every few seconds.

"What's the matter?" Den asked. "You shouldn't be crying. You just had a baby. Aren't you happy?"

"Yes, too happy," Viola said. "These are happy tears. Please, Den, just give me another day to rest, and I'll go to the doctor tomorrow."

"You sure?"

"Yes, please."

"Well, okay. But if you don't feel like going tomorrow, I'm going to get him and bring him here," Den said sternly.

"Okay."

She was relieved. She needed more time to think. She wanted to see Janie, to see how she was. She kept telling herself that the baby was better off without those crazy people at that church. She knew it. But Janie was alone now, and Viola wanted to go to her.

"Den, I'm going to go over to Janie's after I fix something to eat. Can you take me?"

"Sure, but do you think we need to get the baby out yet?"

"No, you bring the baby back with you. I'll only stay a few minutes. I just want to see how she is."

The knock on the screen door broke Den's morning peacefulness.

"Hey, Den. You home?"

It was Sheriff Mills.

"Hey, buddy. What's going on? Am I under arrest?" Den joked.

"No, but we do have some trouble."

Viola panicked. She'd heard the conversation so far. Her knees got week and her legs started to shake. She took the baby into the bedroom nearest the front door so she could hear what was going on.

"Den, it's bad. Real bad."

"What's wrong, Larry?"

"Out at the church—the Pentecostal church. Someone busted into the parsonage there. All the windows were broke out, the doors were torn off the hinges. Brother Casway and his wife were gone. Looked like they moved out in a hurry."

"You mean Brother Caslin?"

"Yeah, Brother Caslin. Anyway, I came down here to get Bick Cole to see if he knew anything. I knocked on his door and no one came. It was open, so I went on in. His wife was lying there bleeding from her head. She's dead, Den. Coroner's already come and got her. Had a big gash right down the side of her temple. She was probably dead as soon as she hit."

"Janie?" Den asked.

"Uh, yeah."

Viola came to her feet and burst out of the bedroom door.

"JANIE?" she screamed in horror. "No!"

Den caught her as she tried to move the sheriff to run out the door.

"She ain't up there," Larry said. "They've took her already."

Viola fell into Den's arms.

"Sorry. I didn't know you folks were that close."

"We're not. Well, I'm not. Viola and Janie got chummy over this summer while I've been gone so much. Just a minute," he said to Sheriff Mills as he led Viola over toward the bedroom. "Get the baby. I think she's crying."

He went back to the front door. "Come on in."

"No, I can't. I just stopped by here to see if either of you had seen or heard from Bick Cole. Nobody can find him. His truck's still up at the house, so I don't guess he's at work."

Viola shivered as she held the baby, her mind churning with the events over the past two days.

"Have you seen or heard from Bick?" Den yelled into the bedroom at Viola.

"No, I haven't," she answered quickly as she wrapped the baby and walked into the front room.

"What do you think's going on?" Den asked.

"Well, I'd say he's hit her one too many times and then one too many times too hard," Larry said as if he'd quoted the line several times that day.

"And the preacher?"

"Well, I've heard things about that church up there. There's no telling what in the hell's happened over there. Maybe they just got a little too much of the spirit. Seriously," Sheriff Mills said. "All kidding aside, they're a strange bunch."

"Yeah," Den said.

"Well, if you see him or hear anything you let me know. Nice little bundle you got there." Larry motioned to the back room where Viola and the baby were.

"Yeah, newest arrival to the Garland clan."

"You folks have a good day," Larry said as he walked out to his patrol car.

"You too, buddy."

"Maybe I'd better stick around for a few more days 'til things settle down here," Den said to Viola when the sheriff was gone.

"Yeah, maybe you'd better," she answered. "S'pose they'll have a funeral for Janie over at the church. We should go down there and find out what the arrangements are."

"No, we're not going anywhere near that place," Den said. "I'll go into town in a little while and talk to the coroner and see where it's going to be."

"I'd like to be there. She was my friend and neighbor."

"We'll see what it's all about. Did you know that Bick beats her?"

"You mean beat her." Viola began to cry.

"Yeah." Den hadn't expected his wife to be so upset. Maybe she was just upset because there'd been a murder. Nevertheless, he felt compelled to offer some kindness about the death. "Maybe we'll go and pay our respects after the crowd has gone?"

"Yeah, that might be best."

"If I go into town, will you be alright here?"

"Yeah, I'll be fine."

"I don't know if I should leave you and the baby here until after they find Bick Cole."

"I wouldn't worry so much." Viola walked back to the kitchen to fix something to eat.

"I keep calling her 'the baby', but are we still set on what we talked about for a girl's name?" Den asked.

"Yes, Doris is her name—after your mother."

CHAPTER EIGHT
Rayes County, Present Day

It was a rare occasion for a job to go as smoothly as this one. The county had sent out bids less than a year before, and already Jim Shanks and his crew were a week into the work. They were optimistic about finishing the excavation before fall so they could move on to the next job.

Jim had spent the last six years with a small crew, trying to find jobs that would keep the four of them afloat financially. It had taken years to find a way into the fiscal court's pocketbook, but now he had it. Jim's brother-in-law had won a seat after years of running for office unsuccessfully. All those years of bailing his sister and her family out of hard times… It was going to pay off.

When the bids came rolling in, Jim was finally taken seriously. His wife Trena had worked on the bid packet for at least three weeks, and Jim had already priced some used equipment for the job. He was just waiting for the answer. It came quickly and pleasantly. Six said yes, and it was unanimous, finally.

Monday mornings weren't so tough anymore with no worries about what wasn't being paid at home. Second notices from bill collectors had become a thing of the past. Trena was happy, the guys were happy, and finally, Jim was on his way to becoming a mover and shaker in Rayes County. But what mattered most was the job and the money.

If only he had just rolled right over that odd-looking stick coming up out of the ground, he might still be working instead of trying to figure out how to stretch the money over another week's worth of salaries and expenses.

He knew it had been too easy, coming this far with no problems at all.

It was the toes that had caught his eye. He should have been looking the other way, but there it was. Up out of the ground came the foot first and then the leg. It was like something from a 1970s horror film. The crew had started from the back of the property. If they'd started from the front, they'd be almost finished by now. No such luck.

Jim turned off the engine and jumped out of the backhoe. Sure enough, there it was. A complete foot skeleton was hanging on the shovel and attached to it was a complete leg. Nothing came after that, but Jim quickly spotted something that looked like a big rock with hair coming out of it.

He called out on the radio for the rest of the guys to come over ASAP.

"What the hell?" Ronnie asked, giving Jim a disgusted look. "Don't ever do that again. I thought you were hurt or something."

"No, I'm not hurt."

"Well, I can see that now, asshole."

"Look," Jim said pulling his cigarette pack out of his front shirt pocket and pointing his head toward the body. He lit up and took a long, deep draw.

"You smartass," Ronnie said, punching Jim's arm. "Don't we have some work to do?"

"You think I put that there?"

"Yes. Yes, I do, dick wad."

"Seriously, Ronnie, I looked up and there was a damn foot hanging off the bucket."

By that time, the entire crew had arrived, relieved that Jim was all right but in awe of the find.

The five of them kicked the dirt around a little with their boots to try to uncover the rest. Some of it just looked like broken limbs from a tree, but some of it—especially the skull—was identifiable once they knocked the dirt off.

After a while, they decided it would be best to leave it alone. It was break time by then anyway. Each found a sitting spot close to Jim and in clear view of the body.

"What the hell are we supposed to do now?" Ronnie asked.

"I don't know yet," Jim said. "If we call the police, there'll be no work today and probably not for another week."

"I wonder if there are more," said Ronnie.

"God, who knows?" said Jim. "It would just figure that it would be on our job."

"I think it's kinda cool."

Jim shook his head. "It ain't cool, Ronnie. This definitely ain't cool."

Jim pulled his cell phone out of his pocket and called his brother-in-law.

"Don, we've got a problem up here."

"You boys might as well go home for the day," Sheriff Rosen said to the crew. "We're waiting for the doc. She's in Frankfort. It'll take her a while to get here. In the meantime, we're going to look around a little bit."

The traffic had started to slow a bit on the highway as the looky-loos caught glimpses of the bright yellow police tape and the patrol cars lining the shoulder of the road. Yellow tape wrapped clear around Jim's backhoe and over the entire backside of the property. Reporters from the only newspaper left in Rayes County, leaped from their cars, cameras in tow. Rosen knew others would follow and, if he was lucky, TV and radio, too. He walked about a hundred feet from the site to try to stop them, although he did enjoy the attention.

Rosen had been sheriff for the last four terms, almost twenty years now. He didn't especially like the press anymore, but he knew he needed them. For that reason, he tolerated them at his crime scene.

Newspapers were in high demand the following day. Almost everyone in Rayes County had one.

Skeletal remains uncovered at spec building site

By Royce Hollin

A crew working at the site for the proposed manufacturing spec building in Rayes County uncovered an entire skeleton during routine excavation of the property.

Police say they do not know the identity of the body or how it got there.

Dr. Elly Burns, forensic anthropologist for the state forensics lab, arrived yesterday afternoon and began gathering evidence from the backhoe that had uncovered the body, as well as from the skeleton itself.

According to Rayes County Sheriff Buck Rosen, the excavation crew alerted fiscal court member Don Bowling after the body was discovered. Bowling called Rosen. When police arrived, they saw the skeleton and immediately called in Burns.

"The body appears to have been here quite a while—a long, long while," Rosen said. "We're going to let the doc (Burns) look things over and see if she can tell us anything."

In the meantime, Rosen said the property would be guarded and not accessible to anyone other than official law enforcement.

Rosen said law enforcement does not believe there are other bodies on the property, but there will be further investigation to alleviate any doubt.

The property, located on Hwy. 80, is county owned. The Rayes County Fiscal Court purchased the property a decade ago. County officials received grants to develop the site for a proposed manufacturing facility that will create 200 jobs once completed.

Rosen said the recent discovery will halt the project "as long as it takes" until police have the evidence they need to conduct a thorough investigation.

Rosen asks that anyone having information about the body to call 555-3728.

Jim and Trena read the newspaper story again. Jim's recently purchased backhoe was right there on the front page of the paper. There it was with the yellow police tape still attached.

"Damn," he said.

CHAPTER NINE

The smell of summer always came through the screen door early in the morning. Maggie would be up by six every day as soon as her eyes opened, with the sun shining through her grandmother's sheer curtains. The rollaway beds that Mamaw had pushed together for Maggie and Denie had parted ways during the night. There were always pillows and covers to pull out from between them before the adventures could start.

The scent of salty bacon and coffee ghosted its way through the house, and as Maggie entered the kitchen, there she was, Mamaw Garland, hair put up neatly in exactly three rolls. Two small ones side by side just above her forehead and one big one in the back. Just like every other morning at Mamaw's house, pans clattered, and the squeak of the oven door meant breakfast couldn't be far away.

"Can I make little biscuits?" Maggie asked her grandmother as she did every morning. Sometimes the answer would be yes and sometimes no. She never knew why some mornings were different than others.

"Yeah, I reckon," Mamaw said, handing over the kneading bowl across the speckled gold and white tabletop.

Maggie kneaded the dough with her little hands just like she'd watched her grandmother do a hundred times before, even though

Mamaw had already folded it over at least fifty times that morning. When Maggie's hands grew tired, she began making balls the size of walnuts to place on the shiny pan. After all of them were placed neatly, three fingers apart—just like Mamaw had taught her—Maggie pressed the side of her fist ever so lightly against each dough ball to flatten them just a bit. Mamaw put the little biscuits in the oven, wiped up the table and went back to her standard position at the sink, washing dishes, pausing to drink from her coffee cup and stare out into the field. Before long, Denie was up, too, stumbling her way to the kitchen.

"Can I make little biscuits?" she asked.

"We already did," Mamaw said and then curled her bottom lip over her top one. "But I guess you want some of your own."

"Yeah," Denie said in a squeaky voice, about to cry.

Mamaw grabbed up the stainless-steel bowl she had just washed and in a minute or two had Denie making her own little biscuits.

"Get in here, Old Man!" Mamaw yelled through the house.

"Den?" she yelled again, this time leaning out through the kitchen door.

Before long, Papaw came to the table. It was always Den or Old Man. Denie and Maggie would find out later their papaw's name was actually Dennis.

He'd been out on the porch swing inspecting the homemade shotgun shells he'd made the night before. He had a machine in his bedroom that Denie and Maggie weren't allowed to touch. It had a cylinder to pour in the tiny pellets and a lever that crinkled the top of the plastic shell into a perfect round pie that looked like all the pieces were cut for exact servings.

The Old Man's hobby was shooting clay pigeons and the occasional squirrel or rabbit. Clay pigeon shooting day was full of excitement. "PULL!" Papaw would shout. His partner would yank the lever, and then in a couple of seconds a shot would ring out. Up against the sky, the yellow and black pigeons would splinter and fall to the ground. Afterward, Maggie and Denie would go out and pick up the ones he missed to be used again. The two of them would snicker and giggle as they picked them up. They called them the shit pigeons, because every time the Old Man would miss one, he'd yell that word almost as loudly as he yelled, "PULL!" When they'd find one, the race was on to see who could say the dirty word the fastest. If Mamaw knew, she'd be pretty mad. But out in the weeds, they were free to say whatever they wanted, almost as loudly as they wanted.

Clay pigeon shooting was an evening event. Rabbits and squirrels, however, were a morning adventure. Denie and Maggie knew that if Papaw wasn't at breakfast and Mamaw wasn't hollering for him, they could expect to watch him skin some sort of a rodent out by the well pump by at least ten.

Maggie and Denie would watch the skins come off the squirrels and rabbits so they could be overly dramatic about how gross it was. Papaw would sometimes sling pieces of rodent their way to make the girls squeal and run away, only they'd come back and watch even closer. Sometimes he'd just act like he was throwing a piece at the girls to hear them scream and run away. If Denie and Maggie screamed too loud or too many times, Mamaw would come out and yell at him, "Den, let them girls alone!"

He'd use pliers to pull the skin away from the dead animal. Most times it was a "clean pull," as he called it, and the skin would come off just like a banana peel. Mamaw never wanted the girls to watch. She said it would give them nightmares.

*

At the breakfast table, Papaw had his own special coffee cup. It looked more like a bowl with a handle to Denie and Maggie. He took the first drink with a light slurp so as not to burn his mouth.

Mamaw grabbed a saucer out of the cabinet, smeared some butter on a biscuit, and sliced a tomato to go with it, just like every other morning. "Is it good?" she asked with a mouthful.

"Uh, huh," Maggie said. Denie nodded her head.

The girls ate their little biscuits and asked Mamaw to choose whose biscuits looked better. It was always the same: no clear-cut winner.

"Well, Denie, yours look a little browner than Maggie's. But some people like their biscuits a little brown. And I guess that's the fault of that old oven."

After breakfast, the girls headed toward the front of the house and out the screen door, letting it slam behind them.

Maggie sat on the porch swing to put on her shoes while Denie sat waiting on the top step. Mamaw sat outside on her white wooden porch chair, comfortable for a moment on the cushions she'd made years before. The fog hadn't lifted from the hay field across the fence quite yet. Maggie could barely see the seeded tips on the grain blowing slightly in the wind as she tied her shoe. The air was cool, breezy, and smelled like Mamaw's dresses after she'd taken them off the clothesline.

"Do you girls want to chalk on the board?" Mamaw asked.

"We don't have any chalk," Denie said. "We used it all."

Mamaw eased her hand into her apron pocket and plopped a brand new box of chalk on the arm of her chair. That red and white package told the girls that a new day of chalking had arrived. Nothing with a surface was safe, least of all the big black board in the garage. The huge piece of black slate had been there ever since Maggie could remember. She and Denie played hangman, connect the dots, tic tac toe, and had even once made an almost exact replica of Pat Sajak's big wheel. The two of them would take turns at being Vanna White. They would sing a song and peck a stick around the chalk-drawn wheel, one peck for each word, until the last word was sung. The song of choice was usually a remake with the words changed.

"The magic wheel goes round and round, it may never touch the ground. If you're the one to hold it last, I fear for you the game is past. You are *it!*"

On the last word, the prize was there for the taking if the letter guessed was part of the puzzle.

The imaginary prizes were sometimes worth hundreds and sometimes even millions. On special bonus rounds, the prize was a new car or a trip to some exotic place. Either way, they always won.

Mamaw stayed inside watching her stories, "Sands through the hourglass." Sometimes she'd be crying for no reason, sitting there in her chair. The stories must have been sad. Now and then, Denie and Maggie could hear the screen door screech and see her emerge from the house to weed the tomato plants, pluck a few tomatoes, or sweep the walk.

The girls romped outside or in the garage all day until they heard their friend Lucy come out the edge of her yard and yell.

Lucy was Mamaw's neighbor and, as luck would have it, exactly a year older than Maggie and a year younger than Denie. They were the perfect trio. Lucy's family owned a dairy farm, and Lucy would work in the mornings milking cows, haying the horses, and cleaning the stalls. When she was finished with her work, she'd come over to play.

Breakfast, lunch, and dinner (with a Pepsi split between the three of them for each meal), and kickball, Badminton, and foot races filled the days of summer until Denie and Maggie's parents returned to pick them up just before school began.

The three of them would play until it was too dark to see or until Rosetta, Lucy's mom, would come to the edge of her yard and yell for her daughter to come home.

Denie and Maggie would drag themselves away from the day and go inside. There awaited some potato chips or a doughnut. Mamaw would already have the snack waiting.

Bath time gave the girls a last chance to fight before bed about whom Lucy liked more. This was a nightly occurrence, as sure as the little biscuits and the chalk.

"Don't you girls splash around in there and get my linoleum wet," Mamaw would peep in and say. Denie and Maggie always splashed and got the floor wet, and Mamaw always cleaned it up afterwards.

Bedtime was the only time the girls ever saw their mamaw with her hair long. Black and shiny, with just an edge of gray around the face, her hair hung even on the bed as she sat straight up. She'd pull down her buns and brush it just before bed. Maggie had asked her a million times why she didn't wear it down all the time.

"I don't want all this mess hangin' around in my face all day," Mamaw would always say.

The girls would crawl into their pushed-together beds as Mamaw tucked the handmade quilts around their feet, then she'd sit on the edge of the bed, and they'd talk.

The walls were empty with the exception of one quilt that belonged to Mamaw's own mother, Denie and Maggie's great grandmother. She died before they were born, but Mamaw told them stories about her sometimes. Mamaw had made it. The colors were vivid and rich. She would stare at it sometimes when she was in the room with the girls.

"When are you going to make my quilt, Mamaw?" Denie asked. "Do I have enough colors yet?"

"No, Denie, still not enough."

"Why not?"

Everyone in the family talked about Mamaw's quilts. They'd say she was an artist. Denie was impatient. She'd asked for her quilt every summer since Maggie could remember. She wanted pink flowers in a grassy field with white clouds and a rainbow.

"We don't know enough about you yet to come up with a whole quilt," Mamaw said. "If we stitch it now, you might only have three colors. If we wait, we can use all the colors."

"Why?" Denie asked.

"I'm going to be watching you while you grow and when you have enough colors, you'll get your quilt."

"When will that be?" Denie begged for an answer.

"When your reds and greens and blues start to make purple and turquoise and orange. What if I make your quilt pink and flowery and you turn out to be a rodeo clown, or an airplane pilot, or an elf for Santa Claus?" Mamaw laughed. "I'd have to re-stitch it. One quilt per customer and only one. When the quilt is finished, it will tell the story of you, and your story is just too short. It wouldn't even keep your feet warm. Speaking of stories, what'll it be tonight, scary or sweet?"

When Mamaw began to tell her stories, it was always like she was offering candy; and in one magic moment could create the hard crunchy kind or make it soft and chewy like caramel.

She had made up hundreds of stories for Maggie and Denie and re-told the classics with a little extra flair a hundred times, too. Her stories were so full of detail, the girls could feel the heat from her words about a hot summer's day. They could feel the weight of catching a magical eighty-pound Catfish that could grant three wishes. They could sometimes even taste the sweet, cold ice cream at the social where Prince Toby of the Mountain first laid eyes on the love of his life, Princess Ruth of the Valley. They were all made-up characters, of course, but very, very real to Denie and Maggie.

*

All through the school year, Maggie and Denie looked forward to summer vacation and spending it at Mamaw's house, three hours away from a home not quite so inviting.

Their parents mostly fought. Sometimes they would hit each other. Nadine, their mom, drank a lot and spent a lot of time over at Mrs. West's house during the day, while Edward, the girls' father was at work. In the mornings, their mother would drive to the liquor store after their dad had left. Then it was on to the neighbor's house. Denie and Maggie played more in Mrs. West's back yard than they did in their own. It wasn't much fun. She didn't have any children. There were plenty of kids in the subdivision, just none at Mrs. West's house.

Mrs. West lived across the street and grew roses red as blood and smooth as silk. They were so tempting and beautiful with their perfume-like smell that Maggie had picked some of them once for her mother. Big mistake. Maggie's mother promptly spanked her as she took them into the house. She had to apologize to Mrs. West.

Through her tears, the word *sorry* was barely audible, but Mrs. West accepted graciously, patted Maggie on the head, and sent her back out to play.

When the girls would come in for a snack, they would break through the haze of cigarette smoke and make their way to the refrigerator for some bologna. The ever-present clink of ice cubes against the glasses could be heard as the girls wolfed down their lunch. Then it was back out to play.

When it was almost time for Mrs. West's husband to come home, the girls and their mother crossed the street.

It was time for Edward to come home, for the yelling to start, and for the worry to settle in for the night.

"Why are these dishes still here?" Edward yelled.

"Because they are," Nadine said dryly.

"There's no supper, the girls aren't fed... What in the goddamned hell do you do all day?!" Edward screamed.

The girls' father made up curse words and strung some together which were never meant to belong in the same sentence. Nadine would follow suit.

"You've been over at her house again, haven't you?" Edward said through clenched teeth, grabbing Nadine by the hair, pulling her head back as she was looking in the refrigerator for something to throw on the table.

Denie and Maggie ran to their room. After the yelling stopped, they came out. Edward was sitting on the couch with his head in his hands, and their mother was in the bathroom.

Denie went over to her father and sat down next to him, putting her small arm across his back.

"What's wrong, Daddy?" she asked.

"Nothing," Edward said in a shaky but loud, stern voice. "Now, go to bed."

Denie ran crying back to the bedroom with Maggie close behind.

Every day was mostly like the rest. Denie and Maggie would stay in their room. Denie would play while Maggie would pray to God.

"Please, God, don't let Mommy die," she'd say over and over. "In Jesus' name I pray."

Maggie's grandmother always told her to say, "In Jesus' name I pray," after every prayer. She told Maggie that if she prayed without using Jesus' name, he might think she was praying to another God and he might not listen. Maggie never really understood the difference between God and Jesus. Once she saw an army of men on the TV news. They were all dressed in green with red stripes on their shoulders. When she heard their feet hitting the ground in time together, it made a noise like drums, and when she saw the guns they carried, it scared her. They looked so serious. She envisioned God as an army like this one, not one man. She thought there had to be a lot of him to take care of the whole world.

CHAPTER TEN

The nurse startled Maggie when she came into the room and bumped against the chair.

"I'm sorry, did I wake you up?"

"No, that's okay."

"How is she today?"

"She's been sleeping since I got here," Maggie whispered. "I tried to be quiet and let her rest. I was just sitting here resting, myself."

Maggie got up from her chair, draped her coat over her arm, and picked up her purse. "I'll just come back later on in the week."

"Now, are you her granddaughter?"

"Yes."

"I thought so. She talks about you and your sister. Uh, Dana is it?"

"No, it's Denie."

"Yeah, she talks about the two of you all the time."

"We don't come as often as we should." Maggie always felt she had to make excuses for her absence, and Denie's, too.

"You should stay and visit awhile. I'll go grab you some coffee."

"No, I think I'll just come back some other time."

"I'm awake now," Mamaw said. "Why didn't you wake me up? I can sleep anytime I want to. I don't ever get to see you."

Maggie put her things down and went over to her grandmother's bed.

Mamaw had been in the nursing home for almost four years now. The arthritis in her hips and legs had her bedfast. Maggie had gone there to see her only about a dozen times, and Denie had come even less than that.

"Where've you been?"

"I've been working and taking care of the house. Just busy," Maggie lied. She hadn't worked in over a month.

"I know, honey." Mamaw pushed her pillow down around her back to sit up and poked the button on her remote-controlled bed for a lift. It always amazed Maggie how unafraid her grandmother was of technology. From a remote-controlled TV to a microwave and now a remote-controlled bed. She just pushed the buttons and went on as if they were just like any other garden tool she'd ever used.

"Everybody's so busy," she said as she adjusted her bed. She always made Maggie feel a little less guilty about not visiting more often. "This whole world is busy, people workin' every day. I don't know how anybody has time to live anymore."

Mamaw's face was flushed pink, and her eyes were still as blue and bright as the afternoon Heavens. Her wrinkles mapped out her face just like always from as far back as Maggie could remember, only deeper now. Her eyes, though... Her eyes always looked so young. When Maggie would see the other patients on her trek down the hall to Mamaw's room, their eyes were different. It was as if their souls weren't even in their bodies anymore. They looked vacant, just wandering, like they'd lost something. But not Mamaw's. Her eyes were always certain, knowing.

"You look good," Maggie said.

"Oh, shush," Mamaw said. "My hair's a mess."

Maggie had to laugh a little at her grandmother. She could always chuck away a compliment like an old pair of nylons, always modest, with never a reason to be. Denie had gotten custody of the old pictures of Mamaw and Papaw. Maggie had looked through them years ago. Back in the day, Mamaw was so tall—almost as tall as Papaw. Her striking black mane and milky blue eyes against her peach skin gave her a starlike quality. Even Elizabeth Taylor couldn't compare.

"I'll be back in a minute to fix your hair, Miss Violee," the nurse said as she closed the door.

Mamaw's name was Viola, but through the years, she came to be known to all as Mamaw or Violee.

"Shew," she said, brushing her hair away from her face. "How long have you been here?"

"Not long," Maggie lied again. She'd been sitting in the chair facing the window for at least an hour.

"I wish you would've woken me up. It's almost time for Doris to come. It's Sunday ain't it?"

"Yeah."

Maggie wished she had left while Mamaw had been asleep. She didn't want to see her Aunt Doris, and had she known her auntie was coming, Maggie wouldn't be there. But now she was stuck. She couldn't leave without Mamaw knowing why.

Maggie hadn't seen Doris much since her mother's funeral, only in passing at the market or in town. She had no desire to see her again. Doris, who Maggie and Denie liked to refer to as The Ice Queen, had no more than stepped out of the car at Nadine's funeral before she started in. It began with an invite to dinner after the funeral. She kept pushing with the lies. She said she'd missed them and would love to spend some time with them. Maggie and Denie knew better. They also knew that was the last thing their mother would have wanted. She always told the girls that Doris's concern was more out of loneliness and not genuine at all. Nadine always told the girls that Doris could have had a better relationship with the family if she hadn't left them for a better life.

"Please, Doris, not today," Denie had said. "I really don't care to help you relieve yourself of your guilt at my mother's funeral. My mother hated you. You know that. She had her reasons, and as far as I'm concerned, they must have been good ones."

Denie began to cry, and Maggie, who had been hiding in the crowd, finally rushed over, quietly saving her sister. Doris had thought she'd caught Denie off guard and vulnerable. She'd probably assumed the emotional time would serve her well to begin a relationship with Denie and Maggie.

"I don't guess you've seen your aunt much since the funeral," Mamaw said as Maggie stared out the window. "But you know, she is your family, and that's something you and Denie are running a little short on with your mama and daddy both gone."

Maggie turned just enough to give her a complacent look out of the corner of her eye.

"Nadine was Doris's sister," Mamaw reminded Maggie. "She misses her, too. She loved her. They were just a little contrary to each other after they grew up."

The two of them were just like Maggie and Denie: only two years apart. Denie and Maggie could never hate each other the way their mother hated Doris. For as far back as Maggie could remember, Nadine had always despised her sister. She had only heard about the two of them being close; she'd never witnessed it.

If Doris missed my mother, she should've stuck around and not left her when she was so young, thought Maggie. *Maybe if she really cared, Mom would still be alive. Maybe having a sister could have helped her with the alcoholism. That's what destroyed her—killed her, really.*

Of the two girls, Doris was the proper southern lady, always wearing dresses and bright red lipstick. Her dark hair was as shiny as a coal diamond. Nadine's auburn hair looked like a rat's nest on most days. She wore no makeup and Maggie and Denie had only seen her in a dress a few times—at their father's funeral or when they'd play dress up and movie star at home. She never complained that day, but anyone could see she was uncomfortable at Edward's funeral, and even more so when she had to act polite with her estranged in-laws.

Nadine and Edward divorced when Maggie and Denie were both in middle school. That was when the fighting stopped for good. And now, with both of them gone, there was no fear of ever hearing the screams and screeches of their marriage remains ever again.

Maggie continued to stare out the window as the nurse came in to pin up the three-bun 'do for Mamaw. The buns were now completely gray. The shiny black hair had been lost over the years. Father Time had only lent it out to Mamaw for a short season for the enjoyment of others, something beautiful to look at like a spring tulip.

Mamaw continued to mumble about Nadine.

"Your mother and Doris used to be thick as thieves," Mamaw said. "Just like you and Denie."

Maggie's eyes were starting to grow warm with tears as she thought of her mother, when she saw Doris pull into the parking lot.

There she was in all her glory: wool skirt, pea coat, red lipstick and all. Whether Maggie liked it or not, Doris was about to trample the memories of her mother with those three-inch heels, which could now be heard clicking down the hall toward Mamaw's room. Denie had taught Maggie how to brace herself and hold on tight for an emotional attack like this one. It wasn't like she had taught a formal class on the subject. It was more a lifetime of demonstrations while Maggie watched from the side. Usually, Denie dealt with all the domestic matters, but she wasn't around. Maggie took one final, deep breath and muttered to herself, "Okay, I'm ready."

"Oh, Mamaaaaa." Doris brushed Maggie's shoulder with her hand and went over to hug Mamaw. "Why, you have a visitor," she said sarcastically.

Doris looked at Maggie as she stood there with her arms folded around her purse. "And to whom might I owe the pleasure?" she asked. "How have you been? We haven't seen you in a while."

Maggie flinched as Doris tried to hug her. The message was received, and the old bird backed away.

Maggie had always hated the way Doris sang her words. It was like she was five years old again, and Doris was going to reach over and pinch her on the cheek. Doris always used to pinch Denie's and Maggie's cheeks. Sounds sweet to tell about a cheek-pinching aunt, but it did really hurt. Doris could say the sweetest words, but Maggie knew she didn't mean them. It was all just a ploy to make up for what she'd done to Maggie's mother. Doris was always trying to subtly blame Nadine for all the troubles between the two of them. She tried to load the accusations with sugar and soft-spoken words, but Maggie knew what they really were.

Her aunt was a sweet, southern sugar-shover with a candy-coated dagger ready to kill the few good memories Maggie had of her mother.

Sometimes when Maggie would run into her in town, she'd say things like, "You know your mother had some problems..."

Maggie would never listen, just change the subject, talk about the weather or something trivial, then say goodbye, leaving her aunt standing alone.

That same perfume Maggie remembered filled the room. Chanel No. 5. Doris's scent of choice. Every time Maggie and Denie would catch a whiff of someone wearing that perfume, they would ask one another, "Do you smell Doris?"

"So, what's going on in your life, Maggie?" Doris interrogated at first and then finished in a whisper, to show her discreetness. "Are you still married? Is Denie okay? Do you need anything? You know, financial help?"

What an odd question? Is she trying to give me money? Maggie wondered. Did she know?

"Everything's fine, Doris. Nothing is wrong. I'm just here to see Mamaw."

"It's just been such a long time, I thought maybe you needed something. Always here to help," Doris said with that sweet, southern tone, sharp enough to pierce even the devil's heart.

"Guilt. Ever heard of it, Doris? Yes, I feel bad for not coming to see Mamaw more often, so I thought I'd drop by today, *if* that's alright with you."

Mamaw sat in the bed, fiddling with the wadded nest of gray hair that had fallen out during this last bout of styling. She looked up from her quiet concentration.

"I asked Maggie to come and see me. I thought she'd be here yesterday."

"Of course. Oh, that," Doris said, looking a little embarrassed. "I'm sorry. I've interrupted. I picked up the things you needed. I'm going to go now. I'll be back Wednesday, Mama."

"Okay, sweetie. You call me later."

Doris leaned into Maggie before she walked out. "If you need anything," she whispered, "you call me."

Maggie shook her head and managed to create a smile for her aunt.

The dramatics of this woman were unrelenting. Always with that victimized look about her.

Maggie watched as she trooped through the parking lot and got into her car.

"Mamaw, I should go," Maggie said quietly. "I'm sorry you had to call and ask me to come down here. I should come on my own."

"Yes, you probably should." Mamaw's tone of voice was different from before.

Maggie was both surprised and hurt—no canned excuses this time in Maggie's defense. By this time, she was tearing up. She picked up her things and started to go.

"Oh, for the love of all that is holy, will you sit down and shut up?" Mamaw said in frustration. "Let's just visit a while."

"No, really, Mamaw," Maggie said, starting to leave the room. "I'll come back tomorrow when everybody's not so upset."

"Nobody is upset but you! Now sit down and shut up, damn it!" Mamaw screamed.

Maggie felt her earth shake. She had never heard her grandmother use such a voice, let alone profanity. Not in a million years.

"Oh, don't look so shocked," Mamaw said. "I'm eighty-seven years old, and I've earned the right to say a few dirty words. Damn it, damn it, damn it."

Puzzled at the outburst and waiting for the punchline to this horrible joke, Maggie put her hands on the chair that faced the window and pushed it over to her grandmother's bed.

"Okay, I'm sitting and I'm shutting up."

"So, how have you been?" Mamaw began as if nothing in the last few minutes had even happened.

"I've been okay." Maggie shook her head, still waiting for the reason.

"Anything out of the ordinary going on?"

"Umm…nope," Maggie replied. "Everything's pretty ordinary. What's the matter, Mamaw?"

"I'll get right to it," Mamaw said. "I heard the newspaper was sold. I heard you lost your job."

"How did you know about that?"

"Doris brought me the Lexington newspaper. There was a story in there about it. You were quoted in it"

"Oh, I see," Maggie said. "Wait a minute, wait a minute. You read it in the newspaper? The competing newspaper? Gee, it's no wonder the company decided to sell. My own grandmother reads the competition."

"I only read it that one time, little girl. Don't get smart with me."

It had only been a little over a month since Maggie had lost her job as publisher at the Journal. The new company wanted their own people at the top seat—Maggie's seat. She felt as if her career had become bottomless with nothing to hang onto. She had started as a reporter and, over the years, had worked her way up to publisher. She wasn't willing to start back at the bottom, but there was no seat for her at the top. The music had stopped, and she hadn't reacted quickly enough. She, who usually took the chair, was now left standing without one. All that clawing and scraping to get to the top had been in vain. There was no comfortable plateau up there as she had imagined, only a quick fall down the ink ravine to the other side, and there she lay in the dirt, with no energy to lift herself up. She hadn't been going out lately. She'd grown tired of having to relive the entire humiliation of it all each time she ran into someone she knew. Here, at her grandmother's bed, seemed safe enough. But even here, the news had reached in with its ugly ink-stained tentacles.

"You told me the last time you were here that you missed writing," Mamaw said. "I say God's given you another chance to go back and do what you love."

"I don't think so, Mamaw. Writing doesn't pay nearly enough."

"It's not always about the money, child. Sometimes it's about doing for others. I never sold a quilt to anyone. I gave them all away, and I never won an award of any kind, but there's not one stitch in that fabric that I ever regretted. I was always happy knowing I had brought a little warmth into this cold world. You can't say that about your fancy publisher job. But your writing—that was your gift to the world. It's just something to think about, little girl."

"I don't know, Mamaw. I'll find something."

"God gives each of us a gift. You shouldn't waste it, Maggie"

Maggie loved it when Mamaw called her little girl. She'd just turned thirty-nine, her children were in college, and she could feel her tired legs sprinting into a midlife crisis. The last thing she felt was young, but it was sure nice to hear it.

Now she understood the reason why Mamaw had called her.

"Mamaw, you don't have to worry about me. We're fine. Chuck still has his job, and the girls are still in school. It's mostly my pride that's been hurt, but really, I'm okay. I hate that you worried…"

"Now, now. Don't tell me I can't worry about my granddaughter. That's what us grannies do."

"So, is that the reason you called me? You were worried?"

"Well, yeah, and I thought since you had some time on your hands now, we could spend some days together. There are some other things that I've been thinking about. Things that I want—I need—to tell my granddaughters about."

"What things?"

"Things that will make a difference in your life and make you understand a little better about why things were the way they were with your mama and your Aunt Doris. I should have told both you and Denie before, but a person puts things off. Now I'm beginning to think I can't put it off anymore. I'm running out of time so I've heard."

"You're not running out of time," Maggie lied for the third time today. This time, though, it was to reassure her grandmother.

"Hey listen, Chicken Little. I'm old and you know it. My time here is short. You know that, too. I'm ready to go, but there's something you and your sister should know about this family. God's keeping this sick old woman around for a reason. He wants me, all right. Don't doubt that. But right now, my load's too heavy, and I'm going to leave it for the rest of you to sort out."

Maggie remembered her grandmother's stories. They were great. She had heard the story of how her grandmother and grandfather had met, their first Christmas together, when her mother was born… She couldn't imagine what this story would be like—a secret.

I probably already know, she thought. *Mom told me all the secrets I could handle before she died. She went out on Daddy. I know that already. He went out on her. I know that, too. Why embarrass ourselves?*

"You don't know everything, little girl," Mamaw said as if she were reading Maggie's mind. "I'm not proud of what I did, but I really had no choice, much like the secrets you keep from your own children, Maggie."

Maggie thought of the many secrets she'd kept and would keep for eternity from her own daughters. The first marriage—all thirty days of it—and the two pregnancies that were never allowed to come full term. They didn't know. Mamaw didn't know. Some of the secrets Denie didn't even know.

"I don't have any secrets from my children," she said defensively.

"Of course, you do," Mamaw said calmly. "We all do."

Maggie thought about it for a moment and decided the old woman was right.

"Yes, I guess we all have some secrets," she agreed and settled back in her chair again.

"I never had a sister, or at least not a real sister," Mamaw began. "But I did have a best friend. We were as much like sisters as any two could ever be—for a short time. I loved her dearly."

"What was her name?"

"Janie. Janie Cole. Our family sort of began with Janie, whether you care to know it or not."

Mamaw got suddenly serious. Her beautiful eyes stared straight into her granddaughter's. Maggie became a little frightened. Did she really want to know? A strong urge to call Denie swept over her, but she fought it. It was probably nothing more than trivial, but Mamaw seemed so solemn, so sad. Maybe it was nothing, Maggie thought. Probably like the time her grandmother took her out to the farm where she and her grandfather used to live and told her the story of how the bank foreclosed on it. It was a beautiful place, not far from town. Now it was being cleared for an industrial manufacturing site.

That property would really be worth some money now.

Something inside Maggie was telling her this was more than just a "days gone by" story.

"Janie's husband, Bick, and your grandfather worked in the coal mines. She and I met when we moved onto the farm next to theirs. We were both only eighteen years old, both pregnant, and a lot like widows. I was widowed to the Black Diamond Coal Mine, sometimes more than a month at a time. She was much like a widow five or six days a week to the coal mines down at Arjay. While our men were working, we spent hours upon hours together that summer, talking, quilting, gardening and such. I wish you could have seen Janie. I can still remember her face. She was freckled a little and had dark auburn hair. She was a tiny little thing, not big as a minute. We were both due to have our babies the summer of 1936—and we both did."

CHAPTER ELEVEN

Maggie heard the dinner cart hit the door and turned around. It was time for Mamaw to eat.

"What do we got today?" Mamaw asked.

"Not sure, Miss Violee. I haven't even looked."

"Doesn't smell too good," Mamaw said crinkling her nose. "Maggie, meet Diana. Diana, this is my granddaughter. Diana makes sure we all get fed around here, and oh my, she makes the best lemon bars. Mmm-mmm."

"So, you cook all the food here and serve it, too?"

"No, child, she brings me dessert from home sometimes. Shhh. Nobody is supposed to know."

"Oh, I haven't seen you here before," Diana said to Maggie. "Live out of town?"

"No, I live here. I just don't get down here much," Maggie said as she shook Diana's hand.

"What are you two fine ladies up to today?"

"We're just going over some family history. I'm telling her some stories. My granddaughter's a writer."

"I, uh, really don't—" Maggie started to correct her grandmother's fib about her being a writer but was interrupted by Diana.

"Oh," Diana said, throwing her hands up in the air. "I love your grandma's stories. She's quite talented at storytelling. If even half of it happened to her, she's lived three lifetimes. I love her tall tales the best, especially the one about the magic catfish and the three wishes. I could sit in here all day and listen to her stories, but they pay me to feed these people." Diana pushed the cart toward the door. "You ladies have a nice evening. Good to meet you, Maggie."

"You too."

Maggie sat there the entire time Diana was in the room, trying to figure out how her grandmother could be so casual about this. How could she just blurt it all out like that?

And again, Mamaw's sixth sense kicked in. "Maggie, I've lived with this for a lot of years. It's not like I'm unemotional about it. It's just that it is and always has been part of my life. It's just normal to me."

"So, you stole a baby? What happened to it? Did Bick come and get it back? He knew it was you, didn't he?"

"Let's not put the cart before the horse. This story isn't over; it's really just beginning. Let's just consider this intermission." The old woman lifted the lid to her food tray. "I am not eating this crap. Could you be kind enough to run down and get me a cheeseburger? I've been needing a cheeseburger forever and a day."

"Sure, I'll get you whatever you want, as long as you tell me the rest of this story."

"Oh, I'm going to tell you. Don't you worry about that. I don't want one of those flat burgers. I want one that looks home-cooked, from a diner. Canady's. They still open? And I want some crinkle-cut fries and some pie. I don't care what kind."

"Mamaw, you really shouldn't be eating like that. It's bad for you."

"Oh, shit, little girl. Look at me. What am I saving myself for?"

Maggie grabbed up her purse. "I'll be back in a few."

It had started to rain a little. Maggie held her purse over the top of her head while she walked to the car.

Once inside, she dug in the bottom of her purse for her cell. *Scroll down, scroll down*—Denie.

"Hello?" Denie answered.

"Hey, what are you doing?" Maggie asked.

"Regular Sunday stuff. I've got about three more loads. What are you doing?"

Maggie could hardly wait for her turn. "Oh my God, Denie. Oh my God." She hadn't even pulled out of the parking lot yet.

"I'm at the nursing home visiting Mamaw. So, she starts telling me a story about her and a woman she used to know and a baby that she took. If you're not dressed, get dressed. I'm on my way over to get you."

"Maggie, I'm not going over there."

"Yes, you are. She was telling me about how she kidnapped a baby when she was young."

89

"God, whatever. I'm not going. I'm busy. Wait—what did you say?" Denie said, apparently just hearing the part about kidnapping. "Seriously?"

"Seriously."

"Maggie, you know this is probably one of her tall tales. Don't get so excited."

"Denie, pleeease," Maggie begged. "C'mon. We haven't had an adventure in a long time. Just humor your poor little unemployed sister."

"Okay, I'll go."

"Listen, call Canady's and order a cheeseburger plate with fries. We'll pick it up on the way back," Maggie said. "I have to get Mamaw some food, and we're going right back."

*

Denie hung up the phone and dialed information to get Canady's number.

While she ordered, she started looking for something to wear.

She had been working at home all day and hadn't even showered or brushed her teeth. It was one of those "bummy" days as she called them, just a day filled with laundry, Lifetime TV, potato chips, and ice cream.

"God, Maggie," Denie said even though her sister wasn't there. "You could've at least given me time to take a shower. Mamaw kidnapped a baby?" She rifled through her closet for something to wear. "I hope she didn't come up with all this just to get a cheeseburger."

Denie wondered if the old woman had finally lost her mind. All those years of vampire soap operas had finally taken a toll. Or maybe it was Maggie who had lost her mind. It did kind of run in the family.

Denie remembered the time her mother had told the girls that their great uncle Charles hadn't really died in an accidental fire. He had actually been burned up in his mobile home by his new mail-order bride. She was Mexican and very young. Evidently, she had gotten tired of the daily beatings, got him drunk to the point of passing out, doused the place with kerosene, and set it on fire. No one ever saw her again. Denie's mom said she'd probably left the country.

For years, most of the family thought it had been an accident. Trailer fires happen all the time, and everyone knew Charles was a drunk. But as time passed, people became more comfortable talking about it, and once the story was out, it made sense.

There was a small investigation, but once the police figured out that Charles' wife wasn't coming back, it just kind of fizzled out.

What was Maggie doing visiting Mamaw in the first place? Denie wondered. Every now and then Maggie would just show up there. She would always say something about doing what her mother would have wanted her to. She'd told Denie once that if Mom were here, she'd visit Mamaw. "I should do it in her place," she'd say. Each time she visited, she'd say she'd come back on a regular basis and then wouldn't. The visits were sporadic at best.

Denie had always thought it was a good thing that at least one of them was overtaken by guilt from time to time. She, on the other hand, had no regrets.

Denie and Maggie had been close as children, but they'd grown apart, as had the rest of the family, after the divorce. When the girls' mother left their father and them behind, too, it just wasn't the same. Their father dated, lived with, and married several women after that. Denie left home, too. She didn't go too far, just across town, and three marriages later, she was still across town. Maggie left home just after high school as well, lived with a man, got pregnant, and was married four times after that. She moved away and came back too many times to count. *Dysfunctional* was the family creed. But now the girls were together again. Both married for the last time with good husbands and children all grown.

"Hello," Denie answered when her phone rang.

"Hey, I'm out here in the driveway," Maggie said from the other end.

Denie grabbed her purse and an umbrella from the entryway closet and shut the door behind her.

"What the hell?" she exclaimed as she climbed in Maggie's car.

"I don't know, Denie. She said she took a baby from one of her neighbors when she was a young girl. It's quite an interesting story. She said she and a friend of hers were pregnant at the same time. Mamaw's baby was stillborn, and she took the other woman's baby because, umm… Janie, that was her name. Anyway, some preacher was trying to kill the baby."

Maggie explained as much as she could about the story her grandmother had just told her. Denie listened intently, exclaiming things like "no way" and "holy crap" along the way.

"You mean the Cole farm, next to Mamaw's house?"

"Yeah, Cole. That's what she said."

Denie remembered driving her grandmother out to see that property several times. It had been gone from the family for years. Denie just always assumed that the Cole farm was a coal farm. How stupid, she thought, that she'd never recognized the difference. Their entire family legacy was built on coal. A coal farm just made sense.

"So, the Cole farm was a family farm owned by the Coles?" Denie asked.

"Yes, Denie. Cole farm. What's wrong with you." Maggie looked at Denie puzzled.

"We're going back to hear the rest of the story. I had to go get Mamaw something to eat. They brought her dinner, and she didn't like it. She told me to get a cheeseburger and crinkle cut fries. Did you call Canady's?"

"Yeah."

Maggie pulled into the parking lot at Canady's Diner downtown. "I'll go in and get it."

Denie sat there in the car. The rain was falling heavy now. She tried to picture this quaint little town her grandmother had called home back in the early 1900s. She closed her eyes and imagined the parts of the story Maggie had just told her.

"Janie. Who in the hell is Janie?" she said to herself.

The sign up on the restaurant looked unfamiliar. *Yaden's Fine Food.* Canady's Diner had changed owners too many times to count, but about a hundred years ago, it had been Canady's. That was what everyone continued to call it, no matter how many times the name changed.

Denie tried to remember what the inside of that diner had looked like when she was growing up. It had a long, white counter that stretched from end to end. Golden flecks speckled it like stars in the sky. The bar stools were upholstered with red vinyl, and the trim was, of course, chrome.

Denie's father had always called the guy behind the counter a soda jerk. He wore a paper hat that Denie and Maggie would always try to duplicate with notebook paper once they got home. They'd play for hours in the bathtub with their homemade soda jerk hats and cups they had gathered from the kitchen. They'd sell each other pop and ice cream topped with bubbles from the bath water.

"Yep, I'd say it's raining out there," Maggie said as she opened the car door and threw two bags on Denie's lap.

"What took you so long?"

"I got us something, too."

"I thought we were in a hurry."

"We are," Maggie said as she put her arm behind Denie's seat and back the car out.

"Mamaw said she had to get herself cleaned up. She said I had a little bit of time. She told me to wait about twenty minutes before I ordered the food, so I went and got you."

"Maggie! She didn't know you were coming to get me?"

"Um…no. Does it matter?"

"Um…yes. What if she doesn't want to see me?"

"She always wants to see us, Denie. What else does she have to do?"

"Are you sure?"

"God, will you just go with the flow, please? Lighten up a little. Geesh," Maggie said. "You kill me. Stop being so goddamned dramatic."

Denie started to reply but decided better of it.

As Maggie and Denie pulled into the parking lot, Denie got a sick, queasy feeling in her stomach. It was the guilt she had avoided for so long. She felt it each time she watched old home movies of her children with her various husbands.; she felt it when she hadn't visited her mother when she was dying; and whether she liked it or not, she felt it now for not seeing her grandmother for so long.

It was just easier not to visit. It reminded her too much of how much she missed her mother.

Once inside, Denie took off down the hall to the right, but Maggie stood in the lobby. "Where are you going?"

"Oh, she's not down here?"

"No, they moved her last year sometime."

Denie followed her sister down a hall, but she stalled as Maggie entered one of the rooms.

"Hey, Mamaw," Maggie said. "I got your food and look what else I found."

Denie poked her head around the corner. "Hey, Mamaw. How have you been?"

"Good," Mamaw said as Denie hugged her. "I think about you all the time and wonder about you."

"I'm sorry it's been so long since I've been here."

"Aww, don't worry about that. You're here now, and I'll just bet I know why." Mamaw shook a wrinkly old fist at Maggie. "You girls never did miss a trick. Thick as thieves still, are ya?"

"Yeah, I guess so," Maggie said.

"Well, it's good to know you girls are still around for each other. I'm an old woman, but you two… You need each other, and you'll need to stay close for hard times to come."

"You mean it gets harder?" Maggie said with a laugh.

"Oh yes, girls. Much harder."

Mamaw had already scraped her plates clean into the garbage and placed her food tray on the nightstand.

"I smell that burger," she said.

Denie pulled the burger out of the bag and laid out the wrapper, placing the fries next to them on top of her grandmother's food tray. She began opening ketchup packets.

"That's enough," Mamaw said with a full mouth already.

Maggie got the other two burgers out and began to eat as well, handing Denie hers.

"Can you believe that rain today?" Denie said, making conversation.

Mamaw tried to carry on as much as her hearty burger and dentures would allow.

Once Maggie finished her burger, she headed toward the bathroom.

"So, how are your children?" Mamaw asked Denie between bites.

"Oh, they're good," Denie said. "One is married now but still no grandchildren. And Timmy, well, I'd rather not talk about that today."

"You know what they say. 'A son's a son till he gets him a wife, but a daughter's a daughter all of her life,'" Mamaw said, obliging Denie's request not to talk about her oldest son.

"Yeah, you've told me that before. I guess Maggie's lucky in that sense, having two daughters."

"Well, I don't know about that," Mamaw said. "There's a whole other set of special problems with girls, believe me. I had two of my own."

"Yeah, I'm sure there are. But Maggie's girls are good. They're both in college now and seem to be doing well."

"I hope they stay that way," Mamaw said.

"Maggie told me the story, Mamaw." Denie couldn't help it. The curiosity was killing her.

"Mmm …" Mamaw said, shaking her head as she chewed her burger.

"Is it one of your stories? Or is it true?"

"Ever hear of Pandora's Box?"

"Yes, I have."

"Well, this situation is a little like that. I could be telling it by choice, but I'm not. God has a way of forcing us to deal with our skeletons, and it seems as if it's my turn. God's kept me around to outlive almost everybody I ever knew. When an old woman starts to think about dying, there are all these suitcases filled with personal things that she'd like to take with her. But the relief in leaving it all here is just too tempting. I'm leaving everything here, every bad memory, every sin, every moment of my life. I'm ready to go, and I'm traveling light as they say.

"People are funny creatures. There's so much in the world that's bad and so much that's wrong. Families need to stick together. We have so much hate…"

"You mean Doris and us?" Denie asked.

"Yes, I mean you two and Doris." Mamaw shook her head and looked up at the ceiling. "You know your mother and Doris used to be just like you and your sister. They loved each other. Couldn't get enough of each other."

"Yeah, and then Doris left home, went up north and left our mother here to rot," Maggie said as she walked into the conversation. "This is not the next part of your story is it? We've heard this one over and over and over."

Nadine had always said Doris went to the "big city" and forgot all about her. She left when she was teenager and didn't return until she was twenty-six. She sent letters the entire time she was gone, but none of them were specifically addressed to her little sister.

When Doris had finally returned home, she'd brought her new husband with her. He'd ended up retiring from the community college in Rayes County a few years back.

Denie's mom said Doris had changed while she was gone. That many years away from home is a long time for someone to stay the same.

Nadine had always wanted to go away to the big city. She was a singer. The girls used to hear her singing in the house all the time while they were playing in their room. Loretta Lynn was her favorite to imitate. She was pretty good. Sometimes she'd sing the Nancy Sinatra song "These Boots are Made for Walkin'." They loved it.

She had a gold sparkly dress and gold shoes to match. When she'd put on her gold dress and shoes and bright red lipstick, the girls would go wild. She'd stand in the living room and give a show. It was as good as any concert Maggie had ever been to. Even the Journey concert where Maggie expanded her mind for the first time wasn't as memorable.

But then when their father would come home, there'd always be a fight.

She'd always wanted out and didn't care about telling him so. He'd ruined her life. She didn't care about telling him that either. She could have been somebody, but he'd ruined it. Now, she was stuck raising his kids and keeping his house.

Their father had always struck back but most times not verbally. Maybe he'd run out of things to say and just started swinging.

The next day the whole thing would start over again. First things first, a trip to the drive-through liquor store and then onto Mrs. West's house. It had become a daily ritual.

Denie was grateful to her grandmother for those perfect summers at her house. The guilt pains in her stomach returned. She had no idea when everything had gone so wrong.

When Nadine had died, Doris came to the funeral and tried to act like nothing had ever happened between them. She wanted to start right away with dinners and visits.

Denie had been very upset, and there'd been a big scene at the funeral. It was a scene that would lead to many years of hatred for Doris. She had evidently told Denie that Nadine was an alcoholic and that Denie shouldn't have listened to the horrible stories Nadine had told about her. Denie despised her aunt after that. Not that she wasn't aware that her mother had a drinking problem, but she knew her mother hated Doris. That was good enough for her.

"Tell us the rest of the story, Mamaw," Maggie said. "I couldn't wait to get back here. Now we've eaten. Let's hear it. I got nowhere to be."

"You, Denie?"

"Nope, nowhere to go but right here."

CHAPTER TWELVE

Mamaw's story continued into the evening. Denie and Maggie had listened intently to a lifetime of memories. In the usual fashion, Mamaw's story felt real. It was as if the sisters had gone back in time and visited there for a while. They had to leave Mamaw there sleeping. Her head had begun to doddle a little, and her eyes closed in moments of slumber as she spoke. The girls left a message with one of the nurses at the front desk.

"Tell her we'll be back first thing after breakfast," Denie said.

The nurse nodded and smiled.

"What about work?" Maggie asked.

"I'm calling in," Denie said with a matter-of-fact look.

The drive back to Denie's house was filled with what-ifs about Bick and the baby.

"This is the most excitement I've had in my life in years," Denie said, laughing.

"Let's make a night of it. We haven't been together for this long in quite a while," Maggie said, pulling into the driveway.

"Come on in and I'll make us some drinks."

Inside, the light on Denie's answering machine was flashing. Her husband Mark was in the front room watching TV.

"Who called?" Denie asked.

"Who do you think?" Mark said, coming into the kitchen. "Well, hello stranger. I haven't seen you in a long time."

"Hey there, yourself," Maggie said.

"I guess y'all are gonna be up a while?" Mark said. "I'm going to retire to the man room."

The "man room" was his and Denie's bedroom. It was really the only place he could have any privacy when his wife was home. He had set himself up with a recliner and a TV, and a view to the back yard from the second-story glass doors didn't hurt the atmosphere.

"I'll see you later, Maggie," Mark said as he kissed Denie on the cheek. "Good night."

Denie stared at the blinking red light on the answering machine and took a long, deep breath. She held it for a moment and then blew it out slowly. "Let me get this and then I'll make us some drinks."

Maggie sat down at the kitchen table and fingered through the sale papers as her sister listened to her son's message.

Hey, Mom. The landlord says he needs the rent by tomorrow or he's going to send an eviction notice to the sheriff. Give me a call when you get home.

Denie's son, Tim, had been in and out of trouble over the past four years or so. His addiction to drinking had eventually led to an addiction to Xanax. He'd lost his job, was on probation, and was now wanted on yet another bench warrant for failure to appear.

Maggie was used to the late-night calls from her hysterical sister. Denie had been trying one of those Dr. Phil lessons—tough love. Maggie would talk her through the dark times when Tim would tell Denie he hated her, that he was going to kill himself, or that she'd been a terrible mother. He was always looking for someone to blame, anyone but himself. Typical addict. Now, though, his biggest problem was money and booze, which were much more tolerable than the pills. Denie had told Maggie at one point that she suspected him of using Crystal Meth.

"Are you going to give it to him?" Maggie asked.

"Yeah, but I'm not calling him back until tomorrow. I'll let him sweat it out for tonight," Denie said. "He's straightened up a lot, but he still can't handle his money."

Every time Maggie listened to Denie talk about Tim, she thanked God that her girls were good kids. She didn't hear from them much unless she called them, but they were stable. Missing them was her biggest obstacle. Denie told Maggie once that she wished she could miss Tim and know that he was doing something good with his life rather than see him every day and have to pull him out of a ditch.

Maggie could never tell her girls no. She knew that if one of them were in trouble, she'd gladly hand over her last dime, or even her still-beating heart.

She had always chalked it up to something her grandmother had always told her. "The Lord will put on you no more than you can stand." If that was true, Denie could stand just about anything.

In one quick moment, Denie changed gears. It was a trait that had been passed down from generation to generation, saved only for the Garland women. It was like a chalkboard had been given to each of them at birth and they could erase all their worries at will.

"What are we drinking?" Denie asked as Maggie continued to flip through the sale papers.

"Um, do you have rum?"

"Yes. And I have some tequila, too."

"God, Denie. What have you been doing?"

"Don't worry. It's aged Tequila."

"Let's make some Margaritas."

"Will do," Denie said, pulling the blender out from its hiding place under the cabinet.

"Before we get started on this—just so you know—yes, I love you." Maggie laughed.

"Smart ass." Denie was a crying drunk. Everyone knew it, especially her sister.

Once, during their first round of marriages, the girls and their husbands had gone camping, and Denie and Maggie had tried their first tequila and their first joint—or at least that was what Maggie told Denie. All night, Denie had professed her love for her little sister and apologized for things Maggie didn't even remember that had taken place in their childhood.

Denie delivered Maggie a Margarita in a wide-mouthed, long-stemmed glass, complete with salt around the rim.

"Ooh, fancy," Maggie said.

"Hey, let's go into the den," said Denie. "Take this. I'll be in there in a minute."

Maggie sat on the couch, licked some salt off her glass, and looked around the room. There they were—the stories of her sister's life. Photographs of her, Timmy, and the rest of the family had hung untouched for years. Just like Maggie, Denie had an empty nest.

"Tim was such a cute little boy," Maggie told her sister when she came into the room. "Too bad he had to grow up to be such a little shit."

Denie ignored the comment. "Look what I've got."

"Oh, my God, Denie. Why do we always have to look at those?"

"I thought it might be fun, especially since we have new things to look for."

Denie had gotten custody of all the family photos after their parents's deaths. She brought them out occasionally and flipped through them. It saddened Maggie to think that an entire person's life—especially two people's lives—could be reduced to a big box of photos.

"Are you staying over?" Denie asked.

"Why?"

"Because I'm basing my decision on whether or not to make another pitcher on that," Denie said.

"Burn that blender up, sister. I'll stay. I needed this more than you know."

The big box of photos was now open. Maggie and Denie had both tried to destroy several of them in years past, or at least hide them. Evidence of all their failed marriages lay inside. It didn't matter now, though. It looked like someone else's life. Now they were just hilarious. Nadine had kept them safe from the girls' ideas of certain destruction.

"Those are my pictures," their mother would say. "Not yours. So, keep your hands off them."

From bell-skirted wedding dresses to straight and strapless, Denie and Maggie could've had their own fashion show if they ever dared to dig those old dresses out of storage.

"Oh, my God, Maggie. Look," Denie said, almost spilling her drink. "It's Leslie."

There he was in his school picture with his Beatles haircut and open shirt, the infamous Leslie Young.

Maggie laughed. "I still say he liked me more. Your boobs were just bigger."

It had been during Denie's ninth-grade year and Maggie's seventh-grade year when Leslie'd entered the picture. Denie had all but one of her classes with him, and Maggie filled the gap with the other. He had to take eighth-grade English over again, and Maggie had excelled to eighth-grade English.

"We thought he was such a fox," Maggie said. "Did he look that young then?"

"No, he couldn't have. No way."

Leslie had just a bit of peach fuzz on his upper lip. His complexion was dark, so the hair above his lip could pass as somewhat of a mustache. His clothes were definitely groovy, and his big brown eyes and long eyelashes made the girls melt. He was a new boy in school that year, which made him fresh meat at

Martin Junior High. He was like a rock star, and Denie and Maggie had both signed on to be his groupies.

"I'm sorry, Denie," Maggie said, looking at her sister sadly.

"Don't worry about it, shit head."

The two had argued all year about Leslie. Notes would be passed to him from Maggie and then from Denie. Maggie had always thought it unfair that Denie had more access to Leslie for most of the day. They had their lunchtime together and spent nearly the whole day walking back and forth between classes together. Maggie tried her best to hate Denie for the entire year— forever, if that was what it took. But it didn't. Maggie had mistaken Leslie's kindness toward her as some sort of flirting. Leslie was just trying to be nice to Denie's little sister.

The whole incident came to a head about two weeks before school was out.

Maggie saw Leslie holding hands with Denie at her locker. She grabbed her by the back of the shirt and slung her to the tile. The two girls fought as the rest of the school, and, of course, Leslie watched. They had fought plenty of times before, but this time it was different. There were no smacks and grabs. This time there were fists and even blood from Denie's lip. When Nadine arrived at the school, both girls were in the principal's office crying and hugging each other. When their mother found out that the fight was over a boy, that was it. The drive home was silent except for the sounds of sobs and snot. Once home, Nadine was livid and through her own tears she spanked the girls—both of them—with one of the leather shoes she was wearing.

After that day, both Denie and Maggie knew the year of Leslie was over for the both of them. Their mother had turned into a raving lunatic. She'd cried, screamed, and tried to explain why sisters should never fight—especially over a boy. They got it. The message was loud and clear. The girls never had that problem again, and Leslie soon was considered a one-hit wonder, fading into the rest of the faces at school.

"God, she was pissed," Maggie said.

"Yeah, she really scared me that day. I thought she was going to kill the both of us," Denie said.

Both girls took one last look at Leslie's picture.

"Whatever happened to him?" Maggie asked.

"Drugs, I think. He's not around here anymore."

"Hmm." Maggie threw the picture back in the box.

The photos weren't organized. Pictures of the girls in their basketball uniforms were mixed in with family photos and pictures of people from their past who they hadn't thought of in years. Some they couldn't even remember. Pictures from a decade ago were mixed in with those from way before Denie and Maggie were even born. One by one, the pictures reminded the girls of days gone by.

"What exactly are we looking for?" Maggie asked.

"Oh, I don't know. Let's see if we can find some pictures of Doris. Look at this one. It's Easter here," Denie said. "Look at Mom. She was cute! And there's Doris with her."

The photo looked like it had been taken at a church. There was a white background of a house with bricks on the foundation and underpinning.

"Let's take this one to Mamaw tomorrow," Denie said.

The girls laid the picture aside and continued with their search for more memories.

"Hey Mamaw," Denie said, Maggie following close behind.

"I'd about give up on you girls," Mamaw said.

"You fell asleep last night, so we didn't want to wake you up."

"What have I told you about waking me up? I've got eternity to sleep."

"I've thought about Bick all night long and wondered what happened to him," Maggie said.

"What've you got there, Denie?" Mamaw asked, avoiding Maggie's statement altogether.

"Oh, we brought some pictures," Denie said. "These are of Mom and Doris, and these are of…"

"Oh, look how precious they were!" Mamaw didn't give Denie a chance to finish. "You know I made those Easter dresses. They were so pretty. You can't tell from this picture here, but your mama's dress was yellow. She loved yellow. And daisies. She couldn't get enough of 'em."

Mamaw held the picture close to her face and looked at every element—every brick, every blade of grass, and every strand of hair. She described each detail of the girls' dresses and how she'd made them. Doris's dress was pink, she said. From the lace to the cotton fabric, she had taken Denie and Maggie back in time once again. The smell of daffodils even overpowered the coffee from Denie's Styrofoam cup.

CHAPTER THIRTEEN
Rayes County, 1945

Doris teared up a little at church when she found out that only children ten and under would be able to hunt Easter eggs. Her mother could see the disappointed look on her face and snuggled her up close.

"Don't worry. We're going to have an Easter egg hunt of our own when we get home," Viola said.

"But Mama, I want Doris to go with me," Nadine said.

"Not this time. Now you go on and hunt your eggs. We'll be watching," Viola said.

Even though Nadine was nine, Doris knew she didn't stand a chance out there without her.

"You go look around the trees first and then under the leaves and inside the bricks," Doris coached her sister. "Don't worry about the eggs in the hard-to-find places. That'll take too much time. And don't forget to look around the bumpers of the cars in the parking lot."

Nadine was off, a little slow to start, but she soon found her legs.

She found fifteen. Not bad for her first time out alone, Doris thought. She couldn't have been prouder if Nadine had been her own child. Afterward, the church ladies kept asking why Doris hadn't hunted. Viola kept explaining to them that the hunt this year was for ten and under, and Doris was now eleven. Doris was embarrassed. She knew her face was red. She wanted to cry. She wished she had left her basket in the car. At least that way it wouldn't look like she had planned on hunting.

"I am really too old to hunt Easter eggs," she said. "It's for the little kids, anyway."

Doris wanted to appear as grown up as possible, but her mother knew her feelings had been hurt.

"Here, Doris. You can have some of my eggs," Nadine said, coaxing her sister to sit down with her and count them again.

"I'll get my dress dirty," Doris said. "You count them. We've already counted them twice. There's fifteen.

"Come on, little gals," Den said, picking Nadine and her Easter basket up in one big swoop.

Viola took Doris's basket, and they headed toward the car.

At home, the girls waited anxiously inside as their father hid the eggs.

"Where did you get the eggs, Mama?" Doris asked.

"From the Easter Bunny of course," Viola said.

The girls had never really believed in the Easter Bunny, and their mother knew it. She'd never really introduced the Easter

Bunny formally into the holiday. It was just something they'd heard about in school.

"No, I colored them last night while you girls were asleep," Viola said. "I thought it'd be fun to hunt Easter eggs at home today, too. And it's a good thing I did, or Doris wouldn't have gotten to hunt at all. That's a stupid rule, and I'm going to tell the pastor exactly what I think."

"No, Mama, don't," Doris said. "He'll just know it was because of me that you're complaining."

"I don't care," Viola said. "Kids these days have to grow up too fast anyway, so why should we force you all to grow up any faster? Eleven years old is not too old to still be a child."

"Please, Mama, don't," Doris begged once again.

"Okay, but I'm going to have to bite my tongue. Maybe next Easter, we won't even go. We'll just stay here and hunt eggs."

"But will we still get an Easter Sunday dress?" Nadine asked.

"Yes, honey. One doesn't have anything to do with the other," Viola said. "I make those dresses for the two of you, not for everyone else."

Doris was trying her best to look out the window to see where her father was hiding the eggs.

"Oh, no you don't." Viola ushered Doris away from the window. "No peeking."

The girls sat at the kitchen table and counted Nadine's eggs again. By this time, almost all of them were cracked and starting to peel.

"Now, don't you girls waste those eggs," Viola said. "If you're not going to eat them, we'll make us some egg salad sandwiches for later."

The screen door slammed.

"Can we go?" Nadine asked.

"Now, you just wait a minute, little missy," Den said. "I've got something to tell you before you go out there. You're not going to believe who I ran into out there."

"Who?" Viola asked, although she could tell he was kidding.

"The Easter Bunny." Den's eyes widened. "He told me while I was out there hiding the eggs that I was taking his job. He said that if I hid even one more egg, he'd see to it that our chickens would never lay another egg again."

"What happened?" Viola asked.

"I punched him square in the jaw, and he took off running into the woods."

Nadine and Doris laughed at their father's story.

"There's no Easter Bunny," Doris said.

"Yeah, I know," said Den. "But it was a good story, wasn't it?"

"I guess."

Nadine was already at the front door, waiting for the word to go.

"Okay, girls, let's get to it," Den said.

Viola watched her girls run all over the yard. Nadine fell; Doris picked her up. She fell again, and Doris picked her up again.

Doris had found all the eggs that had been hidden in obvious places. Now it was time to find the hard ones. She was almost to the edge of the woods when a spot of color caught her eye. She ran over to the stump, and there it was.

"Prize egg—one dollar?" she read aloud. It was in her mother's handwriting. She heard Nadine crying and started to run back.

Den had Nadine up in his lap, and Viola was blowing on her knee. Nadine was screaming. Doris saw that there were only five eggs in her sister's basket, and Doris's was full to the rim. She picked up her prize egg and put it in Nadine's basket.

"Come on, Nadine," she said. "Let's count our eggs."

Through sniffles and tears, Nadine got down from her father's lap. "Prize egg?" she said. "What's this?"

"That egg's worth a dollar," Den said.

"A whole dollar?" Nadine asked in disbelief.

"Nadine, you're rich!" said Doris.

Nadine rolled the dollar out and jumped up and down, holding it high in front of her mother's face.

Den pulled Doris aside. "Hey, little missy. What are you doing giving your prize egg away?"

"She was crying. It made her feel better."

115

"Well, little ladies who love their sisters get a prize today, too." Doris's father reached into his pocket and pulled out a dollar and gave it to her.

"Look, Mama!" she said excitedly. "I got a dollar, too."

CHAPTER FOURTEEN

"Stop looking at me!" Nadine screamed at Doris.

"I wasn't looking at you."

"Yes, you were. Mama, tell Doris to stop looking at me!" Nadine yelled from the bathroom.

"Girls, stop that yelling," Viola said, towels in hand.

"She's always looking at me in here," said Nadine. "I don't like taking a bath with her anymore."

Doris tried not to stare at Nadine's body, but she had noticed that things were beginning to change. Nadine's breasts were starting to get pointed, and her nipples were big. Doris saw some hair on her sister's privates. She had some, too, but not as much as Nadine.

Doris worried. She looked different. She tried to take comfort in her mother's words about how all girls developed differently and at a different rate, but her mother hadn't seen her privates lately. No one had. They were different. Doris tried hard not to look at them, but the harder she tried to ignore them, the harder they were to ignore.

Her chest was flat, not like Nadine's at all, and it didn't appear that it ever would look anything like her sister's. She did wish she could get a closer look at Nadine's privates—or anyone's for that matter. Just to see if it was supposed to be this way.

Maybe, she thought, she was developing faster than Nadine down below, and Nadine was developing faster than her at the top. Maybe, eventually, Nadine's bottom privates would look like hers.

Doris's mother had gotten Nadine a bra and, in the process, got one for Doris, too, even though she didn't need it.

"It's coming," her mother said. "We'll just go ahead and get it now before it does."

Doris stood in front of the mirror. She looked from the front, from the side, and from the back. She hated her body. She pulled a sock out from the drawer and put it inside her bra, then another one. She sucked her stomach in to make her sock breasts appear bigger and more pronounced. She pushed on her womanly parts underneath to hold them down. It hurt, but she did it anyway. Maybe if she pushed enough, they would go back under the skin.

She stood there and looked at her reflection. She was shaped like most of the boys at her school, and she was tired of looking that way. Nadine had curves around her middle. Doris was straight as a stick. As a matter of fact, she thought she looked very much like a stick.

She put on her pajamas and went to the bathroom. She still had her bra on underneath. Stuffing it with a little tissue paper looked more believable than socks. Maybe she could start with a little and then add a little more each week to make it look like a gradual thing. She wished she could add some to her butt. It was so flat.

"Yep, flat as a flitter," she said, turning around in front of the mirror.

She had a perfect sweater—so soft, so fine—but it hung on her like a potato sack, not like the other girls at school. Their sweaters showed every curve, every crack. Some of the girls were so big now, it was a strain on their buttons.

Linda, one of her friends at school, had told Doris that if she wanted her breasts to grow, she should do pushups. Doris had tried it. So far it hadn't worked. Her arms were getting bigger, but not her breasts. She had also tried cupping her hands around each breast and pulling the skin from underneath her arms to make a breast. She would hold each one for at least thirty minutes in hopes that if she did it long enough, it would start to stick out, even just a little. That didn't work, either.

Her little sister was getting boobs, and she wasn't. That was the simple fact.

"Please, God," Doris prayed at her bedside. "Make my breasts grow. I need them really bad. Please, God, please. In Jesus' name I pray. Amen."

"What are you saying over there?" Nadine asked.

"Nothing. None of your business. I don't ask you what you pray about. Now, go to bed."

By the end of the first month, the experiment seemed to be working. She added one-fold over of tissue paper each week, and by the end of the month, Doris felt she had added enough to her breasts to last her for at least a little while. She was happy with them, for now, until they started to come in on their own.

119

Boys were starting to look at her more, or at least she thought they were. Her sweater looked better than ever. It still hung a bit, but now it had something to hang off of. There was a new boy at school this year—Edward. He had moved into the old Cole farm next to hers. His hair was bright blonde, and he had blue eyes just like hers. Smoky blue. He was tall, not quite as tall as she was, but tall enough. Every day on the walk home from school, they would talk a little more. Nadine was always talking enough for the both of them.

Still, that was okay. They both laughed at her as she'd be silly all the way home. It gave them something in common — laughing at Nadine.

Doris's girlfriends at school said they would make an adorable couple. She was just waiting until he might ask her to go steady or even to go to a movie. It became more and more difficult to concentrate on school with Edward sitting in the classroom.

"Doris. Doris Garland," Mrs. Jenkins scolded. "Can you hear me, Doris?"

Oh no, she thought. *Everyone saw me staring at him. How embarrassing.*

"What do you think about the section we just went over?" Mrs. Jenkins asked.

"Uh, I thought it was very interesting."

"And what part did you find interesting?"

Doris's heart began to beat faster, and she could feel her face getting hot.

"Miss Garland, we have not been going over a section. We've been discussing which book we should read for next term. Get your things and go to the office. Once you've told the principal you weren't paying attention, you will write for me one thousand times, *I will not stare at boys in class.*"

Doris picked up her books and didn't make eye contact with anyone. Now Edward knew for sure she'd been staring at him. He would know that she liked him before he told her he liked her.

She knew she'd have to hide the busy work from her mother.

Oh, God. My mother can't know I like a boy, she thought. *Then Nadine will know, and she'll tell everybody.*

After the last bell, Doris left the principal's office and went to meet her friends in the girls' room.

"Doris, are you okay?" Linda asked.

"Yeah, I'm fine," she answered. "Mr. Masters didn't have time to talk to me, thank goodness. He was busy with one of the teachers, making the schedule for next term. I guess I got off lucky."

"Oh, yeah," Linda said. "After you left, old lady Jenkins gave a lecture on boys and girls and feelings and how they should be left outside the classroom."

"Oh, God, *no,*" Doris said.

"Yes, she did," Julia added. "Unfortunately, she did. It embarrassed all of us. Edward looked a little embarrassed, too."

"Linda, go find Nadine and tell her to come in here," said Doris. "I'm not going home right now. I want to give Edward time to leave first. I'm not walking with him today."

Juanita and Julia were looking at themselves in the mirror, much like Doris did each evening. *Hmm,* Doris thought, *at least everyone stares at their bodies.*

"Do you think my boobs are getting bigger?" Julia asked no one in particular.

"Oh, yes," Doris said. "I wish mine were that big."

"You are getting bigger, too," said Julia.

"Hey, what about me?" Juanita whined. "Are mine getting bigger?" Juanita knew the answer to that question. She had the biggest boobs in her grade. They were so big she couldn't even see the ground under her. Boys stared at her all the time. She stood in front of the mirror in the girls' room and sucked her breath in hard until her boobs were even bigger. She rubbed down the front of them and all the way down the shape of her body until she got to her waist.

"Yes," she said. "I think they are getting bigger."

Doris and Julia were both entranced as they watched her smooth her hands over her body. Juanita started rattling around in her purse.

"Do you need a lipstick?" Doris asked.

"No, silly. I've got my period," Juanita said.

Oh, of course, Doris thought. *Juanita gets the big boobs and now she's got her period. Great.*

"Oh, my gosh. When did it happen?" Julia asked.

"Last month. I thought I was the last." Juanita faked surprise. "And now I find out I'm the first?" She knew better. News like this

122

couldn't be kept a secret. If anyone in the group had gotten their period, everyone else in the group would've known first. She was always like that, pretending that she was modest. Everyone knew she was anything but.

"Not yet for me," Julia said.

"Me neither," Doris said.

"Well, I guess I'm just an early bloomer." Juanita took her feminine items into the bathroom stall. "Be out in a minute, gals. This might take a while."

Doris wanted desperately to know what a period was like, but not enough to give Juanita the satisfaction of getting to explain it.

"What's it like?" Julia asked.

"Julia!" Doris exclaimed in a whisper.

"Well, it's just like a dot. You know, like a period. You girls will know soon enough," Juanita said in a condescending tone.

"Did you get any signs that you were going to get it before you got it?" Julia pressed on.

"No. I just got it. Just like that."

All good questions, Doris thought. But the one that nagged at her the most was where did the blood in the period come from? She had looked her body over in search of the place where she thought it would come from. It wasn't there.

"Listen, girls," Juanita said. "Ladies shouldn't be discussing such private things in such a public manner."

Julia looked a little embarrassed. Doris was just glad she hadn't asked the questions. Her day had gone badly enough without having been called out as intrusive by someone she considered to be a friend.

Nadine opened the restroom door. Linda was close behind.

"Oh, my God, Linda. Did you know Juanita got her period?" Julia asked.

"Yeah, didn't you?"

"No, we just now found out," Julia said, puzzled as to why she hadn't been told.

"Is this the big deal? Juanita got her period? I thought you said Doris was in trouble," said Nadine.

"It is me," Doris said.

"You got your period?" Nadine asked.

"No, silly. Listen, I got in trouble today for staring at Edward, and I'm too embarrassed to walk home with him. We can wait in here until he gets a head start on us, and then we'll leave."

"That's stupid, Doris. He knows we have to walk home."

"Well, I'm staying here until I know he's gone."

"Do what you want. I'm walking home with him. I think he's cute."

Doris rolled her eyes. "Well, you go on, but don't you dare tell him what I'm doing. Tell him I went to Linda's or something."

Nadine opened the bathroom door to leave. "I'll tell him whatever he asks me. I'm guessing he won't even ask about you anyway."

"Ugh, she can be such a little witch sometimes," Doris said once her sister was gone.

*

As Doris lay on her bed, writing line after line, *I will not stare at boys in class, I will not stare at boys in class, I will not stare at boys in class*, every now and again, she would think, "Oh, yes, I will. Oh, yes, I will."

"What ya workin' on?" Viola asked, walking into her bedroom.

"Oh, just some homework," Doris said.

"Well, get it done and get to sleep. Nadine's almost finished with her bath. You girls need to get to bed. It's late, and there's school tomorrow."

Oh, God, Doris thought. *There's school tomorrow. I have to walk to school. He'll be there.*

For the rest of the week, Doris went to school early. She told her mother she was helping Mrs. Jenkins with a project, and she stayed fifteen minutes later with the same excuse all week. Nadine went on and walked with Edward, even though Doris begged her not to.

After a week, her mother threatened to go see Mrs. Jenkins. She said she worried about Doris walking to and from school by herself.

"What kind of project is this?" she asked.

"Oh, it's extra credit," Doris said, trying to think of all the things she might be doing for extra credit. "We all get to take a turn helping Mrs. Jenkins prepare in the mornings and clean up after school. We all get a turn."

"Well, enough is enough. I don't want you walking by yourself. I'm going to have a talk with her. She can prepare for her classes and clean up by herself. That's what she gets paid to do."

"Oh, no, Mama. My turn is over. I don't have to do it anymore."

"Are you sure?"

"Yes, Mama. Don't go over there."

Nadine glared at Doris.

*

The next Monday, Doris had to face him. There he was, coming down the road. What would she say? What had Nadine told him?

"Hey, me and Nadine missed you walking with us last week," he said.

"Yeah, we missed ya real bad, sis," Nadine said sarcastically.

"Nadine told me you were helping old lady Jenkins before and after school."

"Yeah." Doris smiled at her sister.

News of all kinds of girls getting their periods began to spread at school. Julia had gotten hers only two weeks after Juanita, and surprisingly Linda had had hers all along. Doris worried she was quickly being ousted from her group. She was the only one left. She knew, however, that the tell-tale sign that a girl had gotten her period was that she started carrying a purse. She'd prayed to God

every night now for not only bigger boobs, but also for her period.
The boobs she carried in her bra were handmade, and the purse
she would now begin to carry would contain nothing but a
notebook and some change for lunch.

She could feel her friends slipping away from her. They were
no longer asking her over to their houses. They all had boyfriends,
and she didn't. There was only Edward, and she was terrified he
would never ask her for anything, let alone to go steady. The extent
of their relationship was just like the one he had with Nadine. They
walked to and from school together every day. That was all, and
Doris thought that maybe that's all there ever would be.

Her friends hadn't asked her outright if she had gotten her
period, and she never made any big announcement that she had.
She simply started carrying her purse. That was proof enough, she
thought.

Meanwhile, Nadine was looking healthier than ever. Her
boobs were bigger now than Doris would ever be able to make her
fake ones look without everyone knowing. She couldn't wait for
school to be out for the summer. Surely, she thought, it would
happen then. Maybe this summer, she would start to sprout like
one of her mama's tomato plants. Yeah, next year, her boobs
would be big and round like tomatoes.

CHAPTER FIFTEEN

Rayes County summers were like the inside of a popcorn kernel at movie time. Nadine and Doris had only one choice for cooling off: the creek in the woods around their house. Their new neighbor had found his way there, too. The water was clear on the shallow ends, but on the deep end, it was just cloudy enough to hide the girls' bodies if they decided to take their swimsuits off. This summer, however, there would be no skinny-dipping. They never knew when Edward would show up at their creek, but they were always sure he would. They had rushed through their morning chores all summer and sprinted to the creek, splashing around, waiting for Edward to come.

"I think I hear him," Nadine said. "I heard something in the woods. Be quiet. Edward!"

"Guess not," Doris said as she sat upon the creek bank, picking weeds.

He was later today than usual. Then again, maybe the girls were early. They had been rushing to get there as quickly as possible. The sun was shining directly over the tops of the trees, casting shadows on the water.

"Why don't you get in?" Nadine asked her sister.

"I don't want to mess my hair up right now."

"Oh, come on. You're going to have to get it wet soon enough anyway."

Doris just shook her head at Nadine and continued to pull tall weeds, gathering them up in her hand and straightening them like a bouquet of flowers. She stared off, at times, into the path that Edward walked every day to get to the creek.

"Here he comes." Doris hurried to get into the water.

She didn't want him to know she had been waiting for him, and she also didn't want him to see her out of the water. Her breasts had begun to grow some over the summer, but still not as big as what she had made them during school. He was sure to notice.

"Hey, where have you been?" Nadine had no fear of seeming overly anxious when it came to Edward.

"Had some extra chores to do. I didn't know we were on a schedule here."

"We're not on a schedule. She's silly," Doris said. "It just gets so hot early in the day now. We come to cool off as early as we can."

There it was: the scene Doris had been looking forward to all afternoon. The sun was shining on him like a spotlight in a theater show. His hair fell around his face, and he slung his head slightly to the right, unveiling his smoky blue eyes. His hair had gotten a little lighter over the summer, his skin tanner. As he pulled the bottom of his shirt up to take it off for a dip in the creek, he uncovered his muscular midsection. Doris tingled all over, and Nadine took a deep breath and then sighed. His arms were dark, and farm work had carved them perfectly.

He's so perfect, Doris thought.

"What's wrong?" Edward asked. "Do I have a booger on my face or something?"

The girls were suddenly brought out of their trance.

"No," Doris said. "What made you say that?"

She knew why he'd asked. She had been staring at him, and he had noticed. She could feel her face getting hot. She scooped up some creek water in her hands and splashed it on her face.

"You don't even have your hair wet," Edward said.

"She didn't want to get it messed up," Nadine teased.

Doris immediately plunged under the water, came back up, and splashed them both as she resurfaced. She knew whoever initiated the water fight got it worst. She didn't care. She wanted to continue the day without Edward noticing she liked him for more than just a neighbor and a friend. This was the only way.

Nadine began to splash Doris, and Edward joined in.

"I'll get you for that. You'll be sorry now," Edward warned.

Doris ran out of the water. Her eyes were soaked, and she could barely see. She grabbed up the blanket and quickly wrapped it around her body, under her arms. She stumbled and then screamed and fell to the ground.

"Oh, come on. It isn't all that bad," Nadine said, rolling her eyes.

Doris looked down at her foot. It was covered with blood. By this time, Edward was out of the water.

"My foot's bleeding," she said.

"Ew, that looks pretty bad," Edward said. "Come up here, Nadine."

He took his shirt to the creek and doused a corner of it in the water, then cleaned Doris's foot and found the problem.

"Oh, no. My toenail has come off," Doris said through clenched teeth.

"It's okay," Nadine said. "Come on and try to get up. We'll go home."

The last thing Doris wanted was to go home and away from Edward.

"No, it'll be okay," she said as she tried to get up.

When she put her foot on the ground and tried to take a step, the blood gushed even more.

"Come on. I'll take you home," Edward said, picking her up in his arms.

He took the shirt and wet it again, cleaned her foot, and wrapped his shirt around her big toe as tight as it would go. It was all bunched up, bloody, and wet, but the shirt was the only available bandage.

He held her legs under one arm, and Doris put her arms around his neck. His skin was finally next to hers. Maybe this wasn't such a bad accident after all, Doris thought. She looked into Edward's eyes.

"You all right now?" he asked.

"Yes," she answered in a breathy voice. "I'm okay."

"Oh, brother." Nadine rolled her eyes and followed behind the two of them as they made their way down the trail and through the woods toward home.

Doris could feel Edward's skin merging with her own with heat and sweat. She wanted to stay there forever. Her toe was throbbing, but she didn't care. She was next to him, and that was all that mattered. His breath was hot as it forced its way onto her chest with each laboring step.

"Am I heavy?" she asked softly, looking into his eyes.

"No, you're okay," Edward said between breaths.

Doris nudged her head closer to Edward's neck. Her breathing was heavy, too, but for different reasons.

Oh, she thought, *he smells so, so, manly.* She closed her eyes and imagined she was lying in his arms after a long kiss, then opened them again to stare at his lips. Oh, they were perfect, too, just like the rest of him. The sun was shining through his long eyelashes. Doris could have died right there. The butterflies had taken over her stomach, and she tingled. Her limbs were weak. All she could think of was putting her lips on his or tickling his neck with her nose.

"Oh," she sighed.

"Are you alright?" he asked. "Don't you pass out on me."

"Oh, I'm not. It just hurts."

"I'll bet it does. That toenail's probably gonna come completely off."

Doris didn't care. All of her toenails could come off and all her fingernails, for all it mattered. She would have given anything for this moment to last forever.

As they got closer to the house, Nadine started to run far ahead of them.

"Hey, wait up!" Edward shouted.

"Looks to me like you all are doing fine on your own," Nadine said.

"Here, let me put you down." Edward seemed embarrassed at Nadine's accusatory tone. "You can lean on me and walk on your good foot."

*

It would be five days before Doris's mom would let her go back to the creek. She said the dog days of summer would set up infection in her toe if she didn't keep it clean. The creek water, she said, was anything but clean.

In the meantime, Nadine spent her days over there, alone with Edward. It nagged at Doris. Each day when her sister would come home with a big smile on her face, she just wanted to smack her.

Nadine was looking more and more like a woman, and Doris feared she could never keep up. She was sure Edward and Nadine were frolicking in the water every day. She was touching him the way Doris wanted to touch him. Summer was getting away from her quickly, and she had no desire to go back to school with all the girls in her group. Hardly anything from womanhood had made its way to her body, and she was sure the rest of the girls in her group would be in full bloom by now.

"Did you see Edward at the creek today?" Doris asked her sister.

"No, he wasn't there. And yesterday he left early. I don't think he wants to be there as much since you're not there. Are you happy?"

"No, and I don't know what you mean by that. I'm going back tomorrow. Will you go with me?"

"Sure," Nadine said. "What else do I have to do? I can't wait for school to start back."

The next morning, the girls got up in a hurry to do their chores, Doris in more of a hurry than Nadine.

"What's wrong?" Doris asked.

"My stomach hurts," said Nadine. "I'm going to go lay down before we go to the creek."

Nadine went into the bathroom, stayed a long time, and then emerged, crying.

"What's wrong now?" Doris asked, annoyed.

"Get Mama."

"Why?"

"Get Mama!" Nadine screamed.

Doris saw it then. There was blood on Nadine's pants. Doris got her mother and then went to the kitchen to cry.

Viola poked her head into the kitchen a few minutes later. "Doris, Nadine has got her monthly. Could you go and get some things from your purse?"

"Sure, Mama," Doris said. "I'll be right back."

The trip to the bedroom to get the pads was long. All Doris could think about was that her baby sister had gotten her period and she hadn't. She knew she was different, but she had no idea why. School was going to start back soon, and she'd be the only one. No big boobs. No period. She might as well be non-existent, she thought. She'd surely lost Edward, and now this. She just wanted to go to bed and sleep forever.

"Here, Mama," Doris said, pecking lightly on the bathroom door. "Here. Do you need anything else?"

"No. Don't you worry, honey," Viola said, obviously aware that Doris was upset. "Yours is coming soon."

"No, it's not, Mama. No, it's not," Doris said softly, leaving the bathroom door open behind her.

As Doris walked back down the hallway, she heard a knock at the front door. She peered through the doorway and saw Edward standing on the other side of the screen door.

"Hey," he said. "I got worried about you gals. You didn't come to the creek today."

"Nadine's not feeling good." Doris was sad—too sad to be excited that he was there, too sad to be excited that he had missed her. "I'd better stay here with her today."

"Aw, come on. Let's go," Edward said. "You're mama's here with her."

"Yeah, but I'll just stay with her today."

"She's not bad sick, is she?"

"No, she's not bad sick, just not feeling good. I'll see you later."

"No, wait," Edward said, holding the door open. "Come on out here a minute. I want to tell you something."

Doris slid out from between the screen door and the frame. She was nervous. He looked serious. She began to sweat, and he grabbed her hand and led her over to sit on the steps.

"You don't mind, do you?"

"No. No, I don't mind." Doris's voice was noticeably shaky.

"I've missed you," Edward said. "I didn't know I could miss you until I did."

He was looking directly into her eyes. She tried to look away but was drawn to his stare.

"I'm glad you missed me." *Oh my gosh*, she thought. *That sounded stupid.* "I mean I missed you, too."

Almost before she could get the words out, Edward leaned into her and kissed her lips, just gently.

Doris was dizzy. The world seemed to be spinning. She lost her balance, almost falling off the step she was sitting on.

"Whoa there," Edward said, laughing a little. "Don't you pass out on me."

Both of them laughed. Doris couldn't help herself. She hugged him. She just wanted him close to her, needed him close to her.

"Hey." He pulled her away so he could look at her. "I think your little sister has a crush on me."

137

"Really?" Doris said with some sarcasm. "I hadn't noticed."

"So, you know."

"Well, she never really said, but yeah I've noticed."

"We probably need to keep this between you and me, at least until she gets over it."

"Yeah, you're probably right."

"Listen, I'll be seeing you at the creek, right?" Edward asked.

"Yep, I'll be there tomorrow."

As he walked away from the porch, Doris began to feel dizzy again. She took a deep breath and closed her eyes. When she opened them, he was still there, walking away. *Yes,* she thought, *that really did just happen.*

She squealed a little and ran into the house, trying not to act too excited. Nadine was in the bedroom, lying on the bed.

"You feel okay?" Doris asked.

"Yeah," Nadine said. "I'm tired. I'm going to sleep."

"I'll be here when you get up." Doris kissed Nadine on the head.

So far, this had been the best and worst day of her life. Her little sister had gotten her period, and Edward had kissed her, told her he had missed her, and said he wanted to see her.

She went to the kitchen to see what Viola had for lunch.

"Sit down here," Viola said. "I want to talk to you."

Doris sat down. *So much talking today, so much serious talk,* she thought. Other than the kiss, she wished she could go back to yesterday when Nadine was still just a little girl and Doris felt almost normal.

"Mama, before you start, I know I'm different than Nadine. I've seen her dressing in our bedroom. I don't look like she does, you know, down there."

"What do you mean you look different?" Viola asked.

"I'm different, Mama," Doris said. "I think something's wrong with me down there. I'm probably never going to get my period. Never, never."

Viola's head dropped to her chest. "Let me take a look at you," she said.

"No, Mama. I don't want you looking at me," Doris said, begging.

"Yes, Doris. I want to take a look."

After some argument and some tears, Doris finally allowed her mother to do the unthinkable—look at her privates.

Once inside the bathroom, Viola tried not to act shocked at what she saw. "You're fine, Doris. Just fine." She turned around to the mirror, picked up a brush, and started brushing her hair.

"Even though it looks different than Nadine? Even though I have this thing—"

Viola didn't let her finish. "Yes, you're fine. We all look different. God made us all different. But just to be on the safe side, I'm going to take you to the doctor, just to see if there's some

139

reason why you haven't gotten your monthly yet. But listen—it's all going to be fine."

"Why, Mama? Why, if everything's fine, do I have to go to the doctor?"

"We just want to check and see if there's some reason why you haven't gotten your monthly. I really expected it to come to you this summer, not your sister."

"Me too, Mama. I'm scared."

"Oh, nothing to be afraid of. You just need to be checked out," Viola said. "I've heard tell of girls not getting their monthlies until they're eighteen. We just need to make sure nothing's wrong."

Doris tried to listen to her mother and not worry, but she couldn't help it. She hated Doc Collins. He had been their family doctor for as long as she could remember. He was old, and he smelled old. The last time Doris had seen him was for the rusty nail she'd stepped on three summers ago, and she definitely didn't want to go back.

The only thing that brought her any comfort was the memory of Edward's kiss. She could still feel his lips on hers and his hand wrapped around hers. She wondered if he would hold her hand now on the way to school and on the way back. She pictured the fall day that he would take his hand in hers. The leaves would be blowing across the road just before their feet. He'd be carrying her books in one arm and holding her hand. Soft, romantic music would be playing in the background, and they'd stop and stare into each other's eyes, and then he'd kiss her.

"What's the matter with you?" Nadine barked. "You look like you're about to pass out."

Doris lay down on the bed for she didn't know how long, playing out this scene with her and Edward on their walks to and from school.

"You feeling better?" she asked her sister.

"Yeah, I'm fine," Nadine said. "Mama told me not to talk about it with you. She said you were upset because mine came first. Believe me, I wish it hadn't."

"Nadine, it's not that I'm upset because yours came first. I'm happy for you," Doris said. "I'm just upset that mine hasn't come at all. I've been waiting a long time. We're going to the doctor just to check on some things."

"That's what Mama said. I've noticed that we're different. I don't know which one of us is right. Maybe we could ask someone or maybe we could try looking at someone else."

"Don't you dare, Nadine. Don't you dare talk to anyone about this. You swear. You swear to me right now."

"Okay, okay. I swear," Nadine said, looking puzzled at her sister's obvious paranoia.

CHAPTER SIXTEEN

Doris came out of Doc Collins' small office and handed the receptionist her file.

"Well, hello, Doris," said Juanita's mother. "I thought that was you going in there while ago. Hope everything's alright."

"Oh, yes," Doris said. "Everything's fine. Just a checkup. I didn't know you worked here."

"Yes, I came in to help Doc Collins out over the summer, and Juanita's taking care of the little ones. It's not that we need the money or anything. I just did it to help him out, you know."

"Yes, yes of course."

Doris couldn't figure out why Juanita's mother would care what she thought about her having a job and working for Doc Collins. She couldn't have cared less. Even so, she got the point loud and clear that Juanita and her family didn't need the money. Doris remembered her parents discussing whether or not her mother should get a job away from home. Her father had said her mother had plenty to do at home taking care of the three of them and should just wipe the thought from her mind.

Doris couldn't imagine her mother working somewhere in town.

"Please tell Juanita I said hello, and I'll see her at school," Doris said.

"Of course, I will, sweetie," Juanita's mother said.

Doris sat patiently in the waiting room while her mother and Doc Collins spoke privately. Neither of them seemed too concerned about the exam. Nonetheless, Doris was terrified. It seemed like she'd been in there forever. She wanted to forget the whole thing and go home. She had simply held her eyes tightly closed like her mother told her to and counted until it was over. She had gotten to three hundred and nineteen. That was how long it had taken. He hadn't touched her at all, only looked. It had been cold in there. Doris was glad to have her clothes back on, glad to be out of that room.

Juanita's mother and the other woman working, who looked like a nurse, had a file opened and were reading. Doris could see them behind the glass. Was it her file, she wondered? *Surely not. They don't look at people's files. That's for the doctor only.*

Every now and then, Juanita's mother would look at Doris through the glass and smile. Doris would smile back and nod her head, then the two of them would go back to looking at the file and whispering to each other. This was taking forever, Doris thought. What on earth could they be talking about that was taking so long? She stared at the walls, counted the dots on the ceiling and the blocks on the floor. She counted the chairs in the waiting room and then multiplied them all, then divided the room and multiplied the number of chairs by the number of blocks on the floor.

*

"Mrs. Garland," Doc Collins began. "I want to be honest with you. This is not something I've seen before, and it's not something I'm comfortable treating."

144

"Why not?" Viola asked.

"Well, when she was born, what did the doctor say then?"

Viola panicked a little but then remembered. "She didn't look like that when she was born. She was perfect. There was no confusion. We knew she was a girl."

"Okay, then," he continued. "Something's happened to her. I don't know what, and it may be nothing. But, like I told you, I just don't know."

Doc Collins searched through his desk drawers. "We have a new doctor coming. He's a specialist, and he'll be working right here in this office with me."

"What kind of a specialist is he?" Viola asked.

"Urologist. In other words, he takes care of these kinds of problems, and I think he can help your daughter."

"Oh, thank goodness," Viola said.

"You have another daughter, don't you?"

"Yes, I do. She's fifteen. She's fine. That's one of the reasons we came here. My youngest daughter got her monthly and Doris hadn't. I got worried. I looked her over and, well, you know what I saw."

"I'll be honest with you, Mrs. Garland. This doctor isn't cheap."

"It'll be okay. We'll do whatever it takes."

"In the meantime, I'm going to prescribe some female pills for her, and that's all I can do. If you want, you can go to Nashville and see him, or you can wait two months and he'll be here."

"I think we'll just wait for him to come here."

"I think that's a good idea. That'll give you time to talk to her and reassure her that everything is going to be alright. Until then, I'd save my pennies. Now, I've got other patients to see. You stay in here as long as you like, Mrs. Garland. And, if you need anything—day or night—you call me. The receptionist outside will give you my home number."

Doc Collins patted Viola on the shoulder as he left the room. She stayed there and stared at the doctor's name he had written down for her, sobbing as quietly as she could into her handkerchief, and remembered the day she had gotten Doris—the words Brother Caslin had spoken and the evil that had taken place on the day she was born. She could barely remember a day going by that she didn't at least remember parts of that day. But today, it was all rushing in at once. Doris was a completely different person than that child who had lain there about to be killed. Viola was a different person now, too, much different from that young woman who had taken that baby and raised it for her own. Maybe it had been a mistake. Maybe she should have left that baby there.

Viola gasped for a breath and looked around the room quickly as if someone were there reading her thoughts. She couldn't think that way. Of course, she should have taken that child. Of course, she should have raised it. Doris was her child, just like Nadine, and that was the way it was. It was meant to be that way.

CHAPTER SEVENTEEN

Doris lay in her bed, watching the sheers flap lightly against the window. She could hear the muffled voices of her mother and father coming from the kitchen. He must have gotten home last night after she and Nadine had gone to bed. She turned her head to the side. Nadine was still sleeping. She looked so peaceful with her mouth gaped open and the blankets tangled around her legs. Doris could hear the clock ticking over her parents' voices. She turned her head back toward the window and watched the sheers feathering against the windowpane again.

Gray clouds were moving slowly across the sky. There were dark splotches with white mixed in. The leaves on the trees outside the window were moving slowly back and forth. Doris closed her eyes and tried to make herself relax, breathing in and out almost as slowly as the leaves were moving, but the voices from the kitchen were just loud enough to keep any slumber from coming to her body. She tried to listen to what her mother and father were talking about. Most times, when the girls would hear their father at the breakfast table, they were out of bed in a second, rushing to get hugs. Doris was glad Nadine was still asleep. At least she didn't have to go look at her father. After what had happened at the doctor's office, she didn't think she could face him.

Doris knew they were talking about the doctor's visit, even though she couldn't make out what they were saying. There was a serious tone to the echoes, not the usual laughter, none of the noise from banging pans in preparation for breakfast. She knew they were talking about her.

Rising up, she rested her weight on her palms, tilted her head back and took a deep breath. She lifted the blankets up off her legs and quietly touched her feet to the floor. Standing by the kitchen door, she hoped to hear something, and looking through the crack of the open door, she hoped to see something.

"Take this and put it in the can," Den said, handing Viola some folded over money. "And keep this out for us." He handed his wife the rest of the cash. "It'll be alright."

She put the money in the can and then went back to her window, staring out over the field. "I know."

Doris's father had a pleasant look about him. He was almost smiling at Viola as he stared at her from his kitchen chair. He picked up his coffee cup and slurped at it a little. The kitchen was quiet for a few moments, and Doris continued to watch them. The floor felt cold to her feet, so she turned to go back to the bedroom.

"I think we have a spy," Den said rather loudly.

Viola turned and looked at the doorway. "Hmm. I think you're right."

"Hey, Daddy," Doris said in soft, slow tone as she stepped out from the doorway.

"What?" Den yelled. "That's it? Didn't you miss me at all? I'm not just a sack of potatoes sitting here. It's me, little Dee! Where's my hug?"

Doris went to her father and hugged him tight around the neck, trying not to tear up, but she couldn't help it. She wanted her father to make it all go away. Surely, if anyone could, he could.

"Well, looky here," Den said. "You did miss me. I guess those tears mean you're happy to see me."

She shook her head but couldn't say anything for fear of breaking down completely.

The kitchen door flew open with a *whack!*

"Daddy!" Nadine shouted, going to her father and nearly knocking him off his chair with a hug.

"Hey, Lil'un." Den put his huge coffee cup back down after taking a big slurp.

Doris watched her sister bouncing all over her father. She stared at him as Viola began to hand out plates of breakfast. His hands were large, even while grasping that giant coffee cup. His right hand would almost wrap completely around his bowl-like mug. His eyes were blue just like her mother's. His face was lined and worn, mostly around his eyes and his forehead. He had worry claws on his forehead between his eyes, or at least that was what her mother called them. She said they looked like the claws of a chicken. She also said they came from hard thinking and pondering. Doris and Nadine knew exactly what she was talking about. When their father thought hard or got angry, it seemed as though he was trying to push his eyebrows together so hard that they would eventually make just one. Sometimes when the girls were in trouble, it seemed as though he would stop and think hard about what to do or what to say. Always deliberate and slow to speak in times of crisis, their father was not one to be taken lightly when it came to bad behavior.

Among his many other talents—hunting, fishing, coal mining, and being a one-truck mechanic—he was also quite the inventor. Doris's father had thought up several inventions and could sit for hours and think up easier ways to do things. Most times, even though his wife thought he was crazy, he'd come up with a way to make a task simpler, whether she liked it or not. Hole-in-the-bag bean planting was a perfect example of how Den could make a task easier. He would cut a small hole in the corner of a potato sack and pour the bean seed in. Rather than laying the three seeds per hole by hand, he'd run his sack along the entire row with the seeds spilling out. Sometimes there'd be just a few, but sometimes there'd be a lot. He was rather proud of his invention. He never knew, though, that once he left for work, Viola would replant them. The girls never told, either. He continued to believe that those perfect white half runners were because of his clever little invention.

As the days went on, Doris began to feel more comfortable about being around her father. Even if he did know what had happened at the doctor's office, he didn't seem to be too worried about it. His behavior made Doris feel like there really might not be anything to worry about.

But the constant reminder that something was wrong came each morning just after breakfast. Viola would slip one of those little pink pills into her daughter's hand, and she'd immediately take it before it was even a thought. Doris wanted to make it disappear as quickly as possible, without anyone even noticing. It was easy most mornings, and most mornings, her mother would hand it to her without even looking at her. Other mornings, Viola would stare at the pill for just a slight moment before handing it to her. Those were the mornings when Doris would wonder how serious the problem really was.

The summer was coming to a certain end. The days of meeting Edward out at the creek were definitely over. It was cooler than usual for September, and the smell of fall made Doris feel as though she should be somewhere else other than home. She longed for school, for her friends, and even for Mrs. Jenkins, the cruel old witch who had embarrassed her last year in front of Edward and the whole class.

Doris thought of him all the time and would take long walks around the edge of the farm to see if she could catch a glimpse of him. She longed for his lips to be against hers again. Every time she'd think of that afternoon on the steps, the butterflies would take over and she'd have to smile a little. She'd run out of clover to pick and for playing *he loves me, he loves me not.* She'd started on just about anything she could see. She'd count the rocks she gathered on her walks and drop them one by one. "He loves me; he loves me not." Of course, she would always go back and do it again if they answer was "not."

Doris had almost taken over her mother's gazing window. She'd stand by the sink and look out over the field and into the sky and dream of having Edward as her husband.

There she'd be washing dishes, and Edward would sit at the table. He'd come over to her at the sink, wrap his arms around her from the back, and kiss her neck and the back of her head. She'd seen her father do this countless times to her mother.

"What in heavens is wrong with you?" Nadine asked, obviously annoyed.

Doris hadn't even noticed Nadine sitting at the kitchen table staring at her while she lost herself in her thoughts, looking out over the field.

"Oh, nothing," she said. "I really don't know what you mean."

"All you do is walk around here like you're in a dream all the time. You never do anything fun. I'm bored. Let's go do something."

"Like what?"

"Why don't we go take a walk?"

"It's rainy out and the grass is all wet," Doris said.

"Who cares? It's a little wet grass. It won't kill you, will it?" Nadine said sharply. Her tone turned more apologetic then. "Seriously, come on. Let's go."

Doris smiled. "Okay, okay. I'll go."

Nadine crashed through tall weeds that made loud, wet, scraping noises against her pants. Doris trod lightly through the, tiptoeing to avoid the moisture.

The fence row was covered with vines tangled around themselves. Doris and Nadine had walked these fields hundreds of times, each time looking for treasures that lay at their feet. Interesting rocks or fallen tree limbs shaped like various objects would catch their eyes from time to time. Once, Nadine had found a tree branch with a growth on it that looked like a bird. The girls had taken it home to their mother. It was still in the kitchen on one of the windowsills.

"I can't wait for school to start back," said Doris.

"Well, I can sure wait for the work, but I'm getting tired of being at home every day. And now that the air's too cold, we can't even go to the creek and swim," Nadine said. "I'm glad you like school so much. Miss popular and all."

"I don't know what you mean. I'm not so popular." Doris knew this was a lie, but she wanted to at least appear a little modest.

"You're popular and you know it. You've got Linda and Juanita and—"

"Just stop right there. They're my friends, and that's why I hang around with them, not because they're popular."

"But you admit they are," Nadine snarled.

"Well, yes. I guess people do like them at school and think they're pretty."

"That's what makes them popular. Just like you. People like you."

"Nadine, you've got to stop worrying so much about being popular. You've got your friends, and I've got mine. I don't know why you and your friends can't start a little group of your own. Then when you get to be older, you guys can be the popular group."

"It's not the same," Nadine whined. "My friends aren't friends like yours. We don't tell each other things. It's all about school. We don't talk about boys and periods and big boobs."

"It's just because they haven't caught up with you yet, Nadine. They will. Maybe this year will be different."

"I don't' know. I doubt it."

"Why can't I just hang around with your group this year?" Nadine begged.

"It's really not up to me. You know you can hang around with me any time you like. You're my sister. But as for the rest of the girls, I can't make them hang out with my little sister."

"I know you can't, but you could at least let me sit with you guys at lunch. Maybe that would make me popular, too."

Doris sighed. "If you see us sitting somewhere, come on over and we'll see what happens, but it's just not normal for girls of our age to be hanging around with someone two years behind us at school. We all have boyfriends and stuff."

"You have a boyfriend?!" Nadine asked.

"Yes, I think I do."

"You mean Edward, right?"

Doris hesitated. "Yes."

"Really?" This time, Nadine's question sounded sarcastic.

"I think so."

"He is not your boyfriend," Nadine said sharply. "He's just our neighbor. Just because you want him to be your boyfriend doesn't make it so."

"It's not like that. You don't know about certain things, Nadine."

"What things?"

"That's none of your business," Doris said, starting to walk away.

Nadine grabbed her sister by the shoulder and turned her around quickly. "Don't think that you're any better than me." We come from the same place—right here. And if people knew what was wrong with you, they wouldn't want to be around you at all—not even Edward. You're a freak like in a freak show! Yeah, I've seen it. It's gross. It makes me sick to look at you, and you talk to me about normal. You don't know what normal is. You haven't even gotten your period."

The moment those words left her mouth, Nadine obviously regretted saying them. Her eyes grew bigger. She'd never seen her sister look so hurt and so mad.

"I'm sorry," Nadine pleaded with her sister. "I'm so sorry. I didn't mean it. God, I'm so sorry. Please."

CHAPTER EIGHTEEN

Doris walked several feet in front of her sister on the first day of school. When Nadine tried to catch up, Doris walked faster. It had been that way between them since that day in the field, Nadine trying desperately to warm up to her sister but getting nothing except ignored.

Nadine heard footsteps coming up behind her and knew it was Edward. She could feel the breeze as he ran by to catch up to Doris.

"Oh, hey Nadine," Edward said, out of breath as he passed her by.

"Hey," she replied, but he wasn't listening.

Doris turned around, closed her eyes briefly, and smiled at Edward as he came up behind her. Nadine had seen that same look so many times this summer from her sister. It was the blank, on-the-verge-of fainting look.

Edward bumped against Doris's shoulder, took her books from her arms, and then took her hand in his.

Nadine glared at their backs for the rest of the way to school. She kicked gravel at them every so often, just close enough to let them know she was still there, but not close enough to hit the backs of their legs.

Nadine wanted her sister to be friends with her again. But she knew after what had happened, there wouldn't be much of a chance right now, especially with school starting back. Now she had Edward, too. She wanted to cry, but she was too mad. She passed big rock after big rock and imagined throwing it at the two of them. She clenched her teeth and stomped over the gravel so that her feet were stinging by the time she got to school.

Lunchtime came quickly on the first day back. Nadine's friends were still immature as ever. All they wanted to talk about was playing tag at recess and kickball after school.

Recess, Nadine thought to herself. *For babies.*

She looked around the cafeteria for a place to sit, away from the children in her class. She was more mature than they were; most of the girls hadn't even gotten their monthly. She held her lunch tray down toward her midsection to reveal how her chest had grown over the summer and continued to search for a cooler group to sit with.

"Hey, Nadine. Over here," said a familiar voice.

Juanita held her hand up and motioned for Nadine to come over.

"Surely not," she said, looking all around her.

"Nadine!" Juanita shouted this time.

Not wanting to look too excited at this once-in-a-lifetime invitation, Nadine sauntered over, moving her head from side to side, trying to seem aloof.

All the girls were there—Julia, Linda, and best of all, Juanita. Only one was missing. Doris.

"Oh," Nadine said. "I don't know where Doris is yet. She's probably coming."

"We're not looking for Doris, you old silly," said Juanita. "We wanted you to come over and sit with us. You just look so out of place with all those other underclassmen."

"Really?" Nadine questioned with a hint of both shock and revelation in her voice.

"Look at you," Julia said. "You've really, well, blossomed over the summer."

"Oh, yeah." Nadine gave them a tight little smile and stuck her chest out so it was more pronounced.

"Speaking of your sister," Linda said, "we saw her and Edward coming into school holding hands."

"Yeah," Nadine said, taking her first bite of food. "I watched them all the way from school."

All three girls drew in closer, all of them leaning forward with their hands under their chins.

"Tell us," Juanita said. "Tell us everything. How did this transpire? Over the summer, I guess?"

"More like the end of the summer," Nadine answered. "Actually, I guess just a few weeks ago." She was starting to feel a little uncomfortable talking about her sister. "Do you guys know where Doris is?"

"Yeah, we saw her in the bathroom just before lunch. She may still be in there," Juanita said.

"Why would she still be in there?"

"She's a little upset," Linda said. "Juanita told her we were having a back-to-school get-together at my house tomorrow night—a sleepover—and she assumed she was invited. I think she kind of embarrassed herself."

Nadine was very confused. "Doris isn't invited to your party?"

"It's not a party, silly. It's a get together," Juanita said, trying to change the subject. "And oh, by the way, you're invited."

"Why am I invited?"

"Well, if you don't want to come then I guess we can invite someone else," said Linda.

"Oh, I know," Julia said. "We could invite Gail. She would be excited to come."

"No, I didn't say I wasn't coming," Nadine blurted. "I'll be there. I was just a little confused."

"Well, being her sister and all, you probably already know, but I'll tell you anyway." Linda pushed her hair back over her ear and moved in closer. "We heard that last year she started stuffing her bra. Well, I won't say who, but someone at this table saw her."

"Oh?" Nadine asked suspiciously, glancing at all the girls one by one.

"Well, it really doesn't matter. It's just that, well, if everyone finds out and she's hanging around with us, then everyone will think that we're stuffing too," Juanita said.

Nadine thought for a moment about that scenario. There was no way anyone could ever believe that Juanita had stuffed her bra. Not even possible. There wasn't enough tissue paper in the world.

"We don't want her to feel bad," Linda added, "but it just isn't right to do such a dishonest thing. And, well, there are other things, too."

"What things?" Nadine demanded.

"Just other things," Juanita said sharply. "We can be friends with whoever we want! Now, are you coming or not?"

"Yes, absolutely," Nadine said. "I'll be there."

After lunch, Nadine made her usual trip to the ladies' room to make sure she didn't have food in her teeth. Just inside the door, Nadine could hear someone sniffling. She walked to the washbasin and looked in the mirror. She heard it again—small grunting noises between sniffles—and could immediately tell that the barely audible voice was her sister's.

She started over to the bathroom stall but stopped herself. She knew she couldn't tell Doris about what had just happened. Doris would tell her mother, and then Nadine wouldn't be allowed to go to the get-together. She was hurt for her sister, but she wanted to hang out with Juanita and the rest of the girls. She would just go on and act as if nothing had ever happened. It was the only way. *Besides,* she thought to herself, *Doris has Edward. I at least deserve some cool friends.*

The next day at school, Nadine felt proud of herself for being invited to the cool girls' get-together. Everyone was treating her differently, it seemed. All the girls in her grade wanted to sit next to her. It was even getting annoying. Obviously, everyone had heard—probably even Doris. On the way home the day before,

Doris and Edward had walked hand in hand, and although Edward spoke to Nadine, Doris never did.

Even when Nadine told her mother the terrible lie that she would be staying over at Virginia's house, Doris never said a word. Nadine knew if she told her mother the truth, she would never be allowed to go. She also knew that her mother would let her go to Virginia's house. Virginia was in her grade and had been to Nadine's house several times over the years. She was really the only person Nadine could think of that her mother would allow her to spend the night with.

After school, the girls gathered outside the door. Linda was the first to get there. Nadine was pleased to see her.

It wasn't a joke, she thought. *I am really going to spend the night with the popular girls. Maybe things are going to be great this year.*

Juanita and Julia came to the doorway, and Nadine got a little tickle in her stomach when Juanita called for her favorite girls to follow her. She never thought she'd be in that line.

She thought of her sister walking home from school with Edward. It infuriated her. She strode defiantly on behind the group of girls all the way to Linda's house.

"So, Nadine, what did your sister say about you coming to our little get-together?" Juanita asked.

"She never really said anything about it." Nadine changed the subject quickly. "Are we going to put on makeup tonight?"

"Maybe," Linda said, disregarding Nadine's trivial question.

"Is Doris, um, okay?" Julia asked.

"Yeah, I guess so. Her and Edward are probably holding hands right about now. I wouldn't worry too much about her." Nadine laughed.

"No, I don't mean just because of this," Julia replied. "I, well, *we've* heard some things about her. Um…about her, uh, as a girl."

Nadine was confused. "I don't know what you mean. As a girl?"

"God, Julia," Juanita shouted. "What she is trying to say is that we heard through the grapevine that your sister had to make a trip to the doctor. Is she sick?"

Nadine realized then that they all knew about Doris. "No, she's not sick. It was just a check-up," she stated flatly, although her heart was racing.

"We know it wasn't just that," Juanita said. "There is something wrong with her. We all know. Don't worry; we haven't said anything to anyone else."

"How did you find out?" Nadine asked.

"Well, we really can't say, but rest assured that no one else know. We got the information firsthand."

Surely, Nadine thought, *Doris didn't tell them.*

"We are really concerned for her," Linda said. "We want her to be alright."

"She's fine," Nadine replied. "She's going to see a specialist. Everything's going to be fine."

"It's just a little weird to us, that's all," Julia said. "I think I'd be interested in knowing exactly what it looks like."

"Julia!" Juanita shouted. "How could you? That's a terrible thing to be interested in."

"Well, actually, I'd kind of like to know what it looks like too," Linda said, holding her hands up defensively. "I'm just being honest."

"Well, Nadine?" Juanita shrugged her shoulders and looked at Nadine curiously. "It seems that our girls want to see."

"There's really nothing to see." Nadine gave them a kind of disgusted look. "I don't think she'd let you, anyway."

"No, I mean, maybe we could see without her knowing."

"How is that even possible?"

"We have a plan," Julia said. "You just take us to your house tonight at bath time, and we'll look for ourselves. We have a right to know just like you do. You're her sister, and we're her best friends. We want to help her. Maybe this has something to do with her stuffing her bra. If we can get to the bottom of this, then maybe we can all be friends again."

Nadine prayed to God the rest of the way to Linda's house that maybe the girls would forget all about this, and they could just put on makeup and fix each other's hair. Nothing else was mentioned for at least a couple of hours after they got to Linda's house. Nadine was relieved.

Once the girls were there, they talked about boys, boobs, and periods for a while, and then they put on their pajamas and went to the kitchen to grab snacks.

"So, what's the plan for tonight?" Juanita asked.

"It's almost dark." Julia looked out the kitchen window. "So, when is bath time, Nadine?"

Nadine was caught off guard. "What?"

"You know, bath time for your sister. When?"

"If I get caught by my mother—" Nadine stopped when the girls gave her condescending looks. "She usually takes her bath around eight-thirty."

"Good. Linda, go round us up some flashlights, and we'll have an adventure," Juanita said excitedly.

"Are we going to walk all the way to my house?" Nadine asked.

"No, silly. We're going to wait for my parents to watch TV, and then we'll take the car," Linda said, as if Nadine should've known. "We take it all the time. My dad really doesn't care as long as we stay on the country roads."

Nadine felt sick. There was a huge lump in her throat. Surely, this wasn't going to happen. Maybe they were just playing around with her. But then she saw Linda rummaging through the laundry room.

"Flashlights," she said when she emerged. "I only have three. Julia, you and Nadine can share one."

Nadine felt sicker and sicker as the clock hands ticked toward eight.

"Come on, girls," Linda said. "Let's go."

They piled into the car, Linda in the driver's seat and Juanita at her side in the passenger's seat. Julia and Nadine were in the back with their one flashlight between them.

Once they reached the end of the road to Nadine's house, they stopped. Juanita got out first.

"Come on," Linda told Nadine and Julia.

"I'm going to go on ahead," Juanita said. "You guys wait here for about ten minutes, and then I'll meet you at Nadine's house. Flicker your flashlight when you get there. Shine it toward the road so I'll know you're there."

"Where is she going?" Nadine asked, watching Juanita run off down the road.

"Oh, she's just going on ahead to make sure it's all safe and no one will see us," Linda answered.

Nadine hung her head and spoke in a low voice. "I don't think I want to go."

"I knew you didn't have it in you to do this," Linda said. "You're just like your sister says you are a big, big baby! Every time we wanted to invite you somewhere, she would always tell us not to. She'd say you'd act like a baby, and here you are acting like a baby."

"Guess she was right," Julia said, taking the flashlight from Nadine's hand.

"No, I'm not a baby," Nadine argued. "I'm going."

"Of course, she is." Linda took the flashlight from Julia and handed it back to Nadine. "I never doubted you for a minute."

They stopped at the edge of the driveway. Nadine could see Juanita far down the road.

Nadine squinted to see Juanita coming down the road. "It looks like she's got someone with her."

"No, it's just a shadow," Linda reassured her. "Keep watch on that window and tell us when."

"Okay, the light's on now," Nadine said. "We can go."

As Nadine started to walk toward the house, the lump in her throat and the knot in her stomach began to grow again. She could imagine Doris just now getting into the bathroom and disrobing. The shade was almost halfway up. If she would just close the shade, Nadine thought, none of this would even matter.

Linda and Julia had both sprinted toward the window. Nadine hurried catch up.

"Okay, now just wait," Linda said.

"What are we waiting for?" Nadine asked.

"Just wait. You'll see." Linda was peeking through the bottom half of the window, just far enough away that Doris wouldn't notice her.

Nadine could see her sister standing at the sink, naked and looking in the mirror, a nightly ritual Nadine had gotten used to over the years. Doris would go over every inch of her face and neck with a washcloth before taking a bath. *If only she would put her towel on while she's standing there,* Nadine thought. But no, she hadn't, and it didn't look like she was going to.

Linda's eyes grew wide as she stared into the window, and without even realizing it, she began to walk toward it in an almost trance-like state.

Then Nadine saw him. Juanita was pushing Edward as she ran behind him.

"It's over here," she said in a loud whisper to Edward. "We don't know what kind of animal it is, but we're all scared to death."

Nadine dropped her flashlight and began to back away from the group. She knew in that moment what all this had been about.

"It was over here by the window," Linda said. "We were all inside having our sleepover, and we heard it out here, and then we saw it."

Nadine was frozen in silence. She couldn't breathe, and she certainly couldn't speak. She could still see her sister standing at the sink. All that was visible was the area from her hips down, but that was all they needed.

Edward looked down at the ground, searching for some kind of animal, scanning up and down the side of the house with a puzzled look on his face. The light from the bathroom window barely shone on the group.

Nadine watched her sister turn from the sink toward the bathtub, toward the window, and in that moment, Linda, Julia, and Juanita pushed Edward up toward the window. His face pressed up against the glass. Nadine heard Doris's scream. They held him there for what seemed like an eternity.

Nadine continued her backward pace away from the crowd, away from the house, away from her sister's screams. She had faded into the darkness. Edward finally broke himself loose from his trance, from the girls that held him to the window, and took off running back toward his house.

Nadine heard her mother emerge from the house. When the back door slammed, she came out screaming.

"Get the hell outta here!" Viola screamed, chasing the girls with a broom.

Nadine had never heard her mother curse, but tonight, she spewed a stream of curse words so loud that it echoed off the mountain. She kept backing away from the house as she watched her mother chase the girls out of the yard and part of the way down the road.

Her half-visible sister fell to the floor in the bathroom and cried incessantly. Her mother ran back from the road, and as she approached the back door to the house, she threw her broom.

Nadine saw her enter the bathroom and hold Doris tight in her arms. Their mother was crying too. The two of them sat in the bathroom floor and sobbed, rocking back and forth together.

Every so often, Nadine could hear her sister wail loudly, "Oh, God, Mama!"

CHAPTER NINETEEN

Doris opened her eyes quickly and gasped for air. Had it really happened? She had asked herself that question several times throughout the night. The terror came in waves as she slept, and each time the horror washed over her, she would wake up, unable to breathe.

She looked over at Nadine's bed. Again, it was empty. The nightmare was real; she was quite aware of that now. She wanted Nadine to be there, even though she knew her sister had brought them there to laugh, to stare. Doris wanted to be mad at her sister, but instead she just felt heavy. Her stomach was sick and empty just like the rest of her body.

Her mother was asleep now. She had to do it—now or never. She wanted to cry some more. Though she tried, there were no more tears, just a dry ache coming from her mouth. Her eyes were still hot and swollen, her nose and mouth red and raw. Without much of a conscious effort, she rose up out of bed and put her feet on the floor. It was as if an invisible force was pushing her. She knew what she had to do. She removed the embroidered pillowcase from her pillow, pulled it up to her face and breathed deeply.

She passed Nadine's bed and began to rummage through the closet. What did she need?

Everything. I need to take it all.

She began to take her clothes off their hangers and fold them neatly on her bed. She shuffled over to the chest and removed undergarments, folded them as best as she could, and placed them in the pillowcase first. Her clothes followed. She wanted to take her jewelry box. There was never much jewelry inside, but the box itself was too special to leave behind. Doris looked in the mirror, brushed her hair, and folded it up on top of her head with pins. She looked older—old enough, she decided, to buy a bus ticket.

If only they hadn't come to the window. If only Nadine had come home instead of going to their party. If only Edward hadn't seen. But he had. All of them had. She couldn't stay here, not anymore.

Since school had first started, Doris could feel their eyes on her every day. She knew by the way she would catch them looking at her that they knew, or at least suspected that she was different. And in some small way, like a storm rumbling in the distance, she'd known it was coming. The air was heavier, thicker, and somehow didn't smell as sweet. She knew.

Her tears were all gone. Only the traces of them remained: the swelling of her face and the redness in the whites of her eyes. They burned and itched. She wanted to cry some more. She wanted to talk to her sister, her mother, to tell them goodbye, but she couldn't. She had to go. Alone. She never wanted Edward, or anyone else for that matter, to look at her again. She couldn't stand it. Not ever. She kept telling herself that her mother would understand. It would be better for everyone. Better for the family, for Nadine.

Doris grabbed her packed pillowcase and tiptoed into the kitchen. It was dark except for the moon shining through the window on the tabletop. She knew exactly where her mother kept the money —in the can on top of the refrigerator. It was the money that had been saved for Doris, for another doctor. She couldn't bear the thought of going to another doctor; she didn't want to know what was happening to her. She never wanted to know.

She laid her packed pillowcase down on the table and reached for the can, pulled it down and opened the top.

Ten, twenty, thirty, forty... She counted the ones and fives separately, then pulled open her purse and put the money inside.

The frogs, crickets, and other nighttime creatures stopped making noises as she opened the front door. It was as if they were bidding her a final farewell with a moment of pause. Doris knew staying would cause the same effect. It would be the same way at school, the same way in town if she stayed, everyone talking and chirping but stopping to stare as she walked by.

She closed the door behind her silently and slowly, then made her way down the road toward town.

Doris knew the buses left early. She just didn't know exactly when. She'd been to the bus station before with her father. He'd said they had the best coffee, and once when they were in town, they stopped for a cup. Doris remembered how her father had shown her the art of coffee drinking. It was her first cup. She didn't like it. But there she was, ordering a coffee.

"There you go, sweetie," said the waitress behind the counter. The woman's hair had been teased at some point during the day, Doris was sure of at least that. But work, sweat, and wind had reduced the puffed-up hair to a lopsided ball near the crown of her head. Wrinkles circled her eyes, and she wore red lipstick that had faded at some point throughout her workday.

She smelled of stale honeysuckle perfume, and some of the mascara from her long eyelashes had made its way into the corners of her eyes. Her hair was a mousy color, and her white uniform had two coffee stains on the collar. They looked almost like the birthmark Doris had on her right thigh. She was smiling, though, and Doris admired her from where she sat sipping on the coffee.

The waitress did everything so deliberately, from wiping the counter to cleaning the coffee maker. She scooted her rag across the counter and shook out the crumbs over a small garbage container under the cash register. She then lifted up the coffee pot with one hand and swiped the damp rag over the eye of the stove. It made a sizzling noise that didn't seem to faze her at all. Doris flinched a little as if she'd just been burned. When she was finished, she folded the damp, stained rag that had surely once been white and laid it next to the cash register as if that was its rightful place.

"When does the next bus leave?" Doris asked her.

"The next bus to where? We have a lot of buses going to a lot of places."

"Um, I'm not sure I remember to exactly where." Doris was shaken a little by the woman's directness. "I was visiting some family here, and I know I have to take two buses to get back home, but I'm not sure where to."

The waitress sighed deeply, interrupting Doris's rambling, pulled out a pack of cigarettes, and smacked it against her palm. Magically, one cigarette popped out the side. She pulled out a match from underneath the cash register, scraped it against the bottom of the counter, and lit her cigarette.

"Oh, yeah. Home." She had an almost reminiscent look about her. "Home is where you can go when no one else wants you." She cocked her head, her hair shifting slightly as she did. "Home is where—"

She was interrupted by the bell on the door to the diner.

"Let me get this one, honey," she said. "I'll be right back."

She left her cigarette burning just below the counter in an ashtray. The smoke billowed up just next to Doris's coffee cup. A man came in and sat down at a booth by himself.

"What can I get for you, sir?" the waitress asked.

"Coffee, please," he said quietly.

"Coffee it is." She put her pen away with her pad of paper and slipped them both back into her pocket. "Coffee runs the world," she said as she walked back from the table to the counter, winking at Doris as she spoke. She grabbed the cup, filled it with coffee quickly, and took it to the man.

"So, you were saying something about home?" The waitress took a long drag off her cigarette and stared at Doris.

"Um, yes," Doris said. "I'm going back home to, uh… I've just visited my cousins, my family here…" She could feel the woman inspecting her thoroughly as her cigarette dangled from her faded red lips.

"You been crying?" she blurted.

"Oh. My cousins. I'm going to miss them terribly, and this mountain air is so bad for my allergies, and—*achoo*." Doris faked a sneeze to change the subject.

"Oh, I see," said the waitress.

"Well…" the waitress leaned in closer to Doris, she had her cigarette in one hand and was leaning in on her elbow. "I hope you get them allergies taken care of when you get home."

Something about how the woman said "home" made Doris feel a little uneasy. It was as if she suspected that she wasn't going home at all.

"That your luggage?" The woman pointed her cigarette at the stuffed pillowcase sitting on the stool next to Doris. "You a world traveler, I guess?"

"Well, no. Just this once, you see, I—"

The waitress cut Doris's lie short, putting out her cigarette in the ashtray and coming out from behind the counter.

"Let's go see when the next bus leaves, honey."

"Okay." Doris got up from her stool, quite relieved.

The chart was confusing, but Doris furrowed her brow and tried to look interested and knowledgeable.

"…and if you wanted to go to Cleveland, then you'd have to take this bus to Louisville and then another to Cincinnati and then to Cleveland," the woman continued without a break.

She said *Louisville* at least half a dozen times in her hurried explanation of the bus routes. It seemed that no matter where Doris went, she'd have to go to Louisville first.

"Yes, that's it." Doris nodded. "Louisville. That's it. And then I get on the bus to Cleveland, but Cincinnati first."

"You're a long way from home, honey. Who dropped you off here at the stop?"

"No one," Doris said panicking a little. "I walked. It's not like I need a babysitter."

"Well, it leaves at six," the waitress said. "You've got a few more minutes."

Doris followed her back to the counter. "How about another cup and maybe a piece of toast?"

"Yeah, that'd be fine."

The woman's fascination about Doris's comings and goings seemed to dissipate as new customers came in.

A bus had pulled in and parked. People were getting off. There was a soldier, a mother and two small children, and others— so many others. The diner buzzed with excitement, and the counter was soon full. Doris picked up her pillowcase and placed it in the floor between her feet, holding it there between her feet while she ate her toast.

Suddenly, it hit her. She was leaving, leaving home, her mother, her father, Nadine... The ache plunged into her stomach again. She went to the bathroom and washed her face.

"Please, Lord Jesus, help me," Doris prayed as she stood there looking into the mirror. "I just want everything to be alright. Please let Mama and Nadine and Daddy be okay."

"Hey, you in there?" someone shouted from outside the door. Doris recognized the voice as that of the waitress. "The bus is leavin'!"

Doris grabbed her pillowcase and ran out of the bathroom. The waitress stood at the doorway, holding the door open for the bus passengers.

"Got your ticket?" she asked Doris as she stepped out of the diner.

"Yes, I got it."

"Good enough. Good trip and all that."

With those final words ushering her out of Rayes County, Doris was pushed from behind by others trying to get on the bus. Her feet were trying to move slowly, but the crowd behind her moved her forward. Before she knew it, she was on the bus looking for her seat, just like everyone else.

Where had all these people come from?

Doris wondered how long she'd been in the bathroom. Maybe they'd been on the bus all along. None of them took note of her at all. It was as if they didn't even see her. Everyone was talking and looking out the windows. They were jostling luggage and settling into their seats.

Doris leaned down a little to peer out the windows and see what was so interesting out there. The sun was just starting to come up over the mountain. It was beautiful. A beautiful Rayes County sunrise. She knew what that meant. She knew at that very moment what her mother was doing, and she probably didn't even realize Doris had gone. She knew her mama was looking out the window, watching the sunrise, sipping her morning coffee. Her mother loved the sunrise. She'd always told Doris and Nadine that it was the earth's way of giving everyone a clean slate every day, to start a fresh, clean, new day. Doris had already thought of her mother's words as she sat there drinking her coffee and listening to the waitress. And now, here it was, staring her in the face.

That new day her mother always spoke of.

CHAPTER TWENTY

Doris was no longer terrified. She was ready. Her eyes were wide. She couldn't take them off the ever-changing landscape that was laid out on the road before her, just in front of the bus. She was beginning to get excited. She was going away. Away from the doctor, away from everyone who knew about her, away from the agony of knowing that Edward had seen everything.

A feeling of relief rushed over her just after the bus left Rayes County. No one on that bus knew her, and she was certainly satisfied with that. Maybe she would even change her name. She would be new—a new person. Doris's eyes grew wider with possibilities. Her legs were still shaking a little, but she wasn't sure now if it was out of fear or excitement or maybe both. Every now and then, she would begin to think of her mother and how upset she'd be when she found Doris and the money were gone. But she would wipe it from her mind almost as quickly as she thought it.

Everyone is better off this way, she thought.

Besides, it all seemed far away now. The landscape changed quickly, from the mountains of home to the rolling hills and then to the flatland. Doris had never seen so many different things, different places. At the last stop, she saw the biggest city she'd ever seen. Later, farther down the road, there was an even bigger city. Each time they passed a town, Doris tried to picture herself living there, but she didn't dare consider staying. She'd bought a ticket to go all the way to Cleveland, and that was where she was going. Cleveland. To almost the end of the earth—or at least the United States.

"This will be our last stop before Cleveland," the bus driver announced over the loudspeaker. "We will be boarding passengers at this stop. Please gather all your items from the other seats and put them under your own seat. We will be making room for new passengers. We will have one hour before we re-board this bus. Please do *not* be late."

The driver stood next to his seat as he spoke, wearing a gray suit and a hat. Doris thought he looked a little like a soldier in that suit, but he was much too fat and much too old for that. When he was finished speaking, he stepped off the bus and escorted the passengers off one by one.

Doris hurried to gather her purse, count her money, and then start walking toward the door. The driver tipped his hat to her as he led her off by the arm.

"Thank you, sir," she said, her voice hoarse from not speaking so long.

"You're very welcome, ma'am."

The streets were lined with stores and diners. Doris had never seen so many places to go, so many places to eat. She tried to fall in line with the other passengers who had left the bus, but they were going every which way, no two or three people going in the same direction at all.

Doris got scared again as she looked up and down the street.

The bus driver must have noticed her struggling for a place to go. "Ma'am? Might I suggest you go into the bus station? There is a nice café and anything else you might need to freshen up a bit."

With that, he closed the door, tipped his hat once again, and walked inside the station. Doris followed close behind. She couldn't believe how many people were there. It was like a festival. There was music playing; people were eating; and there was even a little shop in the building. It didn't look big enough to hold it all, Doris thought. She turned around to glance toward the front door. She didn't want to stray too far. Now she could see beyond the bus. Cars were speeding down the street right next to each other, just like in the movies. There were at least five lanes of traffic, maybe more, and each lane of cars tried to move faster than the others. Horns beeped and people leaned out of their windows, motioning to and yelling at other drivers.

"Excuse me, ma'am," someone said just behind her. "Could you tell me where the shops are here in town?"

Doris was silent, speechless, as she looked at the tall woman. She towered over Doris like a statue. She was beautiful with red hair that was twisted up from behind, and she wore a wool hat with lace coming down in the front over her face. Her light green wool suit matched her hat and black shoes, which looked like they had diamonds for buckles. Doris examined her from head to toe and back again.

"Ma'am," the woman said again. "Did you hear me?"

"Oh, um, I'm not from here. It's my first time here." Doris looked down at her own shoes, embarrassed by her appearance in front of such an elegant lady.

The woman's nails were perfectly manicured, and there was not a hair out of place anywhere. Her waist was tiny, her shoulders broad.

"Oh, dear," the woman said, placing a gloved hand on her hip. "Well, I guess we'll just have to go and find the shops together. What's the fun of traveling if you can't shop and look at new things?"

She put her arm in Doris's, and they headed out of the station and down the street.

"I really don't need to go too far…" Doris muttered.

"When is your bus leaving?"

"In about forty-five minutes."

"Mine too. You wouldn't happen to be leaving on the bus to Cleveland, would you?"

"Yes. Yes, I am," Doris said, smiling. "Are you?"

"Yes, dear, that's my bus, too." The woman's blue eyes sparkled. "We've got plenty of time. Don't you worry about a thing."

Once outside, Doris felt frightened again. Cars rushed by, and the crowd moved so fast she could hardly keep up. It made her dizzy.

"Where are you from?" The woman seemed to know right away that Doris was out of place in the big city.

"South," was all that Doris could get out before the interruption.

"And your name?"

"Doris."

"Amanda," she said, still arm in arm with Doris. "I am so pleased to meet you. But young lady"—she smiled as she pulled Doris's face up with her gloved hands. "You are going to hold your head up high and smile if you are going to go shopping with me. What on earth do you have to be so sad about?"

"Nothing," Doris lied. "I'm just tired from traveling." She had heard so many people during the course of the day use that excuse for everything from overeating to being cross with their children. She could certainly use it as an excuse for looking sad.

"We'll take care of that." Amanda pushed Doris from the side into a café. "We'll get some tea." She stole a table for the two of them just as a couple was about to sit down. "Sorry," she told them, but she sat down anyway. "Go on. Sit down, Doris."

Doris did as she was told.

"Waiter! Waiter," Amanda demanded. "We'll have two hot teas with lemon over here."

The waiter nodded his head, and Amanda turned her attention back toward Doris.

"It's been such a long day," she said. "I've ridden all the way in from Chicago. I've been to every other corner a person can get to from Chicago, but I've never been to Cleveland. Thought I'd try it."

"Why do you travel so much?" Doris asked with much enthusiasm.

"Well, if you must know, it's my husband's fault."

183

Doris noticed the huge diamond on Amanda's left hand. It was hard to imagine that thing had been under a glove all day. She couldn't imagine how it had ever fit.

"Why your husband? Is he sick?

"Yes, he's sick. Very sick. He can't keep his hands off his secretary. It's a dreadful, dreadful disease," Amanda snapped. "We just can't seem to find a cure."

"Oh, I'm sorry."

"Oh, really, don't be." Amanda seemed annoyed at the fact that Doris was showing her pity. "About the only thing that straightens him right up—at least temporarily—are my little trips. I leave for a while, and he gets scared and starts staying home more often. That's why I'm here."

"Why not just leave him all together if he can't be faithful to you?"

Amanda seemed surprised. "Well, you're a progressive little southern girl, aren't you?"

Doris smiled confidently as if to say, *yes, I am quite progressive.*

"But you see, I love him." Amanda pulled out a handkerchief and dabbed a little at her eyes. "I really do. I just want him to get rid of her."

"Have you told him?"

"Oh, dear heavens, no. He doesn't know that I know he's having"—she put her hand up to her mouth and whispered— "an affair."

"Are you sure that he is?" Doris asked.

"Oh, well, you know… A woman just knows," Amanda replied, blowing on her tea. "A woman just knows. He works late all the time, and he's always going out of town." She began to tear up again. This time, Doris handed her the handkerchief.

"Maybe you should talk to him about it. Maybe he thinks you're having an affair with you leaving town all the time."

"Keep your voice down, child," Amanda said, evidently startled that Doris would say such a thing out loud.

"Sorry."

"But now that you mention it… No, no, he doesn't think anything of the sort."

"But if you love him, don't you at least owe him the chance to deny it or confirm it?" Doris asked, thinking she could never travel all the way to Cleveland with this woman.

"You know, I do miss him. I think I'll go home and have a word with him about it," Amanda said, putting her gloves on. "Oh, dear. Look at the time. We have to get you back to the bus."

"You mean you're not going to Cleveland?"

"No, dear, you've talked me into going home. Now, let's get you back to the bus."

Amanda walked Doris back to the bus. It was time to board. Doris was happy to see the driver standing beside the door.

"Did you find everything alright, young lady?" he asked.

"Yes, thank you," Doris replied.

Amanda turned her around before she boarded and hugged her. "You have a lovely trip. You're such a knowledgeable young lady." And with that, she walked back through the doors to the bus station.

"I see you've met our resident socialite," the bus driver said to Doris.

"What do you mean?"

"Oh, she's gotten me before," he said. "She's got some rich husband in Chicago who runs a bank up there. She's always coming to this station, and she always gets a bus ticket, but she never goes anywhere but back home. I think she's got some real problems. Sorry you had to deal with that. You really shouldn't talk to people you don't know."

"Oh no, sir. Really, it's okay. I thought she was, well, interesting."

"Oh, she is." He laughed. "She certainly is interesting. Rich people don't have anything better to do than make up problems for the rest of us to deal with. She really just needs to go home and stay home."

"Yeah," Doris said quietly as she watched Amanda walk back through the station. "Maybe she does."

CHAPTER TWENTY-ONE

It was dark now, and the bus ride was beginning to be a little painful on Doris's bottom. She squirmed in her seat, pulled her pillowcase filled with clothes up to her head, leaned it on the wall of the bus next to her seat, and pushed her head into it. She tried to close her eyes and rest, though she knew she couldn't. It wouldn't be too much longer now, and she'd be in Cleveland. Panic was starting to set in.

She looked over at the seat next to her. An old woman had been sitting there quietly with her hands folded on her stomach since they'd left the last stop. Doris thought long and hard about starting a conversation with her but decided against it. She was sure the bus driver knew what he was talking about when he told her she shouldn't be talking to people she didn't know.

It scared her to think about being late for catching the bus. Amanda had almost made her late. If she'd been left in that town, what would she have done?

It was at that moment that she realized the same thing was about to happen in Cleveland. It was the last stop. She had become so accustomed to being on the bus; she hadn't really given any thought to the fact that she'd have to leave. But no matter what town they stopped in, no matter where it was, she would eventually have to get off that bus for good. That last stop was coming up shortly.

Doris gazed out the window, watching the lights of town after town come and go. Sometimes, in the bigger towns, there were more lights, and sometimes she could see people. The later it got, the more panicked she became.

It was colder there than back home, and she hadn't brought her heavy coat. She should've known it would be colder farther north. What had she been thinking?

I didn't know I was going north until I got to the bus station, she reasoned.

She shook her head and let out a short little sigh. That seemed like such a long time ago—and it sort of was. Almost an entire day had gone by. It wasn't daylight quite yet. In fact, Doris had no idea what time it was. Then she heard that dreaded sound: the bus driver on the loudspeaker again.

"We are now entering the city of Cleveland. Please gather your belongings and prepare to leave the bus."

Those who were asleep woke up and started to get their things together. Doris didn't have much to gather, just one pillowcase and one purse. She ran her hands along her skirt to try and unwrinkle it a bit. It didn't work.

"I'm not ready," she said out loud.

"Well, I was wondering if you could talk at all," said the old woman sitting next to her. "You look ready to me."

"Oh, I didn't mean to say that out loud. My name is Doris." She stuck her hand out to the woman.

"Beatrice. Are you from Cleveland or just visiting?"

"Both. Or I will be doing both," Doris answered. "This is my first time here, but I'm staying."

"Well, welcome to Cleveland," said Beatrice.

Doris considered her encounter with Amanda for a moment; but now she was desperate for a friend, someone who could help her.

"Are you from here, Beatrice?"

"Yes, born and raised," the old woman said. "I was just visiting some folks down south for a few days."

"Oh, that's nice," Doris said quickly. There was no time for pleasantries. "I'm going to need to find somewhere to stay for the night. Do you know a place?"

"Certainly. There's a woman who lets out rooms by the night up here by the bus station. They're pretty cheap. You got money?"

Doris shrugged. "A little."

When they got off the bus, she kept close to Beatrice, right on her heels.

"The place you're looking for is right over there," Beatrice said, pointing at a two-story white house across the street.

"Oh, thank you."

It was late, but traffic still sped up and down the street. Doris had a moment of panic, taking deep breaths to calm herself. There she was, in Cleveland.

Here I am. I'm in Cleveland. Now what? She thought.

Doris was terrified of crossing the street. The cars were going so fast. Everyone was moving so fast. She was jostled a bit by those passing her. They kept running into the bulky pillowcase. She looked at it. It had once been beautiful and white with delicate needlepoint work. Now it was dirty, dingy, just the way she felt. Now that her feet were back on solid ground, she began to feel uneasy about what she had done. Were they looking for her? She was sure her mother and father would be looking for her.

She was also sure Nadine would be happy she was gone. They'd had more trouble getting along this past summer than Doris could ever remember.

"I can't think about that now," she said aloud to herself. Closing her eyes tight, said a small prayer. "Please, Lord Jesus, please help me get through this."

She opened her eyes again, and the traffic seemed to have parted just for her. She began to cross the street—a street unlike any she'd ever seen before.

She was certain that everyone in Rayes County was asleep by now, but not here. This city was bursting at the seams with all kinds of automobiles and people. Businesses were still open. She could see people shopping in them and parking their cars in their lots. Doris couldn't help but be awed by the massive buildings. It was dark, but she could see almost everything. The streets were even brighter than the main streets in Rayes County at Christmas.

Once she was across the street and standing in front of the building, she could she the sign: Rooms for Rent. It was a nice sign. All the words looked the same. It wasn't handwritten, but actually printed. Doris decided it was as good a reason as any to stay there. Under the mailbox attached to the house were the words *five dollars*.

She pushed the buzzer, and a white-haired woman came to the door. The doorway was darkened. The only detail Doris could see was the white hair glistening in the light shining somewhere inside the house.

"Yes?" she said.

"You have a room for the night?" Doris asked.

"Yes. Yes, I do," said the lady. "Are you good people? We only let out to good people."

"Oh, yes. I'm very good people."

The woman stepped out onto the porch. "You from the south, girl?"

Doris jumped back a little. The woman was black. She had never seen a black woman up close before. She'd seen some earlier in the day at different bus stations, but none of them had been running businesses.

"Did I scare you?"

"No," Doris said, "just a little jumpy."

"I asked you a question little girl," The woman put her hands on her hips. "You a southern girl?"

"Yes, I am."

"Where 'bouts?"

"Kentucky."

"'Course. I'd recognize that talk anywhere. I should have guessed without you tellin' me." She ushered Doris into her house. "I got people down there in Kentucky—the northern part, 'course.

You know what I mean. Those of us who stayed down there are plentiful in the north but not so much so in the south. You know what I mean."

The house smelled of cooked cabbage and pinto beans. This woman truly had southern roots. It smelled just like Doris's house when her mother cooked straight from the garden.

The floor was covered with linoleum, but there were foot-wide gaps between the linoleum and the walls that uncovered a shiny hardwood floor. There was a lamp on just next to an armchair in the sitting room. A bowl of popcorn sat next to what looked like a glass of soda on the table next to the chair. A blanket was rolled up there. The woman must have been sitting there before Doris knocked.

She grabbed Doris by the arm and pulled her over to the couch next to the chair.

"Let me get some light on you. We'll put your bag over here next to the door."

Just as Doris sat down on the couch, the woman yelled.

"Whee, Lord have mercy," the woman said, holding Doris's bag up to the light. "This is some fancy needlework here. Delicate. Fine. You do this?"

"No," Doris answered. "My mother."

"Your mother is a talented woman, she is. Now that's some fancy needlework there." She laid the pillowcase at the doorway and came back to sit in her chair.

"Popcorn?" she offered.

"No, thank you."

"I'm Deely," the woman said. "Now, who are you?"

"My name is Doris."

"You look tired, child. You need a bed. Let's get you in one."

Doris was relieved. She was so tired, and the last thing she wanted to do was talk about anything that had happened over the last day.

"Yes. It's five dollars?"

"We'll take care of that in the mornin', child...unless you're gonna take up and leave in the middle of the night. But it's already the middle of the night. I take it you ain't going nowhere but to bed."

"Yes, ma'am," Doris said, bowing her head a little.

"And manners, too. You sure are a Kentucky girl. That's about the only thing I miss about Kentucky. Everybody's got manners."

Deely grabbed her by the arm again and led her upstairs. She talked the entire time about how most people just didn't have any manners and how she sure did appreciate people who did.

Doris opened the door to her room, and Deely handed her the pillowcase.

"You sleep good now," she said. "We can talk some more tomorrow and find out more about you. I like finding out about people."

Doris didn't even open the pillowcase to find her pajamas. She didn't even pull down the bedcovers. She just took off her shoes, laid her head on the pillow, and fell asleep.

CHAPTER TWENTY-TWO

Please don't worry about me, I'm going to be okay here. I love you, but I have to be where everybody doesn't know about it.

Tell everyone I love them and that I'm alright.

Doris couldn't bring herself to even write her sister's name. Every time she thought of Nadine, she felt a raw, gnawing pain in her stomach. It was best just to ignore the fact that Nadine even existed, even though she missed her terribly.

The letter was short. There was no return address. But it made Doris feel a little less heartbroken. Her mother needed to know she was okay.

Doris had woken up several times during the night, not knowing where she was, wondering how she had gotten there. It all seemed like a dream—a nightmare—but each time she looked around the room, she knew it was real.

One letter a month was what she had decided to send her mother, never a return address, no mention of her sister, and they would all be short.

Doris could hear people downstairs. The smell of coffee wafted up into her room. Light shone through the drapes a little, and she knew it was time to face the daylight, time to figure out what she was going to do.

The floor was cold to her feet, and the nightgown she had finally changed into during the night was no match for the northern fall, but they were all she had in her bag, the pillowcase that was propped up against the bed, still unpacked from the night before.

She walked over to the curtain that served as a closet door and pulled it back. There were hangers there, and some cobwebs. The bare wood floor looked unfinished, as did the walls. It smelled of dampness.

I can't hang my clothes in there, she thought. *I'm not staying. I have to find a job and somewhere to live.*

The fear of what she had done overtook her once more, and she couldn't catch her breath. She sat on the bed, too weak to cry anymore.

"Hey, you! Miss Kentucky!" Deely yelled outside the door. "You up?"

"Yes, ma'am," Doris called back. "I'm up."

"Come on down here and get some breakfast."

"Be right there." Doris picked up her bag and rummaged through the clothes she had brought. She decided on the plaid wool skirt and a gray sweater, then brushed her hair and re-did her hairpins, making sure it was put up neatly.

Deely was in the kitchen, walking all around the table, gathering this and that for the morning breakfast. This kitchen was set up all wrong, not at all like Doris's mother's kitchen. The sink was at the back of the room with no window, the refrigerator was on the opposite side of the room, and the stove was next to the window on the far right of the room. From there, Doris could see outside into the street. Cars lined the road, stopping and starting. She had heard noises from the street all night and didn't know quite what to make of it until now. Through that same window, she could see another house, not even ten feet away.

"You comin' in here or not, child?" Deely pulled out a chair for Doris. "I thought you were gonna sleep all day."

"Sorry, ma'am."

"Don't be sorry. People sleep as long as they want when they stay here at Miss Deely's. I just worried that you might be hungry, thin as you are. People as skinny as you can't go too long without food, I'd imagine."

Doris smiled, pleased at being called thin, but unsure about being looked at as skinny. "I wanted to get a letter mailed," she said as Deely poured a cup of coffee for her. "Where do I do that?"

"We can do post here. I'll give it to the mailman when he comes to deliver. Hand it here. I'll take care of it."

"I need a stamp."

"I have some extra. I'll loan you one today, and you can bring me one back tomorrow. That's the way we do things around here. I'd imagine it's much like that where you come from."

"Yes, ma'am."

Deely took the letter from Doris's hands, held it out at arm's length, and looked over her horn-rimmed glasses, examining it closely front and back.

"I have to let them know I've arrived safely."

"Viola. That your mama's name?"

"Yes."

"Beautiful name. Viola." Deely said it again as if to inscribe it into her memory.

"What are you, 'bout nineteen? Twenty?"

Doris hesitated. "Yes."

"Well, which is it? Nineteen or twenty?"

Doris thought about it for a moment and blurted out, "Twenty." If this woman thought she could be twenty, then maybe she could pass for it. It made her feel older, made her sit up a little taller.

"Why, you're still just a baby," Deely said, throwing her hands back in disbelief. "They get younger and younger comin' up here looking for work."

"Yes," Doris said, eyes wide. "I'll be looking for work."

"What kinda work you do?"

"Well, I clean and cook, and I can garden. Just about anything."

"I don't know about such as that, but we do have a lot of factory work up here. Those jobs are mostly for the young men, though. Where do you plan to start looking?"

"I really don't know anything about your town, and I really don't know where to start looking, but I have to find something today or tomorrow."

"Today or tomorrow?" Deely asked, surprised. "I imagine lots of people would like to find work today or tomorrow."

"There are jobs here in the town, aren't there?" The hole in Doris's stomach grew again.

"Oh, yeah," Deely said. "We have jobs. I just don't know about a youngster like you finding work today."

Doris knew she couldn't survive for too much longer with the money she had left. She knew she could stay at Deely's for only one more night at the price posted on the house. She had to hurry. Going home was not an option. She hurried and ate the toast Deely laid before her and drank the coffee. Her purse and coat were ready in the sitting room at the front of the house.

"I'm going to go," she said, walking out of the kitchen.

"You staying another night?" Deely asked as she almost chased her out the door.

"Yes, I'll be back, and I'll bring you a stamp."

"You might check downtown for work. I heard tell they need some help in some of the shops near the college—the lunch shops."

Doris had no idea what Deely was talking about, but she walked down the porch steps, nodding as though she had just understood every word.

Doris didn't know why she was hurrying, and she certainly didn't know to where. The thought of not being able to find work in the next day or so quickly turned her panic into urgency.

Before she knew it, she was out of the sight of Deely's house and in a completely new part of town. She had seen cities before in pictures and imagined how huge they would be. People were walking, talking, and scampering all over the sidewalks. They didn't even notice she was there. Even the people she didn't know back home would nod their heads at her when she passed them in town. These people really didn't see her. Men in long black coats and black hats passed by quickly in the cold autumn air. Doris could feel her nose start to turn red from the cold. She stuck the back of her hand to it to bring some warmth for a few moments and realized how unseasonably she was dressed. No gloves, no hat.

I must look really out of place, she thought.

But again, no one seemed to notice her at all.

There was so much to look at, and as she traveled on, the buildings got bigger and bigger. Glass doors opened and closed. Shoes hit the pavement in time. Windows were filled with beautiful clothes to buy. Signs were everywhere, colorful and bright, big and small ones. It was all going by so fast.

A newspaper, she thought. *That's what I need.*

"Sir? Sir. Excuse me, sir?" Doris pleaded with a man who was walking in front of her. He didn't seem to hear her. She tapped him on the shoulder. He turned his head around, looking back at her, but kept walking. She stepped up her pace to walk next to him.

"May I help you, miss?" he asked in a deep, sophisticated tone.

"I need to find a newspaper."

The man stopped, turned toward her, and smiled. Doris could see amusement on his face.

"My, my, young lady. You are far from home?" he asked.

"Yes, sir, I am. How did you know?" Doris was sure it was the way she was dressed. Her hairstyle alone would tip off anyone that she was not sophisticated enough to be walking in the big city.

"You're a southerner," he said, smiling even wider this time, showing his teeth. "You have a beautiful accent. Very pleasant. Sweet."

"Yes, sir, thank you. I need to find a newspaper—a job."

The man started walking again, and Doris stepped in time with him to keep up. He pointed his briefcase up ahead and across the street diagonally. "Right over there. Good luck to you, miss." He smiled and tipped his hat to her as if realizing she was southern had put him on notice to be a little more polite, just as Deely had said.

Doris smiled back and nodded. She stood there looking in the direction the man had pointed. She could see it, but she didn't really know how to get there from where she was standing. She knew she'd have to do it—cross the busy street—but everything was going so fast. She followed some other pedestrians to the corner. She'd seen others cross the street all morning. She'd join the crowd and blend in as best she could, she decided, and cross the street when they crossed. It had to be harmless, yet somehow Doris was terrified of all those cars speeding by and then stopping, speeding by again and stopping again. She positioned herself right in the middle of a group of strangers waiting to get to the other side. When the cars stopped, she copied the other pedestrians, walking with them. She smelled the gasoline from the cars as she passed them and felt the warmth of the engines. It made her shiver to feel even a little heat in the cool morning air. Finally, she was over to the other side.

"Okay," she said. "Down here."

The newspaper stand was close now. She could find a job in there. "I can do this, I can do this," she said to herself. Then she saw it. *Help Wanted.* It was a small, handmade sign with black lettering. The window where the sign was propped up was cracked at the corner and covered with condensation. Doris peeked inside. It was a small diner, much like the one back home at the bus station. People were eating at tables and drinking coffee at the counter.

She backed up a little to see the sign over top of the diner. *Madessy's* was the name of the place, and it looked friendly enough. It appeared small from the outside, with just enough room for a window and a door. White, half-length curtains hung over the glass window so passersby could see the customers from the street. It was a tall, brick building connected to the other big buildings on either side. There were windows above the diner, but as she looked in again, she could only see the first floor. She searched for an entrance to the windows that were so high above her head, but there didn't seem to be one.

She was afraid to go in, afraid to speak. She'd had no idea until a few moments before that she sounded different. She thought the people *here* sounded different, not her. She rehearsed in her head what she would say when she went in.

What would Mr. Madessy be like? Would he be sophisticated like the man she'd spoken with on the sidewalk? Would he find her accent startling?

She said her lines over and over in her head. "I'd like to speak with Mr. Madessy. I'd like to speak with Mr. Madessy. In her mind, her accent was nonexistent, her diction direct and perfect. Finally, she pushed the door open.

A bell clanged, which brought no attention to her at all. People just kept on doing what they were doing: eating, talking, drinking their coffee. Even the lady working behind the counter just kept working.

Invisible again.

The sounds of the city stopped as the door closed behind her and the bell clanged again. But inside, there were new sounds, crashing dishes and a bell that kept ringing over and over at the hands of a fat black woman. "It's up!" she'd yell each time she put a new plate of food on top of the small counter just beyond the one where the customers were sitting. Now *that* was a bell that everyone seemed to take notice of. Each time she'd ring it, the waitress behind the counter would go straight away to grab the plates and take them out to those waiting to eat.

Doris took her coat off and sat down at the counter, folding it across her lap and placing her purse on top. In no more than a few seconds, the small-framed waitress came over with her pad and pencil out.

"Can I take your order?" she asked through thin pink lips. Her hair was blonde and straight, pinned up in the back. Her voice sounded nasally, like she had a cold.

"I'd like to speak with Mr. Madessy," Doris said in her best northern accent, which she'd just made up out on the sidewalk.

"Mr. Madessy," the girl repeated flatly.

"Yes, thank you," Doris replied.

The blonde girl walked back to the cook's counter and leaned over to the black woman.

The black woman let out a big, hearty laugh and threw her head back. The blonde girl nodded her head in Doris's direction and the black woman looked at Doris, trying to make the smile leave her face. She was still smiling slightly as she took off her apron, placed it on a hook near the stove and came out of the door next to the kitchen and behind the counter.

"Come on over and let's get a table," the woman said when she came out from behind the counter. There were two empty tables next to one another in the far corner of the diner. Doris followed the woman over to the corner and sat down. Just as she did, the blonde waitress came with two cups of coffee.

The black woman began stirring her coffee with a spoon, adding some sugar and some cream from the containers on the table next to the napkins. Her arms were fat, and her skin was the color and consistency of the chocolate gravy Doris's mother would cook sometimes for lunch. Her face was large and her nose, too. Her eyes were black and shiny, like fresh pieces of coal. Her hair was black as tar, pulled up tight and styled in the front, but it glistened in the sunlight from the nearby window.

"So, you're looking for Mr. Madessy, they say?" the woman asked.

"Yes," Doris replied politely, looking around the diner. "Is he not in today?"

She could see a young man mopping on the other side of the room. He was tall and lanky, and one of his eyes was squinted.

Surely, that couldn't be Mr. Madessy?

"Do you know him personally?" the woman asked.

"Um…no, ma'am," Doris stuttered. "I just saw the help wanted sign in the window and wanted to ask about the job."

"Oh, the job." The woman's eyebrows raised a little and she nodded her head. "Well, we do have a job open here, but I don't think we need someone as young as you. What is it you can do anyway?"

"I can cook and clean and do whatever Mr.—"

"There is no Mr. Madessy," the woman interrupted, smiling politely at Doris. "My name is Dessy, and my husband Redd and me own this diner."

"So your name is Dessy Madessy?" Doris questioned.

"No, honey. People called me Ma Dessy for years, and when we took over this place, we just decided to call it Madessy's, 'cause that's what people were calling it anyway. My name is Dessy Jackson."

Doris was embarrassed. She had never given a thought to a black woman owning a diner. She could feel her face getting hot.

"The kind of help we need has been hard to find," Dessy began. "We need someone to be here all the time. We have a room upstairs, and we'd like to find someone to stay up there so we'll have somebody to look over the place all the time—wait tables, clean floors and such."

"Oh," Doris said excitedly, thinking about the room upstairs. "I can do all those things, and I can cook, too. I can make biscuits and gravy, cornbread, and I clean all the time—"

Dessy interrupted Doris once again. "I do all the cooking around here. That's why people come here, and I don't think you'd be happy here, away from your family all the time."

205

"I'm here alone. I don't have any family, and I do need a place to stay," Doris pleaded.

"And we need somebody who's going stay a long time. We don't need someone movin' in and movin' out and then somebody else. How do I know you ain't going to run back home, wherever home is. I assume you're a southerner by the way you talk.

"We decided, Redd and me, that we'd get somebody a little older this time. The last few young one's we've had here have all run off and got married. It don't pay much. The room and food is about all we can give you, other than four dollars a week. It ain't much, see?"

Doris knew the job would be perfect for her; a place to stay, food to eat, and a little extra money each week would be fine with her. But Doris could feel she was losing this woman. She didn't want to hire her for anything.

"Could you just try? I'd be perfect for this job." By this time, Doris's eyes felt hot. The tears were coming, and she wouldn't be able to stop them this time.

"Well, I don't know," Dessy stared at Doris over her coffee cup. "I just don't know." She looked under the table at Doris's legs and then up at her again, as if she was checking for any reason not to give her the job. "Where do you live?"

"I don't really live anywhere right now. I'm staying over at a house just next to the bus station. Do you need the woman's name? You can talk to her. I think she really likes me."

"I'm sure she does. So how long you been staying with her?"

"I just got in last night, but we had a nice talk this morning. I'm going to be staying there again tonight."

Doris fidgeted and began to look around the diner again as Dessy glared at her and sipped her coffee.

"How do you get to the room upstairs?" Doris asked.

"Stairs behind the kitchen," Dessy said, watching Doris's eyes to see what she was looking at. "You say you can bake?"

"Oh, yes, I can," Doris said excitedly.

"Come on in the kitchen," Dessy said, getting up, Doris following close behind.

Once behind the counter, Dessy handed Doris an apron, pointed her to the cupboards, and told her to make a batch. "Just a dozen or so. I want to test you out."

"I thought you wanted to do all the cooking here?" Doris immediately regretted saying it.

"If you work for me, then you'll do whatever I ask you to do, won't you?"

"Yes, ma'am," Doris said, feeling like she had made a breakthrough. Maybe she'd even get the job and, more importantly, the room.

"For now, you just call me Ma Dessy."

With a little more assistance from Ma Dessy, Doris was able to find her way around the kitchen and began gathering her ingredients to make the biscuits. Shortening, flour, baking powder, salt...

"Do you have any buttermilk?" Doris asked Ma Dessy as she was cooking for the next few orders.

"No, child, we don't have buttermilk."

Dessy went to the refrigerator, pulled out a jar of milk, and laid it on the counter where Doris was mixing, then went back to the stove. Every so often, Dessy would look back at Doris to see what she was doing, or maybe *how* she was doing.

Doris was nervous, but she knew what she was doing. She folded in the sweet milk, stirred it a bit with a spoon, and then began to knead the dough. She closed her eyes and imagined she was home again, helping her mother cook breakfast for her dad. Biscuit-making was second nature to all three Garland women. Even Nadine had managed to master the skill.

Doris had just begun to arrange the balls of dough on a pan when an old black man came in through the back of the kitchen. He stopped where Doris was standing.

"Hello, sir." Doris was still amazed at how many black people she had seen since she'd left Rayes County. They were everywhere. She had a teacher once that came from up north and she told her class that black people were plentiful in the big cities, but Doris had still had trouble picturing it...until now. She was right; they *were* plentiful. Doris had never seen a black person in Rayes County, and she began to wonder if any had ever been there at all. For the last two days, Doris had tried to take her mother's words with her, not to stare at people who were different, but she couldn't help it. She couldn't take her eyes off them at times.

The old black man went over to Ma Dessy and whispered to her, but Doris could hear what they were saying.

"I think she'll be fine," Ma Dessy said. "Redd, we need somebody to stay here and watch over the place."

Redd. Ma Dessy's husband, Redd.

She knew if he didn't like her, she would have no chance of getting the job and that room.

When Redd finished whispering with Ma Dessy, he came over to watch what Doris.

"What you makin' there?"

"Biscuits," she replied. "Ma Dessy wanted to see if I could, I guess."

"Well, I guess she did." Redd laughed and looked over at his wife. "I tell her all the time I haven't had a good biscuit since I left Alabama. I see what you're doin' now. You've went and hired you a baker. My wife loves to cook, but she's never been a good baker."

"You shush now and get back on through there," Ma Dessy said, shooing him back through the door.

Doris was starting to feel quite at home with their bickering, it reminded her of her mother and father's trivial arguments with one another.

"Don't pay him any mind. You 'bout done?"

"Yes, they're ready to go in now." Doris put the pan in the preheated oven.

By then, the crowd in the diner was thinning. Only a few people remained, and most of them were standing at the counter paying for their food. The people here were so different from back home, Doris thought. For one thing, not everyone was friendly, only a few. Some were rude and demanding, and the blonde waitress looked exhausted from having to deal with them. Still, she took their money and thanked them for coming to Madessy's and then welcomed them back. She was, at least, polite to them.

Doris hung up the apron Dessy had given her where she found it. She washed her hands, dried them, and then stood by the oven, waiting on her small creations from home to be ready.

The blonde waitress walked by and gave her an odd look. Just as she passed her, she grabbed a hand towel off the stove and came back.

"Here, you've got a little something on your cheek," she said, handing Doris the towel. "I'm Lois. Who are you?"

"Thank you very much. I'm Doris."

"Will you be taking the room upstairs?" Lois asked, pulling a cigarette out of her pocket and lighting it.

"I don't know. I hope so."

"Oh, honey, I wouldn't worry. Ma Dessy wouldn't have let you back here if she wasn't going to hire you."

"Really?"

"I wouldn't be too happy about it before you see that room. I stay with my boyfriend's parents. He's in the service. He hasn't been home in a long time. I miss him a lot."

"Where is he?" Doris asked.

"Oh, he's overseas. In the Army. We're going to get married when he gets back."

The boy who had been mopping the floors earlier came back to the kitchen.

"Hey, Jimmy," Lois said, but he didn't look up. "Jimmy," she said again, sharply this time. She rolled her eyes at Doris. "He's not right, if you know what I mean."

Jimmy came over with his head held low and stood in front of Lois.

"Say hello to Doris," she demanded of him.

"Hello," he said and then quickly went back to his mop and bucket.

"He has mental problems," Lois said, even so loud that Jimmy could hear her. "He came in here one day hungry, and Ma Dessy hired him. She's always hiring crazy people like that. She really shouldn't feel sorry for just everybody. I tell her that all the time, but she won't listen. We've had lots of crazy people working here. We have a lot of homeless people, too. You're not crazy or homeless are you?"

Doris thought about it for a moment. Homeless, yes. Crazy, well, maybe crazy for running away and going to a big city.

"No," she said, looking doubtful. "I'm not crazy or homeless."

"Lois, honey, now you go on and clean up your tables. Doris has some work to do," Ma Dessy said, handing the waitress a cleaning rag.

Doris checked the oven to find the biscuits perfectly done.

Ma Dessy took some jelly and butter out of the refrigerator and yelled at her husband through the back door.

"Come on, kids," Dessy said just as Doris brought the biscuits out of the oven. "Bring those on over here."

Redd came out of the back and joined them at the counter.

211

"Looks like we got a new member of our family, Redd," Dessy said.

"And she can bake. That's all I care about," Redd said as he took some butter and slathered it on the biscuit he'd just sliced open.

Dessy smacked him on top of the head. Lois and Jimmy laughed.

"Thank you, Lord, for this day and for my customers," Dessy prayed. "We are so fortunate to have our good family here with us on this day. Lord, allow us to help your children just as you have helped us so many times…"

Doris watched Ma Dessy pray, even though her eyes should've been closed, and her head bowed like everyone else's. Ma Dessy looked at her with one open eye and continued.

"Thank you, Lord, for our new girl, Doris, who will be living upstairs and watching over the store." She smiled at Doris and then opened the other eye and winked quickly before finishing the prayer. "Amen."

Doris wanted to squeal, but she wanted to appear calm. She already loved these people. It was like the busy streets outside didn't even exist. In here, she felt a little less lost and a little more loved.

Everyone opened their eyes and grabbed the biscuits.

"Mmm… These are good," Ma Dessy said, shaking her head back and forth, closing her eyes tight as she did. "Good, good, good."

Doris thanked them all for their compliments and ate a biscuit herself, complete with a little butter and a lot of jelly.

"You go on over and tell Miss Deely that you are going to be moving out of her boarding house and over here upstairs. She'll be so pleased," Ma Dessy said. "Finish up here and go on; I want to get you started as soon as I can, so me and Redd don't have to worry about this place when we go home at night."

Doris nodded in agreement and thought for a moment. She hadn't told Ma Dessy whom she was staying with, and she hadn't said it was a boarding house, either.

"How did you know—" Doris began to ask, but she was interrupted.

"Miss Deely and me are sisters. So, I figure if you're good enough to stay at Deely's, you're good enough to stay here. My sister's awfully particular about who she lets in. I called her a little bit ago to see if it was you that was staying over there. The story you told me…well, it sounded like her place. She said you were one of those good southern girls, polite and all."

Doris couldn't believe it. It was such a big city, and already she'd met two people who were related. It was starting to feel a little more like home. She looked around the diner. A few people were still there eating.

"Are you closing soon?" she asked.

"Oh no, child, we're just getting started." Ma Dessy laughed. "We still got lunch and supper to go. This is just the calm before the storm."

Redd got up and went behind the counter with his wife. "So, what is your full name, child?"

"Doris Gail Garland."

"Garland, like Christmas garland?" he asked, amused.

213

"Yes, I suppose so. I guess I never really thought of it like that. Garland is a pretty common name where I come from."

"What do you like to be called? Just Doris?" Redd asked.

"Yeah," *Doris will do just fine.*

"Oh, leave her alone," said Ma Dessy.

"He's always trying to find nicknames for everybody," said Lois. "He wants to always call me Lossy."

"I think I'll call you Deegee," Redd told Doris.

"That'll be fine, sir," she said.

"I think we should all just call you Old Goat for short," Ma Dessy said to Redd, smacking him on the back. "Come on, now, we better get back to work."

Jimmy shook his head and got up from the counter. "I work good for you, Ma Dessy," he said.

"Yes, Jimmy, you do." Ma Dessy patted him on the back, then looked over at Doris. "I love my little lost people, Doris. They are my family. The Lord sends them here for me to take care of, and that's what I do. We're all good to each other here. And you'll be good to us, you hear now?"

"Yes, ma'am." Doris got up from the counter and walked behind it to where Dessy and Redd were standing. She reached her arms out to hug Dessy.

"Lord, looky here," Ma Dessy said, hugging Doris tight. Her arms were soft and warm, and Doris could feel herself sinking into her pudgy body. It felt good to be hugged. It felt good to be in her arms. Doris knew the moment she'd heard Dessy pray that she had found home again.

She could feel her life starting to move forward. The new people here and now and a new life felt good. She had a new home, a new job, and she was far away from the shame that had only come two nights earlier. It was all behind her now. The people who knew her secret could never come here, and they would never know where she was. She was going to start a new life with new friends and new surroundings. It was all over now and would be over for good.

Doris was getting excited, truly excited for the first time since she'd left home, left Nadine, Edward, and her friends. No one would ever know anything about why she'd left, and she would never tell anyone about her secret. She didn't want to ruin it all again. Just as soon as she brought her things to the new room, her life would be different. She would become a new person—a new woman with a new life in the big city.

CHAPTER TWENTY-THREE

One letter a month, just like Doris had promised herself she would write. The most recent one was mailed this morning before breakfast. This one was a little harder to write. She wanted so badly to tell her mother where she was—where exactly she was. But again, she mailed it with no specific information and no return address. Most times, it was easier, but today was Doris's birthday. She was eighteen this year, and Christmas would be just around the corner, only a few months away.

The Christmas letter had been difficult to write as well. It had been hard last year sending the letter on her birthday, and this year seemed even more difficult than the last. If she were home, she would've graduated from high school last spring and would be going on to college, or at least that was the plan. She would have been starting right about now. Or maybe she would've married Edward. There was always that chance. Doris thought of Edward often. She wondered what he was doing, if he was happy, if he had another girl.

It was hard to imagine that the world back home in Rayes County had gone on without her, and although she was sure it had, it was just easier to picture everything the same, like time had stopped and it was all just waiting for her return.

It wasn't as if she didn't have enough to keep her busy. She had taken on the responsibility of opening and closing the diner every morning and every night. She had also taken on some of the cooking—just the baking, of course. And she read every night before she went to sleep. Sometimes she'd stay up for hours reading those books. They were fascinating.

Doris had assumed that when Redd and Dessy began to spend a little more time at home and a little less time at the diner, that Lois would be first in line to take on the responsibility of opening, closing, and making sure the bank deposits were made each night, but that didn't happen. Of all the orphans that Dessy had taken in, Doris found that Lois was possibly the most pitiful of all. That included Jimmy.

Doris had expected to someday meet Lois' fiancé. He would have to come back to the States at some point, and he and Lois would be married finally. Lois would expect him in any day, but then he would never come. She and Doris would spend hours looking at catalogs of wedding attire and planning the day. That day never came. Now Doris knew why.

Back in the spring, Doris had expected Lois for work early, but she never came. When Dessy got there, she told Doris that Lois was in the hospital and that she should go over and see her. Dessy never explained what the problem was, only that it happened every so often and usually turned out okay.

When Doris got there, Lois was in the psychiatric ward. She was asleep in the hospital bed and had bandages on her wrists. Doris stared at her for a while and then decided it might be best to leave. As she was passing through the waiting room out front, a middle-aged man and woman stopped her.

"Are you friends with Lois?" the woman asked without waiting for an answer. "We are, well, the family that she lives with."

"Oh, I'm so glad you're here," Doris said. "What happened?"

The woman and man both looked at her as if to say, *you know very well what happened.*

"Where is he—her fiancé?"

"You mean our son?" the woman asked. "He died in a car crash three years ago. We've kept Lois since then. He was about to go off to the service."

"He died?" Doris didn't understand.

"You see," the woman continued. "It's easier for her to just make believe that he's away and coming home soon. But sometimes she has a flash of reality, and when that happens, this is sometimes what she does. Pills—mostly it's pills. She's never done *this* before."

"Oh," Doris said, thinking of all the times she and Lois had talked about him coming home, the wedding, the plans she was making.

"We love her dearly," the woman explained. "She stays with us all the time, and Dessy down at the diner is a saint to keep her on all this time."

"Yes, yes she is," Doris said, still puzzled.

Doris never visited with Lois that day. Instead, she came back to the diner. Dessy hugged her tight. "I didn't want to be the one to tell you, but I'm glad you know now."

It was over a week before Lois came back to work, but when she did, she never missed a beat, talking about the wedding, about him coming home to her.

A whole diner full of misfits is what Dessy had there, only she had no clue what kind of a misfit Doris was.

If she only knew; I'm the biggest freak of all.

It was still there, and Doris did her best not to think about it or look at it. She wished every night when she went to bed for it to just go away. It never did. The thing that made her a freak was still there, attached to her body, a secret. One she knew better than to tell anyone.

"Hey, you," Lois said. "We missed your birthday last year, but this year…"

"SURPRISE!"

There they all were: Dessy, Redd, Jimmy, and Lois. Dessy was carrying a cake with burning candles.

"Get over here," Dessy told Doris as she passed through the swinging door at the counter, heading for an empty table.

"You didn't have to do all this," Doris said, hugging Dessy.

"I know, but last year, we didn't even know when your birthday was. You just let it pass right by."

"Sorry," Doris said. She remembered Jimmy's birthday last year. They had the same type of small party there at the diner. It was then that Dessy had asked about Doris's birthday. Doris was secretly glad she had. Dessy always made her feel so special, so loved. And she had looked forward to this birthday. It wasn't a surprise. Everyone there got the same—the cake, a small gift.

"So, are you going to blow out these candles before they melt all over the cake?" Dessy asked.

It was beautiful with white icing and piping around the edges, roses on top, and a message that said, "Happy Birthday Deegee." The name that Redd had picked out for her during her first week at the diner had stuck, at least with Jimmy, Lois, and Dessy. Her nametag even read, "Deegee." Redd had had it made specially not too long after Doris had started working there.

Doris counted the candles. She couldn't help herself. Along with being a freak physically, she always had these urges to count everything. Candles were an exception, though, she thought, counting the candles on a birthday cake was pretty normal.

There were twenty-one. She counted them again. Twenty-one. It was three years off. The candles quickly reminded her that the life she was leading was all a lie.

"Why do you look so sad, Deegee?" Redd put his arm on her shoulder. "It ain't like you're turning fifty."

Doris laughed, and then the rest of them joined in. "I know Redd," Doris said. "I'm not sad. It's just a lot of candles to blow out. Will you guys help me?"

The group blew the candles out at the end of the song and applauded. Doris got up and took a bow. She'd been looking through the front window every so often, obviously more often than she'd realized.

"Now don't get yourself all up in a tizzy," Redd said. "He'll be here."

Just then, Doris saw him through the window. His long, wavy red hair tossed about as he walked against the wind. Hunched over slightly to keep the air from his face, he was still tall and slender. His glasses had fallen toward the edge of his nose, as they always did. And as usual, he pushed them back up. His pants were worn at the hem, making it obvious that he had walked many miles on the backs of them. His clothing was that of a bachelor; there was no one to take up his pants and no one to match his clothes. It was starting to rain, and thunder could be heard off in the distance. Doris watched him stepping up his pace to cross the street. He looked up at the storm clouds and, as he did, dropped his package in the street. He kept walking at a fast pace before he realized he'd dropped it. Turning around in the middle of the street, he bent down to retrieve it. A car horn blasted, making Doris jump. Her heart raced, and panic took over for a second. She thought he'd been hit. But there he was, popping back up above the car like a jack-in-the-box. He waved at the driver, who was yelling and leaning out the window, and continued across.

Doris laughed a little and shook her head. He was so clumsy. But then again, that was one of the things Doris liked so much about him. He was clumsy, absent-minded, and most times spoke in such educated language that no one could understand him.

"Looks like a storm out there," Freeman Brock said in his best British accent.

"Hey, you. C'mon in here," Redd said, pushing the door shut against the wind. The thunder rolled in high above the building and muffled the next few words Redd and Freeman said to one another.

"For me?" Doris asked excitedly, looking at the tattered package Freeman carried.

"Yes, lady, for you," he said, walking over to Doris. "Had a bit of an accident out there in the wind. Sorry about the wrapping."

"Oh, it's perfect," Doris said as she hugged him. Freeman kissed her on the cheek. It wasn't surprising. He kissed everyone on the cheek when he greeted them, even Redd. The old man had made an off-color comment about it a time or two, but once he realized that Doris had grown friendly with Freeman, he stopped making fun about it.

"Thank God I got here in time for the cake," Freeman said. "But it looks like you've already blown the candles, dear. So sorry."

"It's okay. You're here now."

"Let's open presents and eat that cake before everyone in Cleveland starts piling in here for lunch," Redd said in a gruff yet kidding tone.

"Mine first," Jimmy said. He'd been quiet through the entire party. "Open it Deegee. Open it now."

"Okay, okay, Jimmy. I'm opening it now," Doris said, mimicking his excitement.

The package, wrapped in paper that said *Happy Birthday* all over it, had been tossed around a bit, probably in the pocket of Jimmy's apron.

Doris tore the paper off. "Bob jacks!"

"Yes, we can play on break. I can show you how to play!" Jimmy said.

Doris hugged him tightly. She loved Jimmy. He was so pure, so sweet, so loving and lovable.

He blushed. "Thank you Deegee. I love you too," he said. Jimmy did that often, seemed to read Doris's mind. It was as if he was in tune with his feelings more than anyone she'd ever met. He picked up on every action—a hug, a handshake, a warm cup of milk and sugar that she'd make special for him while she was drinking her coffee. That was probably why Dessy called him special. He was, in every way. He knew when Doris was sad, lonely, and when she needed him to lay his head on her shoulder. "Deegee, you're so pretty," he'd say. Sometimes he'd go up to Doris's room during the day while she was working and leave little notes at her doorstep. *Deegee loves Jimmy,* was mostly what they would say. Sometimes, though, they'd be requests. *Cut my hair, please.* And Doris would. She'd take him into her room and trim his hair a bit. He always wanted it cut. If Doris had honored his request as much as he asked, poor Jimmy would be bald.

"Okay, Deegee, now mine," Lois said, bouncing up and down in her seat.

There was a card attached to the wrapped box. It was a spring flower bouquet in a vase sitting next to a window, where there was spring scenery outside. Doris opened the card.

You are my very best friend, and I want you to be my maid of honor. Happy Birthday, Deegee. Love, Lois.

She looked up at Lois, who was smiling brightly, her eyes glowing. "Well, will you? Will you be my maid of honor?"

Everyone watched Doris to see her reaction. She wished Lois was going to have a wedding. She wished she really did have a fiancé. But the only things she had were false hopes and dreams and a pretend life. Though it saddened those around her that she wasn't well, more often than not, she was happier than the rest of the world —or at least the world that Doris saw.

"Of course, I will, Lois. You always knew I would."

"Yes, I know, but it said in a magazine article that I read that it's always more proper to ask the person, not just expect they'll do it."

Doris reached her hand across the table and laid it over Lois'. "You know I'll do anything you need me to do. Anytime you need me to."

"No need to get so misty-eyed about it, Deegee," Lois quipped. "You save those tears for my wedding day. Now open the present."

Doris pulled a gold metallic hair clasp out of a box. ""Oh, I love it," she said. "Thank you so much, Lois."

"I just knew it would look lovely in your hair," said Lois.

"Oh, I'm sure it will." Doris held the hair clasp to the back of her head and turned around so everyone could see.

"You all are the best friends I've ever had," Doris said, looking around the room.

She looked at Freeman sitting there patiently, waiting to give his gift. He had been holding it in his lap the entire time. When he saw that it was his turn, he looked up at the ceiling and around and began to whistle.

"Oh, is it my turn?" he said, acting as if he didn't know. "The package... Well, it's kind of soiled from the street. I was almost killed trying to get this here for you."

"Yeah, we saw." Doris laughed, as did everyone else.

"Yeah, Freeman," Redd said. "Didn't your mother ever teach you not to play in traffic?"

"Oh, dear. I had hoped no one noticed. I must have looked plenty foolish out there rolling around in the road. Well, here." He handed the package to Doris.

Freeman had been coming into the diner since Doris's first day there. Dessy said he always came, same time, same table every day when Doris first noticed his schedule.

"Sounds British or some other kind of foreign something," Dessy told Doris. "Been coming in here for...well, I guess about the past three years or so."

His name was actually Dr. Freeman Brock or Freeman Brock, Ph.D., Redd told Doris. He wasn't an actual doctor in the medical sense, but a doctor of English or Literature. It was actually both, Doris would later find out. When Doris first saw him with his long hair, she didn't really know what to make of him. But as time went on and she spoke with him each day at lunch, she came to know him as a friend, someone new to talk to. He was smart, so smart, Doris thought.

He was always trying to get Doris to enroll at the college and make a career for herself. Doris would always answer the same way. "Yeah, maybe I will sometime."

When he found out Doris loved to read, he started bringing books. Doris would take one for a few days or weeks, depending on how long it was, and then return it when he was in for lunch. Each time she'd return one, they'd talk about it for a few minutes, and then Doris would continue waiting on other customers.

After a few books, Freeman came not only for lunch, but also for dinner and sometimes even breakfast. Redd was always telling Deegee that Freeman was head over heels for her. Doris would just laugh and say it was Ma Dessy's good cooking that kept the men coming around, not her. And then Doris would joke and say that

Freeman might have a thing for Ma Dessy and that Redd should be a little worried. That would always shut him up.

This was the first time Doris had seen Freeman without taking his order. He had overheard Lois talking to Dessy about the birthday party and had asked if he could come.

"Thank you," she said softly, looking into his eyes as she took the package from him

He nodded his head subtly.

"A book?" she asked.

Freeman smiled. "Just open it, Deegee. I'm not telling."

"It is a book," Doris said after she opened it. "What's it about? There's no title on the cover."

"It's a book about you, my dear lady," he answered.

Doris opened the pages to find them blank. She looked at him, puzzled.

"It's a journal, dear, to keep your most private thoughts, your feelings about things that happen in the world, here in the diner and out there." Freeman waved his hand, gesturing outside. "I received a journal once from an old college chum of mine. It was the most precious gift I ever got. It's excellent exercise for the mind, writing your thoughts."

Doris smiled. She loved it. She got up from her chair and went to hug Freeman. His face instantly flushed red.

"Oh. Oh, my," he said as she released him.

Doris went back to the cake and began to cut pieces.

*

"Coffee?" Redd asked Freeman.

"Sure thing there. Coffee would be fantastic."

"C'mon. We'll get everyone some." Redd motioned for Freeman to join him behind the counter.

"You know, old buddy," Redd started. "Can I call you old buddy?"

"Sure thing, sir," Freeman replied.

"Well, anyway, if you want to buy a gift for a woman, I can think of a lot better than a book full of empty pages."

"Oh," Freeman said, taken aback.

"Women like perfume and candy and…well, flowers. You know. Romance."

"A little soon for that, eh?"

"If you say so," said Redd. "But I've seen the way you look at her. I've noticed you've been coming in here a lot more lately. I've noticed the big tips you give her. Seems to me that you've got more than a friendship going on with our little Deegee."

Freeman stared at Doris as she cut the cake. She was laughing with Lois and Deely. Her smile was like a new sunrise, he thought, the most beautiful sunrise he'd ever seen.

"Hey, you," Redd said, bringing Freeman out of his trance. "It's time to move it along."

"Oh, yes, the coffee. May I help you with those?"

"No, I mean to move it along, if you know what I mean."
Redd winked at Freeman and nodded his head in Doris's direction.

"You believe so?"

"If you don't, some other young man'll come in here and do it
in your place. She's a catch."

"Yes, yes, she is." Freeman gazed at Doris again. "How do
I…?" he started to ask Redd, but he was gone with the coffees
already.

Freeman pushed his glasses back up on his nose and ran his
hands through his hair.

"Breathtaking," he said to himself in a whisper as he walked
back toward the table.

*

"Thank you for walking me out," Freeman said after the
coffee and cake had been finished.

"Sure," Doris said.

"I wanted you to come out here with me so I could ask you
something," Freeman said.

Inside, Redd, Deely, and Lois were all lined up at the counter,
staring at them through the window. Jimmy was still sitting at the
table with the cake, opening Doris's bob jacks.

Freeman reached for Doris's hand and led her over to the
other side of the building.

The storm had come and gone. The sidewalks were wet from
the rain, and the air smelled of clean, brisk fall. The smell suggested
a hint of home to Doris's nose, but the damp air gave her a chill.

"I, um, wanted to ask you if you would do me the pleasure…um…the pleasure of allowing me to escort you to dinner, Deegee," Freeman stuttered.

"Are you asking me to dinner?" Doris asked shivering a little, maybe from the cold, maybe from nerves.

"Yes. Yes, that's what it was supposed to sound like." He laughed.

She paused for a moment and gazed at his eyes through those big, round glasses. He looked terrified.

"Please, don't keep me waiting so long. I, well, I've grown rather fond of you, and when I found out it was your birthday, I had to come."

"I'm so glad you did," Doris said. "I wanted you to come."

He took her hand and held it up to his lips. It was a soft kiss.

"So, will you allow me the pleasure of your company?"

"Yes," Doris said as she gazed at him, his long red hair brushing against his face in the breeze.

"I will be here at seven, then, my lady," Freeman said with a smile. He nodded to her and turned to walk down the sidewalk.

Doris just stood and watched him walk away. She was finally breathing again. She remembered this feeling. It had only happened once before—Edward and that day at the creek. Even so, this was different. She wasn't as nervous as she had been that day. She had never thought of Freeman as anything more than a funny-looking man with big, round glasses, who brought her books and ate at the diner. She hadn't realized until he kissed her hand that she had feelings for him at all in that way. She smiled as she watched him clumsily cross the street and head off down the sidewalk on the other side. She was sure he was trying to walk a little taller. His head was raised, not bowed down like usual.

"Seven," she said to herself. "Seven."

She would have to find something to wear. Dessy could help.

As she walked back into the diner, Lois, Redd, and Dessy were still lined up at the counter. Doris smiled. She tried not to, but the smile wouldn't go away.

"Did that Brit finally ask?"

"Redd, stop that," Dessy scolded him.

"Well, did he?" Lois asked.

"Yes, he did," said Doris. "You should know better than anyone. You were all spying on us."

"Not spying so much as just watching to see what would happen," Dessy said. "It's not every day that a professor comes in and wants to court one of my girls. I just wanted to see how the smart people do it."

"Pretty much just like everyone else," Redd said. "He was nervous as a cat today around you, Deegee. I thought he was going to spill his coffee all over himself. I told him… I told him it was time to do something."

"You did this?" Doris snapped at Redd.

"Well, it was gonna happen anyway. I just hurried things along. I got tired of waitin'. I was just tryin' to help you out a little. We could've gone on like this for another eight months, and I just don't have that kind of time. I'm an old man, you know."

"Oh, shush," Dessy said. "You just like to meddle in other people's business."

"Well, somebody had to do something. And he's gonna need some more help, too. Imagine—a book with no words for the woman you're going to marry."

"Marry?" Doris shouted. "Nobody said anything about marriage."

"Oh, really?" Redd said. "We'll just see about that. Yeah, we'll just see about that."

With those final words, Redd headed to the back of the diner, through the kitchen, and out the back door. Dessy knew what that meant. It was time to go home.

"Well, I'll leave you all to it," she said.

"He wants to take me to dinner tonight," Doris told Dessy.

"Oh, well then I guess I'll need to stay for a while," she said, putting her purse back down on the counter.

"I can take care of the diner," Lois offered.

"No, I've been kind of wantin' to take a night shift anyway," Dessy said. "I like to see sometimes what goes on here at my old diner at night."

Thank you, Doris mouthed. Dessy winked at her and stuck her head out the back door to tell Redd to go on home without her.

"Now you go on upstairs and get yourself ready," she told Doris.

"I really don't know what to wear. I don't know what to do," said Doris.

Dessy acted like she hadn't hear her at all. "Oh, I almost forgot. Me and Redd forgot to give you our present." She pounded a finger on the cash key at the register and handed Doris a ten dollar bill. "You go on up to the department store and buy yourself something nice to wear. You go on, now."

"Thank you," said Doris. "Thank you so much."

"Lois, you go on with her and help her find something pretty."

The two girls barreled out the front door of the diner. Dessy smiled as she watched them go.

CHAPTER TWENTY-FOUR

A soft, silky, blue dress and some borrowed shoes from Lois' backroom stash of dress-up things, in case her fiancé came, was the costume. A little borrowed cash from Lois, along with the ten dollars from Redd and Dessy, had bought Doris the finest dress she'd ever seen.

Lois might not have been all there all the time, but fashion sense was definitely one of her strong suits.

"There," she said, with a last brush stroke of Doris's hair. "Deegee, you're beautiful. Absolutely stunning."

"You think so?"

"Oh, smashing, you are," Lois said in a faux British accent. "Just smashing. And you're going to have a bloody good time, too, my lady. You and Dr. Freeman Brock out for a night on the town, with you in a dress fit for the queen herself."

Both girls laughed. Lois fell on the bed but stopped abruptly and sat upright, looking at the hairbrush in her hand and then stroking her own hair with it.

Doris stopped laughing, too. "What's wrong, Lois?"

"Oh, nothing. Nothing."

Doris watched Lois' eyes turn red and sat down beside her. *Not now*, she thought. *Not tonight.*

"What is it?" she asked again.

"I just wish Robert were here," Lois said softly. "I miss him so much. When he gets back from…from…" She stopped and then started again. "From the service overseas. I'd like for us all—you, me, Freeman, and him—to go out together."

Oh, no, please, Doris begged silently. *Not now. Please, God, let her hold it together.*

It had been months since Lois had been hit hard with the reality that her fiancé was dead. Ma Dessy said some of her doctors thought it would be best if she came to reality permanently. Dessy didn't think so. She would always say, "That child's happier than most people ever have a right to be as long as she believes he's still alive. There's nothing wrong with giving her that happiness. It's the only thing holding her broken heart together."

Doris agreed. Lois was full of life, love, and giddiness. It was almost enviable to think she carried that young, innocent love with her every single day. Well, most days.

"Yes," Doris said, playing along. "We'll do that. We'll all go out together the minute he gets back. Now, how does my hair look?"

"Oh, Deegee, you're beautiful," Lois said. "That dress, that hair."

"Thank you, Lois. I couldn't have pulled all this together without you." She sat down at the vanity and picked up the gold metallic hair clasp that Lois had given her, then held it up to her hair on the right side of her head and then started to put it in.

"What are you doing?" Lois asked. "You don't need that. You don't need anything else. Your hair is beautiful long. Don't pull any of it back."

"Okay, if you say so." Doris set the clasp back down on the vanity.

Lois pulled Doris out of the room and down the stairs. "Let's go show Dessy," She turned on her fake British accent again. "Presenting the royal miss Deegee in all her finery." She held her arm out toward Dessy and Jimmy. "The Princess of Madessy's Diner in downtown Cleveland, here she is." With that, Lois bowed before Doris and then glided out of the way.

Jimmy jumped up and down and clapped his hands. Dessy stood there behind the counter with a look of amazement. Customers stopped eating and watched the display.

"Well, look at you. Our little Deegee," Dessy said. "Well, I never saw anything so gorgeous in my whole world."

"Thank you," Doris said turning around so Dessy could see the rest of her new dress.

"Lois, you're very talented," Dessy said. "Next time Redd—" Dessy stopped and laughed. "Well, if Redd ever takes me out, you are in charge of gussying me up."

"Really?" Lois asked eagerly. "You really think it's good?"

"It's more than good. It's a masterpiece. Oh, lordy, I wish Redd was here to see this. Lois, you better put that Help Wanted sign in the window because when Freeman Brock sees this little sweet thing, he might not bring her back."

By this time, Jimmy had noticed how shiny the fabric on Doris's dress was and began to touch it. He bent down low and felt the hem on the dress.

"Deegee, it's so soft," he said. "Hug?"

He was so taken by the silky fabric that he almost didn't let go.

The bell on the diner door rang then, and there stood Freeman, making an entrance of his own. He was dressed up a little more than usual. His pants were not torn on the bottoms, and his clothes actually matched. He had brushed his hair and even had it back in a little wisp of a ponytail at the back of his neck. He had a sweater draped over one arm and dropped his umbrella as he came in the door. While he was fidgeting with it, trying to pick it up, he dropped his sweater. Doris went to help him, laughing to herself.

"Thank you. I'm so sorry. How stupidly clumsy of me."

Doris's long, brunette hair almost touched the floor as she tried to help Freeman pick up the umbrella and sweater.

"D-d-d," he stuttered.

"Deegee. Did you forget my name since I last saw you today?"

"Um. no. It's just that I've never seen your hair. Or I mean, I've never seen your hair down. It's absolutely exquisite."He reached his hand out to touch her hair and then stopped himself, quickly putting his hand in his pocket. Blinking both eyes, he raised his eyebrows and sighed. "Absolutely exquisite," he whispered as they both stood there in front of one another.

"What did you say?" Doris asked.

"Oh, nothing," Freeman lied. "I said dinner. We're going to dinner."

It was at that moment that Doris caught a glimpse of herself in the glass door of the diner. She looked like someone else, someone beautiful, someone who wasn't a freak. She gazed upon her reflection for what seemed like an eternity. She couldn't take her eyes off that glass. Then, she remembered Amanda from the bus station with her wool suit and hat. Doris had longed to look like Amanda from the moment she set eyes on her. Now she was close. She was no Amanda, but she wasn't Doris either. She felt elegant. For just as long as she gazed at herself in the glass, Freeman was there gazing at her.

Jimmy stepped in and broke the silence, suddenly standing between them. He pushed Freeman out of the way with his shoulder.

"I love you, too, Deegee," he whined.

"Oh yes, Jimmy," Doris said. "I love you, too. I'll be back and I'll bring you something—a present."

"Yes, Jimmy," Freeman said, trying to help. "I'll take good care of her, and I'll bring you back something. We're friends, aren't we?"

"Friends?" Jimmy questioned, but he repeated it with satisfaction after a moment. "Friends"

With that, Jimmy stepped back and let Doris and Freeman head for the door.

"Bring me back something!" Jimmy yelled as the door shut behind them.

Freeman and Doris walked toward the car, and after he opened the door for her, he bent down to the passenger's seat, retrieving a bouquet of roses. He leaned down on one knee and took her hand to his lips.

"These are for the most beautiful woman I've ever laid eyes upon."

Doris stood there holding the flowers, looking at his red hair shining in the light of the streetlamp. She started to wonder what they would talk about at dinner. She wasn't smart; she really wasn't. Other than the books he had lent her, she knew nothing of this man's world, and he certainly knew nothing of hers. Why? Why did he want to take her to dinner? She almost wished he hadn't. She had a bad feeling that this was all going to turn out wrong again, like the way it had turned out wrong with Edward. She wasn't even all that pretty—except for today. Had Lois not worked her magic, she'd be just plain old Doris.

She felt faint. Her knees felt weak, and although she could barely speak, she managed a small string of words.

"I'm not as smart as you," she said quietly as Freeman got back up to his feet.

"Pardon me?"

"Oh, nothing." Doris hoped he hadn't heard after all. "I said thank you."

CHAPTER TWENTY-FIVE

It had been a long drive. Doris had had plenty of time to think about the past and what was about to happen, if anything.

She had sent the box to her mother a month ago with the last line reading, *I'm coming home.*

Doris had been surprised at how small the package was once she'd finally decided to send it—at how small her life had been up to that point, but she sent it anyway.

Freeman had been in the seat next to her sleeping for at least the last fifty miles. His mouth hung open, and he wheezed a little each time he took a sleepy breath. Doris had been trying to stop his smoking without much success since they'd met. This was the result, the wheezing and coughing—smoker's cough, she guessed.

His legs drooped over to one side, lifeless and shriveled. Freeman, who had once been tall, statuesque, had been reduced to a little over four feet tall after the accident. The busy streets of Cleveland had taken her husband's legs. Doris remembered the day vividly. Rain, sleet, and below-freezing temperatures hadn't allowed time for the car to stop quickly enough, and as Freeman was crossing the busy street, he was hit.

Two specialists at the hospital had consulted and then performed two separate surgeries. After months of physical therapy, he wasn't cured, but he was at least better. Half of him had survived. Doris was grateful for that.

They had become close, very close, having dated for over a year before the accident. There had been dinners, movies, ice-skating, and picnics. She'd had some idea that Freeman was thinking of marriage with the way he'd talk about the future—their future. She'd known she would have to tell him about her problem. They'd had moments that threatened to become physical. Doris didn't want him to know, never wanted him to see. She could barely stand to look at it. How could someone else look at it and not be shocked and disgusted by it?

Still, the relationship continued right up until the day he did ask to marry her. A moment that should have been magical, special in every way, had been reduced to a discussion about doctors Freeman knew and medical procedures. Although Doris knew Freeman was an educated man, she was still shocked to find out that he knew something on the subject. She really shouldn't have been. Freeman knew something about everything. Doris now knew its name: ambiguous genitalia.

He called it by other names in other languages. In Kenya, they call it Serer; in India they call it Hijra; and in the Dominican Republic people referred to it as Guevodoche. Even the Native Americans had a name for it—Nadle. He had loaned her the books on Greek and Egyptian mythologies. They were fascinating. Freeman said that if Hermes and Aphrodite's son Hermaphroditus had existed, there had to be humans to model him after. When Freeman described it, it wasn't scary at all. *Ambiguous* was certainly a word Doris could relate to.

"Not as uncommon as people think," Freeman had told her. He said there were many names for it all over the world. In some countries those with the condition were considered special and

were revered above all others. In other countries they were
outcasts, and in some others, the babies were even killed at birth to
keep them from growing into adulthood. In the states, he'd said, it
just wasn't discussed, like it didn't exist. Doris could relate to that
as well. There were times she wanted it not to exist.

But it could be fixed. As excited as Doris had been to hear
that it really could be, she had also been terrified at the thought of
how it would have to be done. Still, for Freeman—for his love and
to be able marry him—she would have done anything.

Freeman had arranged an appointment with a specialist who
practiced in the city. Her fiancé had said this particular doctor was
supposed to be the best. The appointment had been nearing, when
Freeman was hit by the car.

Just like every day, Doris had stood at the diner counter and
watched him clumsily cross the street. The tires hadn't even scuffed
the pavement as the driver tried to slam the brakes. There was just
a thud and Freeman lying there on the pavement. Doris knew her
world was about to change again.

Doris's mother had always said that change happened in
threes. The next two events would prove her right. Lois had one
last moment of clarity in which reality had set in hard. She took
pills again and simply drifted off to sleep to be with her beloved
Robert. At least that was how Robert's parents had presented it to
Ma Dessy and the rest of the crew at the diner. It somehow made
the blow a little less painful.

Redd's fatal heart attack came next, and Ma Dessy closed the
diner and moved in with her sister Deely. They ran the boarding
house together, taking Jimmy in to help with some of the cleaning.
His parents were grateful to Ma Dessy for that. When Doris had
finally met Jimmy's parents, they told her Ma Dessy and Deely

were angels in disguise. Doris knew this already, but it touched her heart to hear someone else say it. The boarding house was a good place for the two ladies. They could spend the rest of their lives taking care of lost souls exiting the bus terminal. Doris guessed God had to put people like that on earth to take care of the misfits who would otherwise be aimlessly wandering.

Doris and Freeman were married during his stay at the hospital. The facility chaplain had performed the ceremony. Those who were left—Dessy, Deely, Jimmy and a few regular customers from Madessy's—came to the small ceremony. It seemed like they'd all known it was the beginning of the end for all of them. A small celebration of marriage would tie up the tragedies of that winter and provide a peaceful ending for a sad story. At least that was what Dessy had said to Doris on her wedding day.

Doris could tell she was about ten minutes from home now— home to Rayes County. The hills rolled the car up and down as she drove. She could feel the tension in her shoulders start to disappear little by little. The mountains in front of her and on each side of the highway went on forever. Doris felt the colors of the trees embracing her as if they were welcoming her home. They were beautiful oranges, reds, yellows, and browns against the crisp, blue sky. So wonderful, so unbelievably majestic, they were still here, still here waiting for her. She'd never given them a second thought while she was away. How could she not have noticed them before? The vision of them now took her breath away. Tears began to fill her eyes. She'd never known how much she'd missed them until she saw them again, comforting her from all sides like a featherbed. She felt completely covered by them, completely safe as she rolled the window down a bit to feel the sweet, cool Rayes County fall. It blew against her wet face and made her skin colder. She closed her eyes and took a deep breath, opened them again. The mountains were still there. She allowed a few more tears to flow as she remembered her childhood in this magical place.

"You're slowing down," Freeman said, rising in his seat. "Are we there?"

Doris glanced at the speedometer. She had slowed to just a little over thirty miles per hour.

"No, not yet but almost," she said softly. "We're almost there."

Freeman was looking around in wonder, taking it all in. "Oh my God, Deegee," he gasped. "I think this is the most beautiful thing I've ever seen, this Rayes County of yours. It's like an ocean of colorful trees. How on earth did you ever leave a place like this? It's…well, it's almost heavenly."

Doris felt comforted by Freeman's talk of Heaven. Just after his accident, he had become very angry with God. All that was over now, though, and it was good to see him humbled by the mountains, something bigger than him, bigger than the both of them.

Doris looked over at him. He could see she'd been crying.

"You know I can never leave here again," she said as another tear made its way down her already wet face.

"I know," he said. "I've always known that."

CHAPTER TWENTY-SIX
Rayes County, Present Day

Maggie had been glancing at Denie throughout the day. She hadn't moved an inch. Her eyes were permanently fixed on Mamaw as the story unfolded before them. By this time, Mamaw had tears in her eyes and was staring off into the space between the girls. She untangled the hanky that had become wrapped around her left hand, swiped at her nose, and took a sip of water. It must have been warm by then, as it had been sitting on the table for quite some time.

"The day the postman brought that package, I set it on the kitchen table and stared at it for a long time," she said. "I didn't know what it meant. It wasn't just a letter; it was something else. I was afraid it was something bad."

"When the Lord finally gave me enough courage to open it, I found the greatest treasure I've ever known. Journals. Fourteen of them. It was pages and pages of my daughter's life, the life I'd missed. There was a note inside the box."

Mamaw had always worn a chain around her neck with a small key attached. Maggie and Denie had never known it was anything more than a gaudy piece of jewelry. She took the chain and pulled it off over her head, her eyes still filled with tears. She motioned to

Denie to come over to the bed and then placed the key in her hand.

"It's in the cabinet," was all Mamaw said.

Denie walked to the cabinet and opened the doors. There it was, the big, locked, metal box. Denie and Maggie had seen it several times over the years. As children, they had always tried to guess what was inside and why it was locked, why it was so heavy. They'd even made up stories of gold and jewels that lay waiting inside that box.

Maggie watched as Denie pulled the box out by the handles on each side. She set it in the chair where she'd been perched all day and then scooted closer to Mamaw to open it.

There it was—the treasure Mamaw had kept locked away all those years. Denie pulled them out one by one and laid them next to Mamaw on the bed. The old woman held the first one in her lap until Denie was done. They all had black covers, and the pages were thick with age. Some were wrinkled, and the edges looked dingy. Mamaw opened the cover of the book she held in her lap and handed Denie a piece of paper. The girls gathered close.

"Read that." It was all she could get out through her tears, and she turned her head away from her granddaughters and over toward the windows.

Mama,

I'm so sorry for leaving. I know now that was a mistake. We've missed so much together. These are for you—my thoughts, my feelings, my life.

I love you so much, Mama. I'm coming home.

Doris

Both Denie and Maggie began to cry as well. They glanced at one another and then at their grandmother, who was still staring out the window. Maggie was amazed at how much she'd taken for granted. All she'd ever known or ever cared to know was that this woman was her grandmother—the perfect biscuit maker, an unbelievable storyteller, a prankster, an old woman who existed only for her and Denie.

But now, all that had changed. For the first time, she saw this woman's life as an exceptional life. Her grandmother was more than just an Easter egg painter and a skinned-knee doctor. She was a woman, a wife, a mother, a best friend, and a brave soldier in the battle of her life and the lives of her children. Maggie took her grandmother's hand and rubbed the wrinkled skin of her fingers. But this time was different. She had taken her grandmother's hand so many times before. She'd pushed the wrinkles back and forth and then tried to smooth them out. Not today. Not ever again. She looked at her shriveled hand in amazement, knowing where those hands had been, what they'd seen. It was almost like if she looked hard enough, she could see the story all over again, see her grandmother as a young woman with her friend Janie during the summer that had changed her life changed forever.

Mamaw turned back to the girls. "Everyone's life is hard," she said through a sob. "You girls know that don't you? It's the love that makes all the pain worthwhile. Love your family as hard as you can, and you'll never regret a minute of your lives."

She nodded at the girls to make sure they understood her message. They both nodded back, swallowing hard and trying to fight back tears.

"You know, I thought the day I got that package was the happiest day of my life," Mamaw said. "Me and your papaw would lock ourselves away every night in the bedroom and read and read until the pages were worn. Your aunt Doris is a lovely writer," Mamaw said, looking at Maggie. "I'd like to think you got some of that from her. Maybe not genetically, but somehow, it's carried on through you.

"I didn't leave the house for all that month, waiting for her to come. I remember it like it was yesterday. The mountains around the house were bright with colors from the trees in the fall. The air was cold and crisp, and I knew in my heart something wonderful was about to happen. I heard the gravel crunch in the driveway and looked out the window. An unfamiliar car was there. I yelled as loud as I could for your papaw. He knew. He knew exactly what it was. We got to the front door right about that same time, and then we were stopped dead in our tracks at the edge of the porch by what we saw.

"There she was. She hadn't noticed us yet. She was no longer our little girl. She was a beautiful young woman. She looked so different, like a stranger, and she had a stranger with her, your Uncle Freeman. We couldn't take our eyes off her, not even to help her get the wheelchair from the trunk. She struggled to get Freeman into the chair and then had a hard time pushing it over the gravel. Still, we stood there, frozen, both of us crying tears of sweet, precious joy. I wanted to keep that moment closed in my heart forever.

"When she raised her head and looked up toward the porch, I saw her like I was seeing her for the first time. In her face, I could still see my little girl. She ran for us, leaving Freeman sitting there in his chair on the gravel. We laugh about that now. It seemed like an eternity until I was able to hold her in my arms. And that, girls, was truly the happiest day of my life." Mamaw nodded her head. "My little girl was home. I didn't know for how long, and I didn't even care. For that moment, she was safe in my arms again."

Maggie and Denie never took their eyes off their grandmother as she told the story of the reunion that day. The tears they'd shared, the laughs they'd had. It was that day that Viola had told Doris the story of who her mother truly was—the story of Janie Cole and the night Viola stole Doris from the barn. Mamaw said she wanted it all to be over. All of it. The truth would be known. She said it was a secret she wished she'd shared with Doris before she'd run away.

"She visits her mother's grave, you know," Mamaw said. "Seems odd to call Janie her mother, but you know, that's what she is—her mother, my friend, my dear, dear friend. She's buried up on Hill Cemetery. Doris goes up there every Sunday after church and talks to her, tells her all the things she tells me. I'm so glad she does. You know I loved Janie like a sister, I'd like to think. She's the closest I've ever had, and I know when I leave this world, she'll be waiting for me. I'm sure she'll have a pocket full of sweet, sweet blackberries straight from Heaven." Mamaw smiled at the girls and winked at Denie as if she were joking, trying to lighten the mood.

CHAPTER TWENTY-SEVEN

"Things had changed. Everything had changed." Mamaw continued to lay the story before her granddaughters. "Your mother had married Edward and already had both you girls. Denie was two years old, and Maggie, you had just been born when your Aunt Doris came back home.

"Oh, your mother was so unhappy. Almost the minute your Aunt Doris left; Nadine started acting out. She was hanging around with a group of girls at school that were drinking and doing things they shouldn't. She never got over the guilt of that night when she brought those girls to the bathroom window—and your father, too.

"I could see it day after day, year after year, eating away at her, but she never said so. She really never said much of anything. She just drank and partied and hated everyone, but your papaw and me knew she mostly hated herself.

"Nadine ended up getting pregnant and marrying your father. That's what happened to most of the girls in that group, getting pregnant and then married at such a young age. Your papaw and me tried to talk to Nadine so many times and keep her out of trouble, but she wouldn't have it any other way. I told Doris that Nadine had married Edward and that they had children, but I think the look on her face when Nadine and Edward came to Sunday dinner after she'd arrived made Nadine hate her even more.

"Your mother started drinking even more after that, and at some point, even without my knowledge, tried to give you girls to Doris. She said she was going to run off and enjoy her life. I loved Nadine so much, but I could just never get through to her. She was my baby, and she'll always be my baby. But I think she truly hated me in the end. Doris was watching you girls almost all the time. Do you remember that?"

Denie nodded, but Maggie gave her a puzzled look.

"Well, of course, Maggie. You were too young to remember, but that went on for about a year. Edward talked to your papaw quite a bit. They were close. So, it was no surprise that your grandfather knew more about the situation than I did. Doris was trying to protect Nadine from me. She didn't want me to find out that Nadine was about to abandon her children. All that came to an end one day when your papaw and Edward had a visit. The two of them were in the garage for hours one Saturday afternoon. Apparently, Edward needed Papaw's help more than we knew.

"Your papaw went to Doris and Freeman's house and took the two of you home. I guess he got pretty rough with Nadine, and even though she was a married woman with two children, he bent her over his knee and gave her the swatting that I believe she'd needed for years. She never stopped drinking, but she did slow it down a bit, and she was at least able to take care of the two of you after that. She blamed Doris for that day, the day that kept her from running off to a new life in the big city like her sister had. She assumed that Doris had told your papaw and me about the plan and that we had intervened. We never told her that it was your father who'd asked for Den's help. It was better for her to hate all of us and not her husband.

"After that, you never got to spend time with your aunt, only my house in the summers." Mamaw smiled like she was remembering those summers when Denie and Maggie were little girls."

"Your mother was an addict—an alcoholic. Summer was a relief to her, when you stayed with me. I always wondered if she hadn't had that time each year to spread her wings a bit, if she wouldn't have taken off and left you girls. I loved your mother. I loved her dearly, my baby, my child. But at that point, she wasn't herself. The alcohol had taken her over; her spirit was gone. I'd lost her, and she wasn't coming back. I knew that for years, but I kept the peace with her and tried to keep her and your father together. Now I don't know if that was the right thing or not. I often wonder. I've always thought it was your mother's drinking that killed your father. We all know that's what eventually killed her, but before their divorce, your father's spirit had been broken as well. He was a shell of a man for loving her, for staying with her for the sake of you girls.

"Your mother turned you against Doris. She had to have someone to blame for her own miserable life. We could have helped her if she'd let us, but she wouldn't, so instead, we helped the two of you. When you stayed at my house during the summer, your aunt would come and visit you then, bring you things to keep at my house, so your mother wouldn't know. The big black chalkboard out in the garage? That was from her. The two of you got so much enjoyment out of that.

"Doris told me time and time again she'd wished that Nadine would just leave and let the two of you stay with her. That became a new point of resentment between the two of them. One wanted children so badly she could barely stand it, and the other just wanted to be free of all responsibility. I would always tell Doris that she shouldn't wish that on our family again. No one else needed to leave. We all needed to stay right here in Rayes County and help each other."

Denie had looked like she wanted to speak for the last several minutes. Finally, she did. "Mamaw, I love you, but I can't sit here and listen to you talk about my mother this way," She began to cry. "She was a good woman. She loved us. Yeah, she drank. Everyone back then did, but you're sitting here calling her an addict!"

Maggie could see the enlightenment through Denie's tears. She knew her sister better than anybody, better than Mamaw. As the old woman continued to talk about Nadine's actions when she drank and her desire to be anywhere other than wherever she was at the moment, Denie understood. Maggie saw it: the look of understanding and empathy for a mother who had gone through what Denie was now experiencing with her own child. She loved him—there was no doubt about that—but the love now had to be different. It was a tougher love. She couldn't let him get too close anymore. He had already destroyed her heart several times, and so many times, it had to heal. It was still scarred but nonetheless healed. Maggie had helped her sister through a lot of those times. Denie didn't want to see it, but Maggie saw it clearly. The addictions that had taken their mother's soul from their mamaw had also taken Tim's soul from her sister.

"I see it in your face, child," Mamaw told Denie. "You're scared, you're hurt, and you're desperate to get him back. Sometimes you think he'd be better off dead than in the shape he's in. You think it'd be better for everybody. It's a hard fact to face, but until he's cleaned up, he's not your child. He belongs to his drugs."

Denie gasped for air and sobbed, holding her hands over her face. "Oh God, Mamaw, what do I do?"

"Let it out," the old woman said, reaching her arms out to her oldest granddaughter. "Let it all out."

Denie lay there in Mamaw's bed like a child, and Maggie began to wonder how long her sister had needed this comfort, this allowance for a moment of weakness. Maggie had seen her simply go through the motions of life so many times where Tim was concerned. She'd seen her sister pick her son up at jail and pay his bail. She'd then show up to court with him and run into friends or people she worked with on a professional level. She always held her head high, ignoring the stares of disapproval once they found out why she was in court. Maggie had gone with her to the probation office, only to find out that once again her son had been a no-show and violated his parole. Again and again, there were bench warrants put out for his arrest, and again, Denie would find him and plead with him to turn himself in. It was an endless cycle, and one that was beginning to take a toll on Maggie's sister.

She could see it at times, but mostly Denie was the rock in Maggie's life. She was strong while Maggie was weak. Maggie would give up and Denie would trudge on, not even knowing where she was going. When Maggie felt the least bit lost, she'd just stop moving all together. In Maggie's eyes, Denie could handle everything. But for the first time in a long time, she was watching her sister fall apart. She didn't quite know what to do other than stand there helplessly, crying and watching the scene play out. She imagined that this must be how her sister felt most times in her life, with no one to turn to in a crisis, no rock.

She had seen her sister get emotional about her son's situation, but Denie would always immediately straighten herself up, wipe the chalkboard clean, change gears, and align her posture as if to say, "I am in control." This was, after all, a true Garland woman's way.

That wasn't happening this time. Maggie watched as her sister, her rock, crumbled there on the bed into a million little pieces with Mamaw fitting them carefully back together one by one.

"You need to help your sister," Mamaw told Maggie sternly.

"I try," she said through her tears.

"Sometimes you need to be the strong one for her. She's carried you many a mile, and now it's time you carry the load."

Denie rose up and looked at Maggie. The look in her eyes shook her. She looked like a child.

"No, Mamaw. It's okay. Maggie helps me. She helps me so much."

"Maggie helps you, talks to you, but just like so many other things in her life, she avoids the truly painful parts. When your mother was ill, she couldn't bear to look at her. When your father was ill, she did the same thing. You girls are there for each other, and for that I am grateful, but there could be more."

Maggie hated to hear the truth. Hated it. She had no tolerance for grief, no tolerance for true, raw emotion, especially when it came to her own affairs or those closest to her. If she pretended that everything was okay, then it was. She had known for years that she had become the poster child for denial. She chose only to believe what would hurt the least. She had become a liar—a liar to herself. When her mother had died, it'd been easier to think of her as just being away. When her father had died, she'd done the same thing. With no acceptance of the truth, there would be no pain.

She knew her sister had been in trouble for a long time, but she chose to believe that Denie was the strong one.

She can handle it. She's tough, she thought.

And then the homemade excuses just kept coming. For so
many years, Maggie had practiced a motto that was a lie.

She's strong; I'm weak.

She's smart; I'm stupid.

She's brave; I'm a coward.

She knew her grandmother was right. As hard as it was to
hear, she knew that motto was an old one. It was time to step out
from behind her sister's shadow and take the lead. There was no
truth to this self-imposed mantra. It was an excuse, an excuse to do
nothing, to feel nothing.

CHAPTER TWENTY-EIGHT

It was hard to eat with a lump the size of an orange in her throat, but Maggie had made the decision to take her sister to eat, take her home, and stay the night. The next day was Sunday, and she had a plan for them.

"I've made a decision, Denie," she said, keeping her posture straight and looking at her sister directly.

"Yeah?"

"Tomorrow, we're going to Janie Cole's grave, and then we're going to Doris's house to eat dinner. She asks all the time, and I think we should go. No, I mean we're going."

Maggie was taking control of the situation as best she could. She really wasn't used to bossing her sister around yet, but it was coming. Denie was eating roast beef and mashed potatoes, her favorite. Her mouth was full, so she couldn't say much.

"You don't have to go, but I think you should, or rather I *know* you should," Maggie said. "You can even sit in the car if you'd like. You don't have to get out. I'll handle everything."

Denie swallowed her food and took a drink of her tea. "Maggie, we've had a really emotional past two days. Do we really have to cram it all in at once?"

"Yes, we do."

Denie gave Maggie a look that said, *whatever you say*, and continued eating.

"Denie, do you remember a lot about Aunt Doris keeping us?"

"Not a lot, really, but I do remember Mom and Doris fighting a lot. I think I might remember the day that Daddy and Papaw came and got us. It could just be a phony memory. Children sometimes tend to do that, you know."

"Nothing? Really? You seemed certain when Mamaw asked you earlier."

"Well, I do remember we had a playroom at her house. You were too little to play, so you were mostly with Doris. But I had a lot of nice things in there. I seem to remember a lot of pink. And of course, the smell of Chanel No. 5." Denie laughed. "I know that when Doris would come around at Mamaw's, I'd always feel guilty if I acted like I liked her at all. Mom had always told us that she couldn't be trusted that she destroyed everyone's lives that she touched. It was easier just to vilify her and keep things right with Mom. I guess you took your feelings about Doris mostly from me."

"Now that I think about it, you're probably right," Maggie said. "I don't really have any terrible memories of her, just what I've heard."

"For that, I guess I should say I'm sorry," Denie said. "But it's hard to like someone your mother despises so much. I mean your mother is always your mother."

"Yeah," Maggie said. "But don't be sorry. I think we've spent way too much of our lives thinking that somehow we could've been better or done things differently, and that would have made Mom happy."

Denie knew Maggie was right. The only thing that made her mother happy was a drink or two or three. She was miserable—a miserable person while they were growing up and an even more miserable person before she died. Denie knew from the stories Mamaw had told her that her mother was an addict just like Tim. She'd been there, done that. There wasn't one thing about her mother that she'd heard today that surprised her. It was like the story of Viola and Nadine had been passed down to Denie and Tim. The faces had changed, but the scenario was all just the same.

Maggie knew what her sister was thinking about. She could tell by the worried look on her face.

"You know, Denie, I'm sorry if I haven't been there for you where Tim is concerned."

"But you have, Maggie. Mamaw doesn't know."

"Don't kid yourself," Maggie said. "She knows everything, and she's right. I'm going to go have a visit with Tim, and I'm going to see if I can help him."

"I hate to say it, but I don't think it would do any good," Denie said with some hesitation.

"Doesn't matter. I'm going anyway."

"I'd really appreciate that."

Maggie was surprised to hear her sister say that. It was almost like Denie had been waiting for someone to talk to him, someone besides her.

"I think it would be good for him coming from someone else, you know," she continued. "You could talk to him about his future and maybe get him excited about college or at least trade school. You know, Maggie, you have a lot of contacts. You might be able to lead him in the right direction."

Maggie was even more astonished that she not only wanted her to talk to Tim, but that she had faith that Maggie might be able help him.

"Thanks," Denie said.

And in good Garland fashion, Maggie changed the subject. "Hard to believe that Doris was Dad's first girlfriend."

"Yeah, it is," Denie said. "I can't believe no one ever told us until now."

"Well, we all keep secrets from our children," Maggie said. "The girls think I've only been married three times. I just pretend the other one never happened. It was short and over really before anyone knew. No one ever mentions it to me, even if they do remember."

"I guess you're right," Denie said. "Just think. Someday we'll get to reveal them all from our nursing home beds. I think everyone should have to experience what we have this past week."

The girls both laughed and shook their heads.

"But you know?" Maggie said. "Mamaw never told us what happened to Bick Cole."

"No, you're right. She didn't," Denie said, surprised that she hadn't noticed. "She got all the way to the end and never mentioned him again."

"Maybe she forgot," Maggie said.

"Not likely. In case you haven't noticed, that woman's got a mind like a steel trap."

They sat there for a moment and thought about what could have happened to Bick and why their grandmother had left that part out.

"I guess maybe he just ran off," Maggie suggested.

CHAPTER TWENTY-NINE

The road was curvy, and the blind hills made Maggie take extra caution. She'd been to Hill Cemetery before, not actually in it, but she'd at least driven past there. There really hadn't been much to do in Rayes County when she was a teenager, and it wasn't much better now. When it came time to skip school junior and senior year, Maggie and her friends would always drive to some out-of-the-way place.

There were plenty of those in Rayes County. They'd park the car and drink the day away. Although she'd never participated in any, Maggie was sure the end of the road on the way to Hill Cemetery was full of memories of first kisses, consummated teenage relationships, and maybe even a few conceptions—children who would now be about the ages of Maggie's girls.

She never remembered it being this far. She had already passed two railroad tracks and a dozen old, broken-down mobile homes. Some were lived in; some had broken-out windows, and Maggie hoped no one lived in them. When reporters from the big city dailies would make references to Rayes County being one of the poorest counties in the state, Maggie would cringe. It angered her to have the stigma of poor and uneducated attached to the place she loved so much. Sometimes, though, when Maggie's eyes met scenes like these, it was hard to deny that the reports could have some merit to them. Still, this was part of Rayes County,

Maggie reminded herself, the part that made the county interesting and sometimes volatile. Crime in Rayes County was never absent from the newspaper's front page. In fact, going an entire week without a murder or at least an assault would have been odd.

Denie had been quiet for the entire drive, staring out the window. Maggie wondered what she was thinking about but didn't ask. It seemed like a good day for simple, quiet reflection, and she guessed that was what they were both doing, taking a few moments to absorb all the new information they'd been given.

Maggie wasn't at all sure how this go at a new relationship with their aunt was going to come off. Maybe Denie was thinking the same thing as she sat there quietly, the bumps and curves jostling her on the passenger's seat. Maggie glanced over at her sister as often as she could without running off the road. The sun shone through her long eyelashes; her face still looked as soft and creamy as ever. There were times when Maggie was sure that Denie looked the younger of the two of them, but then she reminded herself that smoking had probably aged her years ahead of her time. Maggie looked at her sister's hands, searching for any sign that she was aged a little more. There was none. Her hands appeared to be smooth as silk—no sun damage, no wrinkles. Maggie shook her head when she saw Denie's fingernails. She didn't have any. For as long as Maggie could remember, Denie had bitten her nails to the quick. It looked painful. Even so, the nail biting didn't hold a candle to most of Maggie's vices. The smoking she'd stopped, but the others, especially drinking too much on the weekends, had increased. She worried sometimes that she'd end up like her mother, but she decided that as long as she was concerned, she might become an alcoholic, she could keep it in check.

The lane entering Hill Cemetery was concealed even more so than Maggie remembered. Large trees and bushes on either side of the narrow way made it hard to see. The kudzu had taken over this holler, just like every other holler in Rayes County. The leaves were starting to wilt a little, but not so much that Maggie couldn't make out shapes in the vine coverings.

When the kudzu covered electrical poles lining the highway, Maggie thought they looked like big monsters. Tree monsters. She remembered thinking so as a child, and she still thought it now. It was interesting to look at the vine-covered objects and see dinosaurs, giants, and trolls. Maggie marked it all up to an overactive imagination, or at least that was what her father had always told her.

Some cemeteries in Rayes County were dedicated to just one family, others to just two or three families. Maggie's mother and father had both been buried at a cemetery near town, the same place her grandmother would be buried, in the empty spot next to their grandfather, Dennis. Several Rayes County families were buried there. You could almost trace a family tree simply by taking a stroll around those gravestones. Maggie didn't like cemeteries, but when she was forced to go, she'd always try to imagine what people's lives had been like by the engravings on the stones. *Our Beloved Mother* was the engraving Maggie and Denie had chosen for their mother's stone. *Our Loving Father* was the inscription chosen for their father's. Did it sum up their lives? No. She knew that, but what else could you say in five words or less? Maggie had never known anyone who was buried at Hill Cemetery. It was an old cemetery in comparison to the rest of them. Some of the tombstones dated all the way back to the 1800s. She had read an article about some kids who'd vandalized some of them a few years back.

The gravel popped out from under the wheels of the car. The climb was almost straight up.

"Gee, I wonder why they call this Hill Cemetery," Denie said with the sarcasm Maggie loved so much.

"Yeah, I know. It feels like we're going to flip over backwards," Maggie said, navigating an unexpected curve.

Finally, the car emerged from nature's canopy, the road leveled, and Maggie could see a few tombstones through the front window.

"Look. There he is. There's Freeman," Denie said, pointing to the right.

They got out of the car and stood, leaning against the hood.

"You don't have to go," Maggie said.

"Why would you think I wouldn't go?"

"I don't know. I was just saying if you don't want to go, you don't have to."

"Come on." Denie started to walk away without even looking at Maggie.

There he was. Freeman Brock. Maggie had always thought it sounded so educated. The two names just flowed well together. She remembered that when she was little, the sight of Freeman had scared her. They'd barely spoken at all when she was a child. Freeman would try to talk to her sometimes, but Maggie just tried to avoid him as much as possible. She always thought of him as being in pain. No one ever bothered to explain to her that he couldn't feel his legs, only that they were hurt. That was one of the reasons she couldn't stand to be around him for too long. She thought he was in constant pain because his legs were hurt. His wheelchair alone was enough to make Maggie feel uncomfortable, and his long hair was different from anything Maggie had ever seen. But when she went off to college, she saw a lot of professors who looked like her Uncle Freeman, like old hippies who hadn't seen a hairdresser since the seventies.

Maggie couldn't see Doris anywhere near Freeman. He was sitting there alone at the top of a ridge. The hair that had escaped from the small gray ponytail, just barely reaching the back of his coat, blew wildly in the wind. His glasses rested on the tip of his nose, and his head was leaned back. He looked like he was enjoying himself in the breeze. The coat he wore was obviously a selection his wife had made for him. All of his clothes, for that matter, must have been chosen for him. Although his name may have sounded like he was put together and flowed well with the universe, it just didn't seem possible that a professor type could match his clothes as perfectly as he did.

Being outside felt good. It made Maggie feel alive, which she thought was a little ironic considering where she was. The leaves had fallen but were still colorful on the ground. The sky was a perfect fall blue, and the air was just cool enough to send a shiver through her every now and then.

Freeman lowered his head then and turned toward the girls, who had been standing there for a few moments. He smiled as though he had been expecting to see them all day, like it was no surprise at all.

"What brings you two up here on this fresh mountain Rayes County Day?" Freeman took a long inhale, raising his arms as he did.

Maggie laughed and looked over at Denie, who was chuckling, too. He sounded like a poet, or at least someone who had once been a poet and had forgotten how to do it. Or maybe just someone who had always longed to be a poet. He smiled at the girls after his long, deep breath as if he knew he was an amusing fellow but didn't care.

"Where is she?" Denie asked without so much as a hello.

"Deegee? She's down there." He raised his arm and pointed down the hill.

Doris was camouflaged, standing there in all her glory, or at least that was what Maggie would have called it a few days ago. She was wearing a light green and tan wool suit with a matching wool hat, looking perfect as usual. The only thing that blew her cover completely was the striking dark hair beneath her hat. The rest of her could have been claimed by the fall colors that surrounded her.

"I'm glad you girls are here." Freeman nodded, looking at the two of them. "I truly am. Your aunt will be happy that you're here."

The walk down the hill toward Doris was an obstacle course of gravestones. There was no pattern. It looked as if someone had just buried people at random, like they'd simply picked a spot and said, "Here." Some of the stones were old and weatherworn. Others looked new, which was a surprise to Maggie.

Doris stood beside a stone about the height of her knees. She touched the top as she stared out across the field. She turned as though she was startled and saw the two of them coming toward her.

"Wait," Denie said, holding out an arm in front of Maggie.

They stopped as they watched Doris turn completely toward them. She looked puzzled and then, as though she was lost deep in thought, stared at the ground for a few moments. With her head still down, she turned back to the gravestone in front of her.

Denie and Maggie stood motionless as they watched their aunt pull a handkerchief out of her purse and lift it to her eyes. She wiped one eye and then the other as she stared at the tombstone; then she turned again and held out her arm as if taking an invisible hand in hers. The girls went to her then, each taking one of her hands.

Through her tears, Doris managed to be polite. "How are you girls today?"

Denie nodded her head. "Good, good."

"Yeah, good," Maggie agreed.

"It's such a glorious day," Doris said looking up at the sky. "I'm—we're glad you're here."

At that moment, Maggie wasn't sure if the *we* Doris was referring to included Freeman, her dead mother, or both. Doris turned again, this time with her nieces' hands in hers, and looked toward her mother's gravestone.

"This is her," was all she said.

Maggie wasn't surprised that Doris didn't mention Mamaw's breech of her secret, and she wasn't surprised that her aunt wasn't questioning whether their grandmother had shared the journals. She was, however, a little surprised at what happened next.

"So, are you girls coming over for dinner today?" Doris asked as if nothing had just happened.

Maggie let out a small laugh and just looked at her aunt for a moment. Their eyes met. It was an understanding, a healing and a warmth that rushed over Maggie even in the cool fall air.

The three of them walked hand in hand back up the hill toward Freeman. He was staring back up at the sky again, head back, gray hair blowing in the wind.

"Wait," Maggie said, turning back for a moment.

The gravestone wasn't old like so many of the rest of them, Maggie thought. It was newer. She had to see it again.

Janie Cole
Dear Friend and Mother

There was another stone close to Janie's, a small lamb. Denie and Maggie noticed it at almost the same time. They glanced up at each other and then back at the concrete lamb. It took them only a moment to realize whose child this was. No one spoke, and the three of them turned again to walk toward Freeman.

CHAPTER THIRTY

Maggie had seen the red message light flashing for the past several days. She didn't want to know what was on the answering machine. She didn't care. Chuck and the girls had been calling on the cell phone. Whoever was leaving messages on her machine could wait until she'd had time to deal with it…or wait until she *wanted* to deal with it.

It was Monday morning, and the rest of the world was at work, busy with the things of life. Maggie was still in her pajamas at almost ten o'clock. She passed the flashing red light again as she'd done so many times that week. Yawning as she and her fluffy slippers slid across the kitchen floor to the fridge, she grabbed a Diet Coke and yearned for a cigarette to go with it, just like every other morning since the day she'd quit. People had told her to drink coffee. "You have to replace a habit with a habit," they'd say. Where were those people this morning? Since she'd lost her job, she'd lost most of her friends as well. She knew at this point that believing that her co-workers were her friends was a mistake. Maggie was sure they didn't want to be seen talking to her, didn't want anyone knowing they had been in touch with her. She knew the drill well. When someone got fired, laid off or quit, steer clear. No one wanted the management thinking they were disloyal or in cahoots.

She wanted to call Denie, but she was at work with the rest of the employed world. She had no idea what she would talk to Denie about other than the events of the past few days.

Mamaw's story. Maggie and Denie had talked it to death. There wasn't much left to say.

She pointed the remote control toward the TV and began to flip channels so fast she couldn't even tell what was on. The message light was still flashing.

"Okay! Okay!" she yelled. "I know. There's a message."

She rolled her eyes as she pushed the button.

"Maggie, this is Sheriff Rosen. I've been trying to reach you. I heard about what happened with your job. I'm sorry. But I've got a job in mind for you, if you'll give me a call."

"Job? Rosen?" Maggie looked at the dog, Daisy, like she had answers.

She pushed the button again.

"Maggie, please give me a call. I need to talk to you..."

Maggie hit the delete button. Same message from Rosen.

She pushed the red light again.

"Maggie, stop ignoring me and call please. I have something..."

She hit the erase button again.

"What in the hell kind of job does he have for me?" she asked the dog sarcastically. "Is he going to deputize me?"

Maggie laughed, and Daisy left the room.

"Oh great. You too, huh?"

Maggie pulled up the sleeve of her robe and chased Daisy down the hall.

"See? See? I don't have leprosy. I'm just unemployed. Lots of people are unemployed."

Now I'm arguing with the dog. Get a life, Maggie. Get a grip. Get a job.

Maggie and Rosen had gone way back, even to when Maggie had first started as a reporter at the Journal at age twenty-five. Rosen didn't look much different than he had then, Maggie thought, but he was getting old…too old to be the sheriff, most people thought. The only loyal people he had left were those on his payroll, the deputies and the clerks who worked in the office. They all loved him. People were starting to say they needed a new, younger man in office. The days of bootlegging had come to an end since the county had been voted wet, and most thought Rosen was out of his league when it came to the newer offenses like methamphetamine, cocaine, oxycodone. They thought he had served his purpose, and it was time for him to move on. Maggie's editor at the Journal had even written an editorial to that effect. That was the last time Rosen had bombarded the answering machine with messages.

Although Maggie had gone to college to study journalism, her real education began with Rosen. He was a hard nut to crack. For the entire first year of her career, he never gave her anything more than a press release. He made no comments about cases or investigations. Then she had him.

The Hamilton murder case.

Hamilton had been a federal employee, and it was suspected that his murder had something to do with a federal case. The FBI came in and excluded everyone from the scene, including Rosen. For an entire day, Rosen was stuck on the outside looking in, just like Maggie, on the other side of the yellow tape. The other reporters got their sound bites and left. Maggie stayed in hopes of getting in. Rosen was there with her. It was during that entire day and night that Maggie and Rosen formed a solid partnership. When the FBI finished and left, Rosen took Maggie behind the scenes. She wrote the story from the sheriff's perspective while all the other media mentioned nothing but the FBI and said things like, "Due to the lack of training from the sheriff's department, Federal Agents had to intervene." Maggie's story barely mentioned the FBI. It made Rosen look like Captain America.

Even after that, they had their ups and downs, like the time Rosen tipped her off that someone would be arrested at the Union Bank, and Maggie made the mistake of calling to ask for a comment. The bank teller who was going to be arrested for a weekend of hell-raising that had included a hit and run didn't know he was about to be arrested. He tried to leave, but Rosen caught him in the parking lot. It was then that Maggie learned how a reporter could be charged with aiding and abetting a criminal. Thank goodness Rosen had only threatened Maggi. She really might have gone to jail.

Still, Maggie missed those days. That was truly when she'd been happiest, out there in the field telling the stories. Even before she'd lost her job, she still envied her employees in the newsroom, so young, so excited about coming to work every day. Meanwhile, Maggie had her hands in budgets, corporate meetings, and figuring out ways to cut expenses.

She had started out in college majoring in accounting. She was horrible at it, so she'd changed her major to journalism. Ironically, there she was as publisher at the Journal. A simple bean counter.

Maggie should never have climbed so high on the proverbial corporate ladder. That way, maybe the fall wouldn't have hurt so badly, or at least it would have been less humiliating, less noticeable. Maybe it wouldn't have happened at all. Maggie had never fired one of her reporters; they had always left first to go on to bigger and better things. She should have stayed exactly where she was, scribing the news of the day, playing cops and robbers and pretending to be a private detective combing through old rap sheets of hardened criminals. But she didn't. She kept climbing, rung by rung, until—*snap*—it all came crashing down.

Really, a job was the last thing Maggie wanted. If she left the newspaper business completely, the industry would win. She didn't want them to win, but she couldn't go back. Taking another job would be admitting defeat. She wasn't even sure if she could do anything else. She'd been newspapering for her entire adult life.

Daisy was back in the room then, wagging her tail and nudging Maggie's hand as if to ask, *Am I still in trouble?*

"Well, Daisy," she said, bending down and taking the dog's face in her hands. "I guess I'll take a shower and go see Rosen."

CHAPTER THIRTY-ONE

Maggie hadn't been in the courthouse in years, but it looked exactly the same. The grout in the tile floors that lined the halls was still dirty. Some of the dirt was probably left there from when Maggie had clonked in here years ago after being at the Foley murder scene. It had rained that day, and there was mud everywhere. Once the body had been removed, she'd followed Rosen back to his office to get comments from him and a cup of hot chocolate, not necessarily in that order. They had kept the chocolate mix there just for her.

She saw several faces now—familiar faces—and she waved hello to all of them. They were ghosts from her past. They all looked so much older. Some new people were there, and it made Maggie feel a little territorial. How could they have hired new people without consulting her first? This was *her* courthouse.

The smoker's room was nearby. Maggie could smell it, the room built to accommodate those who were slowly killing themselves. The state had passed a new law that there would be no smoking in public buildings, but the county judge had decided to compromise and allowed a small room off in the back of the courthouse. There were a lot of smokers in Rayes County, and the judge figured those smokers had a lot of votes to swing his way. Evidently it had worked. He was still in office.

Maggie wanted a cigarette today worse than ever. She had even fake-smoked a straw before leaving the house. She looked pretty stupid, she'd thought when she'd caught a glimpse of herself in the toaster. Chuck would have gotten a huge kick out of seeing her if he'd been home. He was supposed to be home during the middle of the week. She had so much to tell him, and none of it was appropriate for phone discussion. There was way too much to say. She had told him, though, that a lot had happened. He said he couldn't wait to hear all about it. He'd been so supportive since Maggie had lost her job, telling her not to worry, that it would all work out. It was the company's loss, he'd say, and all the other things people were supposed to say when things like that happened.

Being with Mamaw had been a nice distraction…one that Maggie had needed. It seemed as though Denie had needed it, too. But now it was back to the real world, and Maggie was right in the thick of it, in the Rayes County Courthouse, ready to meet with Buck Rosen about a job of some sort.

Who knows what this is all about? she thought.

"Well, hello, Maggie." It was Claudia Campbell. She'd been Rosen's front-line woman since the day he'd been elected, way before Maggie's time at the paper.

She got up from her chair, walked around in front of her desk, and gave Maggie and hug. "Well, I haven't seen you in years, young lady. Where have you been keeping yourself?"

"Here and there," Maggie said, hoping this wouldn't turn into a conversation about losing her job.

"You have a seat right here and let me get you some coffee," Claudia said. "Cream and sugar?"

She'd forgotten. She'd forgotten that Maggie didn't drink coffee. How could that happen?

Maggie was furious. She'd been forgotten, old news. Even faithful, loyal, polite Claudia had forgotten all about her.

Maggie forced a smile. "Black will be fine."

"Sheriff Rosen has gone upstairs to the Circuit Judge's office, but he'll be right back."

"That's fine," Maggie said, pretending to sip the coffee.

Claudia talked about the new roads that were being built around the county, her children, Maggie's children, Chuck, her husband, Rosen's family, and even her new kittens. Maggie was glad to be talking about anything and everything other than the big purple elephant standing in the room.

Then suddenly, and without any grace or invitation at all, Claudia jumped on the elephant and began riding it around.

"Oh, dear, I heard about what happened to you at the paper," she rattled quickly, as if she were afraid she'd be interrupted. "And after you'd been there for so long! We just think it's awful. You know, I have half a mind to call that new publisher and tell him what I think of his corporate mumbo jumbo."

Maggie had no idea what Claudia was talking about, and somehow without saying a word, she was able to get that point across.

"Oh, dear?" Claudia said. "Have you not been reading the editorial page?"

Maggie shook her head and pretended to take another sip of coffee.

"People are very upset that the two newspapers are now just one. There's been some things said. That new publisher wrote an editorial about revenues and expenses and how one newspaper could better serve Rayes County and about how, as a new company, they needed to have their own management in place. I think he was referring to getting rid of you…" Claudia stopped herself. "Oh, I'm sorry. I didn't mean—"

"It's okay, Claudia," Maggie interrupted. "Don't worry about it."

With that, Claudia dismounted the elephant and went back to her desk. It was silent in the room other than talk of the weather, and both women were relieved when Rosen finally showed up. Maggie could've thrown him a parade just for walking in the door.

"Well, it's about damn time you showed up." Rosen put his hands on his hips, glaring at Maggie disapprovingly. "I only left you a hundred messages."

"It was fourteen," Maggie said flatly.

He laughed. "Fourteen, huh?"

"Yeah, fourteen."

"Come on back here. I need to have a talk with you." Rosen motioned for Maggie to follow him into his office.

"I'm just going to leave this here," Maggie told Claudia, referring to the coffee cup.

"Oh, that's fine, dear," said Claudia. "I'll get it."

Maggie started to sit down, but Sheriff Rosen grabbed her hand and pulled her toward him, hugging her hard.

"I haven't seen you in a long, long, long time," he said. "Once you got the fancy job, you stayed holed up in that office, never a peep from you. What have you been doing?"

"Not much of anything. Sleeping late, going to bed late, watching a lot of television. It's a lot like being a teenager." Maggie laughed.

"I'd imagine so." Rosen cracked a smile and then repeated himself. "I'd imagine so."

Maggie looked around the office to see newspaper clippings everywhere. Rosen at an old booze bust. Rosen holding a few stalks of marijuana. Rosen holding up confiscated pills. There were so many newspaper clippings of him on the walls, she could barely tell what color the paint used to be.

Maggie looked for some of her own stuff that he'd hung up there. Some things looked familiar, but she couldn't remember if she'd written them or if one of her employees had since she'd become publisher. She couldn't see the bylines and couldn't remember any of the photos, so she finally gave up trying to figure it out.

"Look at these walls," she said. "Remember when 'no comment' used to be your favorite line?"

"Oh yeah," Rosen said. "But there was this reporter one time that told me if I didn't let the people see what I was doing, they would think I wasn't doing anything at all. Do you know whatever happened to that young lady?"

Maggie remembered that day—the day of the Hamilton murder case when Rosen had been thrown out by the FBI. What should have been his murder case had been claimed proudly by the Feds. That was the day Rosen had cracked for her.

"Oh, I think she's still around," Maggie joked. "A little older and a little slower than the one you used to know, but she's still around."

"Maggie, we do miss you around here," Rosen said. "Only got to talk to you when we had a problem with one of your reporters."

"Yeah. I should've come around a little more."

"Aw, that's alright. I'm sure you had plenty to take care of."

Just then, Claudia opened the door and interrupted. "Sheriff Rosen, the county judge is here to see you."

"Tell him he'll have to come back later. Or tell him I'll come by there tomorrow morning."

Wow, thought Maggie. *Rosen turning down a visit from the county judge. This must be serious.*

"How are the kids?" the sheriff asked.

"Good."

"And Chuck?"

"Great." She gave him a look that told him to get to the point.

"How's your grandmother, Mrs. Garland?"

"She's okay. I've seen a lot of her this week. She's doing really good."

"Maggie, do you remember some of the stories we worked on together?"

Rosen got up and walked around the room. He motioned for her to follow him. One by one, he pointed out stories that he and

Maggie had been involved in together. Now that Maggie had a closer view, she could see almost all the stories were hers.

They talked about the murder at the factory, the gay man who had been beaten to death and then dumped at the landfill, the woman who was convicted of duct-taping her husband to the bed and then setting their mobile home on fire.

One by one, Sheriff Rosen and Maggie pointed out stories that they remembered. She was having a good time reliving old scenes that had played out in times past.

"What are you working on now?" she asked excitedly.

"Well, we've found a body over at the site where they're puttin' up that spec building."

"Ooh, a body," Maggie said. "Sounds interesting."

"You seriously haven't heard about this?"

Maggie shook her head no.

"You are really out of touch."

"I really have no desire to buy a newspaper, and TV, well, I'd rather watch something a little less depressing than the news."

"This is a very interesting case, Maggie. We've got these guys out there working on leveling the ground at the site—excavation type work. Well, they're digging around out there with the big equipment and backhoes and such, and they find a man's body. Strange thing is that the doc—you know, Elly Burns—says the body is over fifty years old."

"Wow, so it's a cold case?" Maggie asked.

"To say the least, yes. It's cold. Might as well be frozen."

287

"What are you going to do? How on earth are you going to find suspects in a case like that?"

"Well, the first place I looked was at the property valuator's office to see who used to own the property — you know, who might have owned it fifty years ago or more—and I found that the property was owned at that time by Viola and Dennis Garland, your grandmother and grandfather."

Maggie's mouth gaped open. She felt sick. She couldn't speak.

This is why he brought me here, she thought. *There's no job. He wants information about the property.*

Maggie chose to remain silent and let him finish.

"Then I get this call from your grandma," Rosen continued. "Mrs. Garland says she has some information about the body we found on that property, says I should come over right away."

"My grandmother called you?"

"Well, she talked to Claudia. I've been trying to reach you. I figured you might need to go with me to talk to her. I don't know how old Mrs. Garland is now, but I figure either eighty or really close to eighty. Maggie, I don't want to go over and question an old woman about an old murder, but Claudia says she keeps calling and keeps insisting that I do. I just wanted to let you know before I do, so that you won't think I'm doing anything behind your back."

"I've been with her for the past few days," Maggie said, looking puzzled. "She never said anything about information about the... Yeah, the spec building property is on the land that Mamaw and Papaw used to own, but I don't know. I guess she would've said something..."

And then she stopped. Like an ice-cold bucket of water had just been thrown on her, it hit her. "Did she say anything else?"

Rosen didn't answer.

"Did she say anything else?" Maggie demanded.

"No, she didn't. Just that she had information. Really, I'd just like to talk to her and wanted to know if you'd like to be there when I do?"

"Are you sure, Buck? That's all it is? You just want to talk to her?"

"Of course. What kind of an old so-and-so do you think I am?"

"I'd like to talk to her first if you don't mind," Maggie said, looking him straight in the eyes.

Rosen knew what Maggie meant by that, and he knew she would do anything to protect her grandmother…or anyone else in the Garland family.

CHAPTER THIRTY-TWO

Rosen and Maggie pulled in the parking lot at the nursing home at the same time. They met at the front door.

"I'm going to go in and talk to her first, right?" Maggie reminded Sheriff Rosen.

"Yes. You talk to her first, just like we said back at the office. Nothing has changed." He was becoming aggravated at Maggie's distrust. "I'll be sitting right here in the waiting room until you come out."

He picked up a remote control and leaned back on the overstuffed couch. "I think I'll try to find a game to watch. Did you see this? They got a big screen."

Maggie rolled her eyes at the sheriff and tromped off down the hall to her grandmother's room.

Oh, God. What has she done? Has she lost her mind, telling the sheriff she has information about a dead body? Maggie's thoughts were coming too rapidly for her to fully comprehend.

Should I call Denie and Doris? There's no time. I can't wait for them to get here. What if it is? It can't be. But what if it is? What if it's him? She never mentioned him after the story. Maybe the old lady has lost her mind and she's making up things, and maybe even the story wasn't real. It didn't seem real. But I saw it, Janie Cole's grave with the baby's grave marker beside it.

Suddenly she found herself in her Mamaw's room.

"Well, hey there, you. I'm so glad you're—"

Maggie interrupted her grandmother. "Did you call the sheriff and tell him you had information about a dead body?"

"Well, why would they tell you about that?" Mamaw asked. "That's my business, you know. I'm still able to talk to whoever I want about whatever I want."

That was the confirmation Maggie needed. "Mamaw, tell me. Tell me what you know before Sheriff Rosen comes in here. That way, I can see if it's anything we need to worry about."

"Is he here? Is Sheriff Rosen here? It's about time they showed up. I was wondering if they really wanted to solve this crime or not," Mamaw said.

"Yeah, he's here. He's in the lobby, waiting for me to talk to you first."

"Well, that's the craziest thing I've ever heard of. I need to talk to him about this, and you don't need to get involved."

"Involved with what, Mamaw? What is there to be involved in? What kind of information do you have about this body?" Maggie begged for information, anything. "Please tell me this doesn't have anything to do with Bick Cole, Mamaw. Please, tell me you didn't—"

You need to hush that mouth of yours, young lady," Viola interrupted sharply. "I am telling you nothing. Now, you might as well got get the sheriff, because I don't have to say another word to you. You go on now and go get him." With that, Viola pretended her mouth was a zipper and she was closing it up.

"Mamaw, please tell me what this is about before you talk to anyone else."

Viola shook her head no.

"Please, Mamaw. I'm not asking for much. Just tell me what you're about to tell the sheriff. I'm your granddaughter. Why not tell me, and I'll tell him?"

Voila shook her head again, this time more forcefully. She pointed toward the door, ordering Maggie to go out and get the sheriff.

There was something about the whole thing that made Maggie feel sick. She just knew something bad was about to happen, that everything was about to change.

Her grandmother always said bad things happen in threes. She'd lost her job, then she'd found out about Doris and Mom, and now this.

"I just know it," Maggie said to herself as she walked slowly toward Sheriff Rosen. "I just know it's bad."

Rosen got up from his seat. "I thought you'd never come back," He seemed to notice the look on Maggie's face then. "What's wrong? What happened?"

"She won't talk to me. She won't tell me why she called you, won't tell me what information she has. She won't even speak to me at all now. She's zipped her lips. She says she'll only talk to you and that it's none of my concern." *Tell me what to do*, Maggie begged him with her eyes.

"Don't worry, Maggie. I can handle this. You go back in there with me, and we'll get the story together," he said. "I've been dealing with stubborn old women all my life."

CHAPTER THIRTY-THREE

Maggie cautiously entered her grandmother's room again. Their eyes met. Mamaw's weren't bright today. They'd faded into a stormy gray. The anger that Maggie had seen just moments before was gone, replaced by a sadness that filled the entire room.

"Where's the sheriff?" Mamaw asked softly.

"Right here, ma'am. I'm right here," Buck said, stepping out from behind Maggie.

"I'll need to talk to him alone, you know." Mamaw looked at Maggie and nodded her head toward the door.

"I'm staying," Maggie said as defiantly as she could, still being careful not to anger her grandmother.

"Sheriff Rosen," Viola began, "I am still of sound mind. I am still a citizen of this county. Just because I'm an old woman here in a bed and my body's eat up with arthritis doesn't mean I need to be protected."

She sighed angrily, and Maggie could tell she was also a little hurt.

"My granddaughter has no place in this conversation we're about to have. She needs to leave."

"With all due respect, Mrs. Garland, I'd appreciate it if you would let Maggie stay," Buck said. "I trust her above all others in this county—other than my kin—and some of them I don't trust as much as her. I'll have to have a witness to whatever you're going to tell me about this body, and she already knows that's why I'm here."

Maggie was surprised at the ease with which her grandmother transitioned into the story. Buck had taken his hat off at the door; he now held it in his lap as he sat, leaning toward Maggie's grandmother.

"You know I almost drowned once when I was very young…eighteen," Viola started. "Me and a few others were down at the Lily Pits. You know where I'm talking about?"

"Yes, Mrs. Garland. I've heard my father talk about the pits," Rosen said with interest.

Maggie remembered her father talking about the Lily Pits, the coal pits that had been dug when the big companies had come in and raped the county, robbing the earth of her diamonds. At least that was how Maggie's father used to describe it. Huge manmade holes filled with water were entertainment for teenagers in the summer, but they were undoubtedly a reminder to landowners of what could have been if they'd only had the foresight. Maggie's father had also told her about a boy who'd drowned there.

"I've always thought it would have been a blessing if the two of us had just gone down together." At this, Viola looked at Maggie with watery eyes. "Yes, it probably would have been a blessing—a blessing for us all."

"The two of you?" Buck questioned.

"Me and my baby," Viola said, turning to the sheriff.

The word *baby* was barely audible as Mamaw's chin began to tighten and her tears began to flow.

"It was my first child. I was about seven months along," she continued. "Me and Den—you remember my husband Den?"

The sheriff nodded his head.

"He saved us, saved us both. From what, I'll never know. I've always heard that after you go down the third time, you usually don't come back up. The last thing I saw was Den as I went down for the third and last time. He was about twenty feet away. Something had wrapped around one of my feet, and my other foot was slipping. I couldn't gain any ground. I had my hand up out of the water, and he saw me struggling.

"It had been a fearful seven months for me. I was always scared that something was wrong with the baby. It was like I just knew. Something was telling me that a bad time was coming. I wasn't as happy as I should've been, I thought. I was just going through the motions, you know, of being excited about that baby coming. But that baby never got to be a part of my family. Even though Den had saved us both from drowning, he couldn't save us from the pain that would come about later."

Maggie knew the story well. In fact, that was all she'd been able to think about over the past several days. Now, someone else—someone outside the family—was about to know. Maggie was almost sure of the ending, the ending she and Denie never got to hear. It was the one loose end that had never been tied up neatly in the family saga they had been told that week.

As the story unfolded before Sheriff Rosen, Maggie began to feel a little uncomfortable. Mamaw was telling the abbreviated version, of course, and there were new things Maggie hadn't heard before. At one point, her grandmother talking about her love for horses and how she'd ride sometimes. Maggie was amazed at what she still didn't know about this woman. The stories were like the colors in a kaleidoscope, ever changing, always more to see.

"While me and Janie Cole were in town that day," Mamaw continued, "we saw Melvin Langley. Have you ever heard of him?"

"No, ma'am, I can't say that I have," Rosen said.

"Well, he was a…well, he was simple, kind of slow, and he dressed in women's clothes: hats, scarves, sometimes even nylons. I never knew who his parents were, never saw them, never really heard anyone talk about them. Langley was just by himself, a person in town everyone made fun of and teased. Oh, they teased him awful." Mamaw shook her head and wrinkled her forehead as if she had somehow tapped into the pain Langley felt. "I always felt sorry for him…wanted to help him in some way. He was in town that day that me and Janie were. Janie couldn't stand the sight of him. She thought he was the worst kind of sinful. Me and Janie were watching some property being auctioned off at the courthouse steps. Langley was sitting on a bench nearby.

"I had a few dollars in my pocket that day. While Janie was watching the Taylors' property being auctioned, more people gathered around to see who was bidding. We were all kind of shoulder to shoulder at that point, so I slipped around the back and laid two dollars on the bench next to Langley. I knew he had to be hot, thirsty, like the rest of us. It was so hot that day, had to be nearly a hundred degrees. I had to sneak and do it. Janie would have never approved. To her, Langley was bent on splittin' Hell wide open. I loved her so, but in Janie's eyes it was either Heaven or Hell, and she was sure Langley would be sitting at the right hand of Satan when he died."

Rosen sat there just like Denie and Maggie had done when Mamaw had told the story to them. He was still, motionless as he stared into the old woman's eyes.

CHAPTER THIRTY-FOUR
Rayes County, 1936
The Reckoning

For the first time in what seemed like days, Viola felt clean. She and the baby were in the bed now, safe, warm. The baby was nursing.

As she sat there with feather pillows against her sore back, she looked at the child taking its milk. It was so delicate, so precious, so clean and fresh. Viola rubbed the baby's little hands back and forth across her cheek. She was tired, but she couldn't rest. Her entire body was throbbing as if the blood in her veins was trying to rush as quickly as it could to get to the soreness underneath every inch of her skin.

It felt good to be still—to just be still.

As she sat there, she looked around the room. There was no trace of anything that had happened the day before. It was all gone, everything back in its place.

Out of the corner of her eye, she saw a shadow, a figure passing by the window. It looked like a person, though Viola knew it couldn't have been. No one had knocked on the door. If it were Den, he would have come in.

She picked up the baby, cradling it in her arms, and walked to the back of the house, looking out each window as she went.

She didn't see anything. It was probably just her imagination, she thought. Her mind was playing tricks; it was the exhaustion. She could barely move her feet more than a few inches at a time. She was so sore. She could feel gushes between her legs with almost every step she took, but it was becoming less and less as the day went on. She was grateful for that. She knew she was healing.

She heard voices coming from the back of the house then. There was someone by the window, she thought, rushing to the back door and peeking out to see who was there.

She held tight to the doorknob, but it was suddenly yanked from her hand. She and the baby almost fell off the steps as they were pulled out into the open.

"And there she is! Miss Jezebel herself!" Bick Cole screamed at her, his face not more than two inches from her own. He held her arm tight, pulling her into his stinking liquor breath.

"Stop it! Stop it! Viola screamed. "You're going to hurt the baby!"

Viola realized that was why he was there. He knew. He'd seen her, seen her take the baby.

Bick staggered as he held her arm tight. He looked like he was about to speak but couldn't think of what to say.

"Baby?" he whispered, his hot breath on her face. "Baby?"

Although he had stopped screaming, his voice and his demeanor almost seemed sinister now.

"Bick, you've been drinking. You need to go home," Viola stuttered through her terror. "You don't drink, Bick."

He let her arm go and shoved her into the side of the house, pointing his finger in her face now. "You don't know anything about me, Viola Garland, you little whore. You little Satan worshipper. You little—" Bick stopped, coughing now, bent over and gasping for breath and then raising back up.

"That's my baby. You know that's my baby!"

Viola couldn't breathe. Her chest tightened, and she could feel her grip on the child tighten.

"Where's Janie? I need to see Janie, Bick. I need to see Janie. I have to talk to her," Viola begged, trying to reason with him.

"You'll not see my wife anymore," Bick slurred and pulled something from his pocket. "And you'll not be to my house anymore either."

Viola saw it leave his pocket. He gripped it tightly and held it close to her face. It was her hair—*her* hair. A large chunk of her hair. Viola's scalp began to ache as she looked at it, remembering that her hair had gotten caught in the fence when she'd taken the baby.

"How in the hell did I happen to get this?" Bick had her by the arm again, holding the hair over her face. The baby was crying, screaming, as Bick had it pinned between himself and Viola. He loosened his grip on Viola slightly and looked at the baby, putting the long lock of hair back in his pocket. "I think we both know how I got it, Mrs. Garland." He was sinister again, speaking almost in a whisper. His breath was rotten with the smell of liquor, his clothes wet with sweat.

Over Bick's shoulder, Viola could see someone coming from the woods behind the house. It looked like a woman. She couldn't see clearly. Bick was jerking her back and forth and hitting her hard against the side of the house.

It's Janie, she thought. *It has to be Janie.* Viola started to call out her name and then caught herself. Bick hadn't seen her. *Oh, God,* she thought, *if she comes over here, he'll kill her and maybe the baby, too.* Viola froze with fear. The baby screamed as she held on tight with the one arm she had free.

"I'm going to take my baby now," Bick said. He spoke quietly and glared into her eyes as if he could see straight through to her soul.

Viola felt cold and sick but held her grip tightly on the child as he released her arm to take the baby. "No, no, no!" She squeezed the baby to her chest, both arms wrapped tightly around it as Bick tried to pry her arms apart.

CLANG!

Bick's eyes rolled around and as he fell into Viola. She pushed him off of her.

Langley was holding the shovel high above his head, ready to hit Bick again as he lay there lifeless on the ground.

"Don't hurt Miss Viola! She's going to have a baby!" Langley slobbered as he spoke.

Viola was shocked. Still holding the baby tight, she looked around the other side of Langley for Janie. She wasn't there. She had never been there. It had been Langley coming out of the woods.

She looked down at Bick, who was bleeding from his mouth and ears. He was choking on his own blood, starting to turn pale.

Langley started to come down with the shovel again, and Viola didn't stop him. She watched as he hit Bick over and over with the shovel. She held the baby tight and began backing away.

Over and over, Langley shouted, "Don't hurt Miss Viola…Miss Viola…baby!"

Viola was sure that Bick was dead by now. "Stop, Langley. Stop! Stop!

He looked up at her as if he'd just seen her for the first time, and without even acknowledging what he'd just done, spoke in his childlike voice.

"Miss Viola, you have a baby."

"Yes, Langley, it's a baby," she stuttered. "Now, put that shovel down. Put it down."

Langley dropped the shovel and looked at Bick, face contorted with worry and grief. "I hurt him, Miss Viola, but he hurt you. I hurt him. He's got bloody." He pulled the scarf from around his neck and tried to wipe the blood from Bick's mouth.

"No, Langley," Viola said, glancing frantically around the mountains to make sure no one had seen what had just happened. "You come over here." She took him by the hand and led him over to the steps. "I need you to hold the baby. It's crying. See? I need for you to rock the baby back and forth and make her stop crying. You sit here and rock the baby, Langley. Don't go anywhere. Just sit here and rock the baby."

Langley looked at the child as Viola handed it to him. "Aww," he cooed. "It's a little baby, Miss Viola. I've never held a baby before. Nobody ever let me hold their baby."

"You hold my baby, Langley. You rock her until she stops crying."

Langley rubbed the baby's head and began to hum to her. "I'm rocking the baby, Miss Viola. It's gonna stop cryin' now."

"Yes, Langley, yes. Rock the baby."

Viola thought for a moment about what to do. She looked around at the mountains again to see if anyone was there—no one, no one anywhere. She looked at the shovel. It was bloody. Bick was bloody. It was everywhere.

The well.

The rock and dirt were piled up next to the well still, and the shovel that had been stuck in the dirt now lay bloody next to Bick.

She pulled back the wooden well cover, just a bunch of wood pieces Den had nailed together to cover the hole until he could get it filled in, then looked over at Langley. He was in his own world with the baby, cooing and singing and rocking. He was wearing a skirt today. It, too, had blood on it, as did the blouse. Viola would have to give him something to wear and get rid of his clothes.

She had asked God's forgiveness too many times to count over the last day, but she continued to pray and tell herself that Janie would be better off if she just thought Bick had run off. She told herself that she and Janie would raise the baby together as Viola's baby. She could take care of both Janie and the baby, and no one would ever have to know about any of it.

Viola no longer felt the soreness in her body. She had to get rid of him. She picked up Bick's feet and began to drag him toward the well. Langley stopped rocking and looked up at her for a moment. Viola nodded her head at him. "You have to keep doing it, or the baby will cry."

Langley continued rocking and cooing.

Bick's body hit the bottom of the well with a thud. She watched him there for a moment, sprawled in the rocks and dirt, then went over and picked up the bloody shovel and started covering him over with lime she had gotten from the smokehouse. Then came the rocks and dirt.

Viola cleaned up the shovel, the blood from the ground, and washed her hands and arms. She took Langley and the baby in the house, gave Langley a dress to wear, and cleaned him up a little. As Viola washed his face with a cloth, he smiled at her with childlike features. Viola had never seen Langley this close up. He was a beautiful boy with long eyelashes and soft skin—so innocent.

She showed him to the door and sent him off with some leftover biscuits she'd made a few days before.

"I have to give you something," Langley said as he was about to leave. "You left this in town." He handed Viola the two dollars she had laid beside him on the bench.

"You walked all this way to give me that two dollars?" she asked. "I wondered what you were doing all the way out here. I've never seen you out here before."

"No, I have to stay in town. My mama says so." He still held the two dollars out in front of her.

"Langley, I gave those two dollars to you. You keep it and buy yourself something pretty."

CHAPTER THIRTY-FIVE
Rayes County, Present Day

Sheriff Rosen was still staring deeply into Mrs. Garland's eyes, not moving.

Mamaw looked away from Sheriff Rosen and over at Maggie, waiting for a reaction, but there was none. Maggie wasn't shocked by the information she'd just heard, only saddened and worried about what might happen next. She and Buck locked eyes at the same time.

Mamaw raised herself up in the bed a bit, then put her wrists together and held out her arms toward Rosen.

Her eyes were shut tightly. Her shriveled little hands and her tiny little wrists shook as she tried to hold them steady. Sheriff Rosen did nothing.

Mamaw opened one eye to look at him. He was smiling.

"Mrs. Garland, please put your hands down," he said, looking at her with amusement. "So, you think the body we found was Bick Cole?"

"It is, isn't it?" Mamaw asked. "It had to be. I put him in the well."

Buck looked over at Maggie, his eyebrows raised in question, as if he didn't quite know what to say next. She knew from the pleasant look in his eyes that everything was going to be okay.

"That body that we found—the one over at the spec building—ma'am, it was a woman's body," Sheriff Rosen said. "It can't be the person you're talking about. It's a missing person we've been looking for. That body's not more than a few months old."

"But … but, the newspaper said it was a man and it was a body that was over fifty years old. It has to be…"

Sheriff Rosen picked up a newspaper from Mamaw's nightstand and rolled it up as if he were handing it to her.

"Don't believe everything you read in this newspaper," he said. "You know since Maggie stopped writing you can't believe anything in here. They're always getting something wrong."

Rosen laughed and patted Mamaw's hands. She still looked puzzled but seemed to accept the explanation he gave her.

"Maggie, is your grandmother on any type of medication?" he asked, trying to play serious, but Maggie knew where he was going with this line of questioning.

"Yes, she's on medication. She has arthritis in her hips."

"Don't talk about me like I'm not here," Mamaw said, angered at the two of them ignoring her.

"Beg pardon, Mrs. Garland," Sheriff Rosen said, "but, there's been no crime committed here, and we have all the information we need on this body. So, unless you have some information about the woman we found, I really need to get back to work."

"Well, no, I don't have any about a woman...a missing woman..."

"Good day, ma'am." Buck Rosen put his hat back on and said goodbye to Viola Garland. "Care to walk me out, Maggie?"

"I'll be right back, Mamaw," she told her grandmother, who was still sitting on the bed, searching to find an answer.

"Sheriff Rosen?" Viola called out. "What was the name of the construction company that found man the other day?"

"Oh, that was Shanks'," he said, not realizing he had just validated Viola's confession.

She raised her brow and nodded her head. "Good enough. Good enough."

"Have a good day, ma'am," Rosen said, and he and Maggie left the room.

As they walked down the hall to the front doors of the nursing home, Maggie started to speak. Buck shook his head and held his finger to his lips. In the waiting room, Maggie spoke.

"That body wasn't a woman, and you know it, Rosen," Maggie scolded him. "And Mamaw's not stupid. She knows you're lying. She knows when everyone's lying. She's not likely to let this go."

Rosen spoke as if he hadn't even heard Maggie. "That job I was telling you about...you know, the one we were supposed to talk about today?"

"Oh, yeah." Maggie smiled. "I almost forgot."

"I heard there was a reporter's opening at the newspaper. As I understand it, it's the police beat."

"Are you saying that I should—"

"I was told that you were offered the job when you were demoted but turned it down. I'd like for you to reconsider."

Maggie was a little surprised. "I don't understand why you would want me to... How can I go back? I've been humiliated, degraded. I just—I just don't know."

"Maggie, you know as well as I do that elections are won and lost in the inkwells of newspapers all across the country, and especially in Rayes County. The political machine here thinks I'm too old. Next time out, I don't think they're going to support me financially like they have in the past. I've heard they've got some young punk lined up to run against me next time. You need to take this job. I can make you famous. You'll get exclusives—only you. Not the TV, not the radio, only you."

The more Maggie listened to Rosen, the more she understood. He was going to open every cold case in Rayes County and solve them, and he needed her help.

"Don't get me wrong," he said. "I know I'm getting old...probably too old to do this job for too much longer."

"You're not that old," Maggie said, but she thought about it for a moment and realized that Rosen had to be about fifty.

"This case, the one I heard here today," Rosen said. "That will be the only unsolved murder case left in Rayes County by the time I'm done. But I don't want the state police or the FBI coming in here and taking all the credit. That's what you can help me with."

The thought of working as a reporter again excited Maggie whether she wanted to admit it or not. It didn't pay all that great, not like a publisher's job, but still. It was her first love and always would be. She knew about all the unsolved murders in Rayes County. Everyone blamed Rosen and his deputies for most of unresolved cases, and she knew he was right. Whenever the sheriff's department did do something good, the state police would come in and claim the glory. She'd seen it happen hundreds of times.

If she agreed to do it, if she even considered it, this would be the only unethical thing she'd ever done in her career as a journalist, as a newspaper woman, as a slave to the trade, most people in the business called it.

But she'd done the ethical thing. She'd played by the rules, stood up for what was right and good.

What did that get me? Nothing.

All those cold cases hanging out there in Rayes County…exclusives on all of them… It was still good reporting, not all that unethical to make a trade right here and now. If she had to start over, this was certainly the way to do it. She knew more now, so much more than when she was just a kid trying to cover a city council meeting. Of all the elected officials in Rayes County, she had always considered Buck to be one of the good ones. He was always the "what you see is what you get" type. Still, she had to be sure.

"You know you still have to play by the rules," Maggie warned him. "I can't print lies."

"Oh, I know," he said, "and I don't expect you to. I just want a fair shot. No lies, just solved cases."

"Buck, why don't you just retire and hang it up?" Maggie asked. "Aren't you tired of it all? The games, the politics...?"

Rosen looked at her strangely and let out one small, breathy laugh. "I don't quit for the same reason you won't quit, Maggie."

He looked back toward the hall they had just walked. "Me and your grandmother..." he said. "We're the same. We're after the same thing."

"I don't understand what you mean."

"Sure you do. You wanted to go out on your own terms, didn't you?"

Maggie nodded her head, remembering the day she'd lost her job. She would have preferred to have left on her own, saved her dignity.

"Me and your grandmother want the same thing. We want to go out on our own terms."

Maggie smiled at him, her eyes quickly filling with tears, as she nodded in agreement. "I'll see you next Monday morning," she said as he got up to leave.

He winked at her. "Good girl."

Maggie watched Rosen walk toward the door. *Always the lawman*, she thought. She'd never seen him wear anything else but that uniform. He always looked the part. Then it hit her.

"Hey, Rosen."

Sheriff Rosen turned around.

"Where's your badge?"

"Oh," he said, looking down at his chest where his badge should have been. He looked surprised that she'd noticed. "I must have left it at the office."

ABOUT THE AUTHOR

Melissa Newman, Ed.D. is an award-winning journalist, a novelist, and professor of communication. She has committed her career to making Kentucky's Appalachia a better place to live, work, grow, and thrive.

Melissa earned her doctoral degree in Educational Leadership & Policy Studies from Eastern Kentucky University. Her master's degree is in secondary education and her bachelor's degree is in business management and communication, both from Union College. Her ongoing research, rooted in Kentucky's Appalachia, studies methods of raising hope in communities through the erosion of negative stereotypes and reveals economic implications for individuals and regional populations.

"Sister Blackberry" is her first novel, originally published in 2009 and then re-released in 2022 under a new imprint.

www.melissanewman.net
www.martinsisterspublishing.com